Tangled Magic

BOOK 1 OF THE GODDESSES INC SERIES

Desert Cats
PUBLISHING

STEFANIE SANTONE

This book could only exist with many thanks
My beloved Aunt Ruth
1956 – 2022
Thank you for getting me off my ass
even if you didn't know it at the time
and...
Mom
Because you never stopped believing in me
especially when I stopped believing in myself

Contents

Chapter One

N ever go home.

    I know the phrase is 'you can never go home' and it has these bittersweet implications which bring tears to even the most stoic of hearts. After what I've been through the past few weeks, it's now 'never go home.'

If I hadn't gone home, my best friend wouldn't be trapped in a haphazard circle of salt, inches from certain death. I wouldn't be staring down a literal Hel Hound—you know, Hel Hounds? The approximate size of a rhinoceros and the shape of a Doberman on steroids? One of those. Oh, and let's not forget about my brand-spanking-new co-workers in the extinct volcano, battling for their lives. That is, if they weren't already dead from the friend of said literal Hel Hound.

Cerberus's big brother growled a low rumble that caused my heart to freeze while the odor of decay and rotting meat made my stomach roil. I searched the bare copper ground before settling on the only thing bigger than me. The tree branch, more of a stick, really, cut painfully into my hands when I gripped it, but I didn't care.

I wanted to be here. Okay, not right here where I'm going to become Fluffy's chew toy. But I wanted to know things I had no business knowing.

And now I was going to die.

I guess that's not much to go on. Let me try again.

The name's Aspen Sommers. Until three weeks ago, my life as a graduate fresh out of Arizona State was perfectly normal. I felt ready for grad school, the world, and possibly a new therapist.

Summer had come upon us as hot and fast as any sex joke you started making out of that sentence. Maybe not for most of the Western Hemisphere, but Tempe is in the middle of the Sonoran Desert of central Arizona. The thermostat on my dash already showed near tripled digit heat when I started my trip.

I'd packed up my dorm, checked my grades—passed, thank you, merciful God—and skipped my graduation ceremony to get on the highway after morning rush-hour. My roommates said they'd deal with the cleaning. To be honest, I didn't care if I got billed for the questionable minion-yellow stains in my roommate's bedroom. I needed to be home.

Cacti and low, dead sagebrush zipped by me on the highway out of town. It didn't take long to get out of the Phoenix metro area, which Tempe cut a sliver south of Sky Harbor Airport. It's a college town hooked into a big city with a sprawling suburban area, giving the benefits of all three.

Also, all the shittiness of them.

I had been prepared to stay in the mild shittiness for another few years to complete my master's. Until two days ago, I got the call that changed my already rapidly evolving life. Dad rushed through the conversation because he and Mom were preparing to leave the hospital. Sometimes my mom's multiple sclerosis flares left her in bed for days. She needed strong drugs and had a standing order at the small local hospital for pain control. The fear in his normally warm voice caused me to drop the tinfoil hat for the end-of-term-graduation party.

They were going home after a week-long stint in the hospital, much longer than normal. They hadn't told my younger brother and I because of finals, they claimed. My older sister knew, but only because she lived so close by. Maybe I should appreciate that I only almost failed one test instead of five because of this. The other four were because my boyfriend broke up with me.

Thanks, Marc.

Dad needed someone to help Mom. He needed someone who didn't have a job, summer sports, or a child. Someone who had been rejected from graduate schools and sat on the waiting list at ASU because of spotty attendance over five years.

He didn't say that. In fact, he said nothing beyond, "Please, we need you."

Mom had taken care of me when I was sick, even after I turned eighteen and knew everything. How could I not do the same for her?

I knew I'd never be strong enough to put up with what she did for me. The up all nights, the crying spells, and worse, the hospital stays. To this day, I don't know how she did it. MS, however, is well known for progressing. They were called 'flares,' and often when they ended a new baseline of pain existed.

I shook myself free of my lingering fears and regarded my current choice. Up ahead the I-17 was the obvious, easy way to go home. However, if I took the alternate way through Sedona, I could take the 89A up, spiral around a little, and meet the road to Cora Alma to go west. I checked the clock. 10:30. There was plenty of time to get to Mom's appointment at noon, so I weighed my options. Red rock and pine trees sounded better than more flats, brush, and boring asphalt. The town of Sedona was fun to drive through. It held a certain charm, having been founded in the early 1900s around the same time as my home of Cora Alma.

I checked the thermostat again and grinned while cracking the window. A wonderful 75F. As I drove further north, even here in Arizona, it got cooler. It's a desert, folks, but only part of it. The oak and juniper were still brush-like in appearance, standing maybe a few meters tall, but they were thick and strong. The further up I went, the greener and taller everything got. It may not have been sprawling redwoods or anything, but as an AZ native, I appreciated every single tree. Wildfires scarred the land too often for me not to. Big trees basically don't exist in the city. Except palm trees.

"Mmmrrr..."

No, that wasn't my stomach. It was my beautiful, adorable, lovable—

"RRRRRRRAAAA..."

—complete jerk of a cat—Carrie. Short for Carrot, named so for her bushy ginger tail. She picked me at an adoption event at a big box pet store. My then boyfriend and I were there to pick up food for his own cat when her paw snared my pant leg.

Those crystal-clear blue eyes spoke to me so deeply that Marc laughed openly in the store. Then on the entire way home, too.

Damn, I missed him.

Tears welled up again and I let them plot their course.

"It's okay, Carrie." Yes, I talk to my cat like she'll answer me. So what? "We're almost home."

The smells of pine sap and dirt flooded my nose and the cool mountain air dried my tears. The summer ahead was going to be different than the ones I'd spent in Tempe, and I couldn't wait to discover how.

Sedona's colorful mix of palm readers, expensive jewelry shops, and food streamed by, all situated in late 19th century wood façades that had no business being as charming as they were. Crowds of tourists flooded the streets, converging upon the various food joints and holding up too expensive t-shirts from outside racks to see if they would fit. Others climbed the steps to find some of the more eclectic shops, like the everyday Christmas one.

A grumble in my stomach reminded me I hadn't eaten, and the tourist traps weren't helping. My cat growled in response and I laughed lightly. "It's only another twenty minutes to get home. You'll make it, I promise."

From her cage she gave me a grumpy *'mrwr, mrwr, mrwr'*. Though I don't speak cat fluently, I'm pretty sure that meant I would pay for this later.

Before we started the perilous path of the 89A, I glanced back and checked on my other precious cargo. Crates filled with jars of water held the fruit of five years of labor: cuttings of my plants from the garden in Tempe. Of course, those were all originally cuttings of the plants of my childhood home back in Cora Alma. The home my parents sold before the end of the school year when Nana gave them her house.

Crap. They really, and I mean really, planned this move while telling no one.

I let that go, for now at least, and turned my attention to the 89A. Rather than speeding up, I slowed down, easing into the narrow, tight curves as I traversed further and further up. Here, right outside of Sedona, was where the forest bloomed. Trees as tall as buildings grew, and a recent rain smell hung in the air. Each slow curve was a bit of a thrill as the canopy of green overtook me. My gaze darted back and forth at the sharp corners as I eased forward. Slow and steady here. For being a relic of the nineties, Old Bessie kept pushing on, and I shifted against the well-worn cloth seats with a little pride in that.

The road straightened and I didn't lose a single cutting in the sharp spiral that lay after Sedona. Even my cat purred in contentment, not noticing the change. I sped up, joining the flow of traffic. Though it took some work to unclench my jaw.

I had barely celebrated my heroic climb when a streak of white flashed in front of me. Coming at me at sixty-five miles an hour was a doe. A silver-white doe, red eyed, terrified and—SHIT!

My brakes squealed and locked. Three tickets and a defensive driving course taught me to turn the wheel into the skid. My cat shrieked from her carrier, held in place with the seatbelt, but still not a comfort to her as we crashed. Water sloshed over me from behind, drenching me completely. I came to a screeching halt after less than a second.

With my heart stomping through my chest, I dared to look over my dashboard and almost cried, and not just because I had to peel my hands off the steering wheel. One of the many brush patches that lined the highway had been kind enough to stop me. Not the animal. Or worse, the red rock cliff on the other side of the brush.

An albino doe, almost silver with the characteristic pink-red eyes, blinked at me from the driver's side, about fifteen feet away. She shimmered like a desert mirage, out of focus and fuzzy. Was I seeing things? Maybe the doe was incorporeal? Maybe I'd hit my head.

The doe kept her stare locked on me. She cocked her head and I swore for a moment she studied me. Weren't deer usually more fragile than this? You know, bounding off as fast as rabbits before they saw the real danger?

Then, someone honked.

"Get off the road, ya dumb broad!" a voice screamed at me. I responded in kind, letting out a scream as I came back to the real world, my heart beating rapidly and still soaked by seedlings. I stuck my head out the window and the wind pushed my black hair into my face even as I tried to hold it back, only to groan in frustration. My car sat partly in the lane, and because it was a two-lane highway, a line of cars had already formed on both sides of the road.

They didn't get out to help or even ask if I was okay after my accident. Tourists.

The doe took off, bounding into the brush, vanishing into an invisible forest world. I wanted to run off with it as soon as I got a look at my car. Branches had raked scratches into the paint on Bessie's hood right down to the silver of the bumper. I banged my head on the steering wheel and let out a shriek of frustration, hitting it several times as horns blared.

Chapter Two

When I finally pulled up to the house the shadows were beginning to lengthen. Dad's work truck sat in the driveway, but Mom's SUV did not. They were at her appointment without me.

Great. Just great. My first test as a caregiver had failed so epically, a hollow pin pricked in my chest. I tried to swallow it down, but that only allowed it to bloom with each passing moment, threatening to overtake me if I didn't acknowledge and solve it.

Ah, guilt. My old friend.

I didn't have a garage door opener, but I did have a key. I pushed rocks away, searching for the familiar jagged red rock nestled among many in front of the house. Okay, so technically I had a way to break in. But if you knew where they kept the spare... anyway. After a few seconds I fumbled through river rocks only and a shot of panic-driven thought caused me to freeze.

What if they hadn't put it out yet? What if they were counting on me to be here and—

Before the thoughts took off, I pushed away more river rock to reveal the palm-sized simple black stone. My shoulders sagged from the release of unknown tension.

A few short steps up the deck which encircled the house on either side, the bright red front door loomed. My nana's dad built this house for 'many grandchildren to come' when Nana was pregnant with Mom. He and my grandfather had collaborated on it, fought over it, but ultimately they built it just in time for Grandpa to die and for Nana to move and never remarry.

She'd held onto the house, having it periodically cleaned and what not, but it sat empty for fifty years, slowly rotting away—I assumed. Dad offered for her to come live with us in her old home, but she claimed that it was amassed in weird energy and simply wasn't suitable for her. Like that somehow explained anything. It was always 'weird energy' with Nana.

I wrinkled my nose at the odor of fresh paint as I safely heaved Carrie into the house, leaving her in the carrier. I threw open the windows and left the door gaping open while I brought my things into the entry. I didn't dare release Carrie despite the verbal abuse I continued to take for it. I'd take the verbal abuse over the blood loss any day.

May was planting season, well, the end of it, but not for me this year. I got a good look at the toppled milk crates I had stacked so carefully with live plants and cuttings and I wanted to cry. Not only had the water sloshed out, but they had toppled over, and were lying on their sides and even upside down in places, meaning I hadn't actually secured them. I sighed into a particularly droopy bunch of celery sprouts, wishing I was able to breathe life back into them.

That's okay. I can handle this. The garden from my childhood and years at college was a complete mess and would probably die from shock. It was nothing I couldn't handle. I continued to stomp down the pain in my chest and took in damaged seedling after damaged seedling with my suitcases.

Sometimes I thought I heard them whisper, 'Don't worry!' or 'You'll save us!' But in reality, these stories I told myself were just that: stories to help me feel better. Tomorrow I would have to talk to Dad about a way to start mulching things.

After what seemed like too long, I closed the door and got my first good look at my new house. Two stories and, according to Dad, I would have three of four bedrooms upstairs to myself. The master bedroom downstairs fit perfectly for Mom; she couldn't really do stairs these days. Dad told me he even talked Nana into moving in with us. He took it upon himself to build a small suite behind the house so she could move in and not live with the 'weird energy.' Though Dad said she wanted to be closer to family, I knew a dumb cover up when I heard it.

It was younger Aspen's dream. No bratty brother and annoying sister to share the house with.

Now, as I looked up the stairs to those bedrooms, I felt lucky and a little free having the entire upstairs to myself ninety-nine percent of the time, especially since I had my own room for the first time in five years. I kicked my shoes off and closed the door behind me. The cool tile chilled my feet, even with socks on. I quickly closed up the rest of the house and let Carrie out, who I swear was Carieta N. White at prom by the way she caterwauled.

The fluffy-tailed horror skidded out and eventually stopped in her tracks. She turned to me as though to say, 'Seriously? What is this?' She lowered herself, tail bristled and ears turning for any sign of shenanigans before slinking around the corner into the living room, her belly close to the ground.

So *dramatic.*

I took my socks off and crimped my toes in the new carpet, rejoicing in the feel of my new home. How did my dad put this house back together, take care of his business and my mom with her appointments, all while keeping it from me and my siblings?

Only the sound of my breathing came as an answer to me.

I pushed open the swinging door to the kitchen. I let it go and it closed after me with barely a whisper. Hmm, Carrie wouldn't be able to open that. Good to know.

Three cups of coffee, still warm, were on the counter next to the newspaper. Three meant Nana had been here, too. With a sigh, I scanned the headlines. Boring, bad news, boring, a drowning, ugh—politics...

Okay, so today wouldn't be a good day to actually read the paper. That crap was only the first page. Instead, I flipped to the horoscope section for Aries.

> *'Don't forget that your needs matter, but others sometimes need more. Share your energy with them unconditionally.'*

Great. Way to rub it in, Universe.

My stomach grumbled way louder than Carrie's yowls, reminding me that before off-roading, I'd been hungry. I dropped the paper and instead foraged for something healthier than the candy shops that set me off before the accident. I helped myself to a no-sugar-added peanut butter and jelly sandwich on a bagel from the fridge.

Even though I chose crunchy peanut butter and cherry jelly, one of my comfort favorites, it had the consistency and taste of unflavored mochi. I read the jelly label again and blanched at 'sugar-free' and not 'natural sugar'.

I tried not to confront it, but I'd failed as a daughter and as a caretaker by not making this appointment. I was so stupid. The I-17 would have been faster with fewer animals and honking tourists.

Before I spiraled any further down that rabbit hole, the back door opened. A familiar, almost too bright head of red hair came into view. She wore jeans and a Diamondbacks T-shirt with pink sneakers. Her mouth proudly declared her fine laugh lines and I loved how they gave her the appearance of wisdom and life well lived.

"Aspen!" Nana cooed at me as though I hadn't seen her last week. We were at the old house when I dropped off some of my things, thinking I would be moving back there for the summer.

"Aspen, Aspen, Aspen!" She grabbed me from behind and held me tight, her perfect French manicure tapping against my chest as she shook me back and forth in a slight wave. "Did you see the stars knew you had a duty today? Tried to tell Flo you'd be running late. He's never wrong."

Flo was my mom and 'he' was Nana's psychic. He had a history of giving exceptionally vague predictions that might be true of any situation, anytime, anywhere. Like I said, the *appearance* of wisdom.

I grinned and grabbed her hands, giving them a squeeze. "He also said I was going to get into graduate school."

She tsked and let me go and I continued with my tasteless sandwich. "You're going to apply again next year, aren't you?"

I mumbled an affirmative, making sure to stuff my mouth with the last bite of PBJ.

"Then there's still a chance, dear, a chance. And since he said it would happen, I guess it's going to."

Yeah, and there was also a chance that I'd thrown five years into a biology degree only to end up working at another coffee shop.

Or worse.

Instead of following up or hanging around, Nana squeezed my hands and jogged over to her purse hanging on the wall.

"I stayed to have a look at the work Bob's done, but I have got to get back before lunch today. I was late yesterday and only managed because I have my mini fridge hidden under my TV."

She sighed dramatically, and I desperately tried to keep my grin hidden. She wasn't fooling anyone in her assisted living home. She'd been staying there to recover after falling and breaking her leg and hip at Christmas and the rules were stricter than she liked. She was looking forward to moving somewhere new, I supposed.

"I wanted to stay because I figured you wouldn't be long after Flo. Little longer than I thought, but not long at all. Don't go into the building out back yet, nails everywhere, everywhere. Enjoy the backyard, dear!"

An odd thing to say, but Nana was an odd woman. I glimpsed a taxi in the front. She probably thought I forgot and called for it. My heart twisted, but she'd said it herself, she wanted to be here for lunch. Soon, here would be her home. While Nana is a bit weird herself, she's also awesome.

I glanced at the folded $100 bill she'd tucked in my hand. Really, really awesome.

I cleared my dishes and wiped down the counters while Carrie played with bugs through the front windows, making little meeping sounds at them. My lips turned up. I didn't like how this had happened, but I would try to be okay with the what.

Shrugging, I grabbed my two suitcases and dragged them up the stairs which creaked under the heavy weight. Otherwise, everything seemed relatively modern.

Up the stairs I paused and laughed. The loft between the two sides of the house was haphazardly stacked full of furniture from my old room. It opened up on each side to two bedrooms and a bathroom. I peeked into the closest one and had to nod appreciatively, then the next. To my surprise, each bedroom seemed big enough to hold two twin beds and some extra furniture. I knew I'd have a lot of room, but this wasn't what I expected from Dad's description.

I guess Nana and Grandpa really had planned to have a big family.

The bedrooms were each connected by a Jack-and-Jill bathroom between them. The new plumbing fixtures sparkled, and the counters were a nice off-white that wouldn't easily stain.

I glimpsed myself in the mirror and squeaked, dropping a suitcase on my foot in shock. I swore more viciously than normal and hopped on one foot into the bathroom, tangling my fingers in the knots of my hair. I think I growled. That's what I get for rolling down the window and not tying back my hair. Additionally, there were bags under my bloodshot grey eyes—lack of sleep for two days will do that—and I looked paler than usual, probably from the run-in with the deer. Nana had said nothing about my appearance running along the lines of 'stuck my finger in a socket'.

What a great nana.

I staked my claim and unloaded the case into the room on the right. I pushed my bed into my room and set it up across from the window before also grunting and groaning and pushing my reliable wooden dresser, bedside table, and lamp into the room.

"Aspen?"

I threw the comforter down and yelled back. "Upstairs, Mom!"

"What happened to the car?"

I groaned and wound my way past Carrie. I really hoped they wouldn't notice that. I ran through a bunch of scenarios in my head as I went downstairs and followed the voices to where the garage opened into the kitchen.

Dad entered, closing the door behind him as he haphazardly carried a box into the house.

"Cool, what did you get?" I asked as Dad set it down and Mom hugged me. I kissed Dad's cheek and looked at the front of the box. "Something... oh." My breath left me in a *whoosh* and my throat dried up. The box showed a bright red walker and a woman with grey hair and even greyer clothes smiling as she used it. "It's, um, that bad?"

I couldn't tear myself away from the image of the walker and the too-cheerful woman, at least thirty years older than Mom. It wasn't time for this yet. Right?

"Not yet," Mom said with a chipper voice as she kicked off her shoes. "But the doctor warned us we should be prepared. It's not always a steady decline like you would think." She paused and when I didn't answer, changed the subject. "How was graduation, dear?"

I winced. Rather than getting my name called and a stupid card handed to me with a handshake, I had been in a ditch while volunteers pushed my car to safety.

"How's the car?" Dad deadpanned and I winced again. Too embarrassed to tell him I'd avoided a deer right into a small tree, I wracked my brain for a plausible excuse, anything before remembering something and mumbled, "Marc took it off roading a-a couple of weekends ago?" Not a lie.

"What? The boy scratched your paint like that, broke the headlight, and then broke up with you a week later? Cheezus," he muttered his favorite not-a-swear-I-swear. Then a pause. "What a dick."

I snorted at his quick snap. Throwing Marc under the bus felt like the best way to hide my heartbreak and incompetence, even if it made Dad break his no-swearing rule.

"I guess you can get it fixed after you get a job," Dad said as he wandered off into the kitchen.

My face must have betrayed my confusion because Mom followed him and motioned for me to come. I did, because I don't mind working. I worked at the coffee shop on campus for five years, but I thought I'd have the year off, aside from helping Mom, of course.

Time to think, to grow, to—

"You want me to work at the bakery." I realized immediately.

Both of my parents avoided looking at me directly.

Morning Sun Bakery wasn't ours or anything, but we considered it 'in the family.' David and Rachelle, the owners, both worked for Dad before they started the bakery about ten years ago. It had been a smash and after the initial bitter feelings were over and done with, even Dad thought so.

For me it means I would be on my feet for shifts that lasted up to twelve hours. Staffing a cash register, taking orders, assisting David with baking and Rachelle with cooking. Cleaning, listening to the customers scream even when doing everything right... I'm not against hard work, and I'm used to long days. Compared to the bakery, the coffee shop had been a cakewalk. People were too busy to talk or be mad or do more but grumble and leave. People here, in this tourist trap of a town, did not grab n' go. They stayed. They dug their heels in. They hated everything and wanted it all free, yesterday, free, and did I mention free?

"No."

Mom grabbed my hands. I tried to avoid looking at her directly, knowing she had mastered the guilt look years ago.

"David would let you off whenever you needed it. Even minimum wage would help with the gas bill."

Minimum wage.

"No."

"But—"

"I'm not saying I won't work. I'll find a job." They exchanged looks and before Mom laid on the guilt trip, I plowed forward. "I've got a degree now. I can get a real job. Something at an office or... something." I finished with a wave of my hand. As though that would end the conversation in my favor by magically procuring a job. A BS in Biology would do nothing in a tourist town.

Dad took the lead after a beat. "Two weeks. You have two weeks to get settled in and find a job." He and Mom exchanged another glance, and he sighed. "Or at least some leads."

I twisted my shirt in my fingers, the fabric reminding me that I was here, in the moment now. I held myself steady. "Two weeks," I agreed.

Dad's phone buzzed, thank God, and he grabbed it and clipped into his business line. "This is Bob."

Mom smiled at me and took my hand as he wandered off to speak to whoever had the emergency. "Always something," she tittered. "Come on."

Mom had only lived in the house for two years before her dad died and Nana moved to a small apartment to raise her daughter. Because The Cards told her to, probably. She led me to the back porch, a soft smile on her face the whole way.

Nana's suite sat about fifty feet behind the wraparound back porch. It seemed to be ninety percent complete if the outside was to be believed. In between emerald-green grass, something I wasn't used to seeing after rocks and bigger rocks in Phoenix, flourished in clover. No fence in any direction, just a tree line with an excellent area for relaxation and...

"Whoa," I gasped as she led me beyond the suite.

Chapter Three

The trees, fruit trees now that I got a good look, were part of the large, overrun garden. The chaos of fifty years of overgrowth was somehow contained in the back half of the yard. Or my dad had done some major work he wasn't going to tell me about.

Probably the second one.

There were three sheds, two of them dilapidated, and one that seemed comparatively untouched by the elements. Wooden raised flower beds arranged in a four-by-four pattern took up the most space, though it was easy to see why I hadn't been able to tell they were there until I got closer. Alyssum. Sweet alyssum covered every bed like a carpet, spilling and entwining together. I expected to see one or two colors, but I saw buds of pink, purple, white and every shade between.

"My daddy planted it," Mom said with a smile, touching one of the delicate white blooms. "I know it's basically a weed, but it's not like he would have known that. And they're—"

"Nana's favorite flower." I grinned as I checked the topsoil of the nearest bed. It needed to be updated. Otherwise, it didn't seem like the last fifty years of abandonment had done much besides cause the beds themselves to fall into disrepair. It would be easy to get some wood with Dad one day, some nails, potting soil...

I must have been lost in my world for longer than I thought because the next thing I knew, Mom's voice broke through my head.

"—we're going to have more problems with the trees, but they're salvageable."

My mouth dropped as I followed her gaze. I had realized they were fruit trees, yes, but if anything I figured they were all apples, not the dozen species that I saw before me. I started grabbing at branches to study the leaves.

"There are two each of about ten types of fruit." She rattled off a few that she seemed certain of, which didn't surprise me. Mom loved to garden. I was the one who dialed it up to eleven.

"Any cherries?" I asked.

She jerked her head and started walking in the same direction. I followed, taking in the mature, sturdy trees around us. Some were grown in strange ways. A particularly gnarly apple tree with low branches was the worst I could see. From the looks of things, they would all give perfectly good fruit with some care and pruning.

Mom put her hand on the closest tree and I smiled. Her favorite, and also mine. If I did anything with my degree, it would be to grow the perfect pit-less cherry. Perfection on a stem.

My phone chimed. Well, to be precise, a monster groaned and screamed. I grabbed my phone from my back pocket and swiped the screen.

"You haven't changed it from that yet?" Mom shook her head, giggling.

> *r u home yet???*

I didn't have to hear my best friend Isa aloud in order to hear her accusatory tone. After all, I had told her I would be home by now.

Another groan and scream.

vallejo or bust

I typed my reply and put the phone away. "Sorry, that's—"

"Yeah, yeah. Isa."

I hesitated, feeling the pull of my bestie but also the want to make up for being such a bad daughter. Mom, being Mom, seemed to sense my hesitation and cocked her head to the side with a questioning smile on her face.

"Should I—I mean, can I...?"

Her puzzled smile turned into a chuckle. "Of course!"

I kissed her cheek and started back toward the house. Before getting too far, I turned to the overgrown alyssum, the orchard of trees, and back to Nana's so-called suite. It would be a lot of work. I might not even get enough done to plant anything by the end of the month, but I would do my best.

"This is all ours?" I asked, scarcely believing I had so much to work with.

"My daddy hoped he and Mama would grow their own food, maybe even raise chickens and goats to help with that, too. I was supposed to have a lot of siblings." Her smile turned wistful for the life Grandpa always promised Nana. The life that included her, this house, and this garden.

Before too much sadness settled over the garden, I jogged back to the house, leaving Mom with her memories and me with a feeling of guilt in my stomach for putting a friend before my family.

I rolled up to Joanna's Valle, or 'ValleJo's' as some of us called it, less than fifteen minutes after Isa texted me. Isa's mom and Jo were good friends, which meant we got free tacos and soda any time we showed up. We always ordered something else on top of it, like fried ice cream.

Never take advantage of someone's kindness. Free food any time you wanted was a kindness you did not abuse.

Sure enough, after I pushed in the well-worn dark wood door, the scent of onions, cheese, and simmering pork smashed into me like a cat skidding into a wall. I loved it. An after-lunch lull had settled so the room was about half full and the volume mirrored that. Quickly adjusting to the light, I scanned the area for a familiar face.

I made a beeline for the table nearest the kitchen door. I approached quietly just making out a head of dark brown hair that fell way too far down her back.

"You're not stealthy at all," Isa scoffed just as I raised my hands in hopes of covering her eyes from behind. I deflated and dropped into the chair across from her, shoving my purse on the chair next to hers.

"I don't know how you know it's me. It could have been literally anyone." I made a face at her, like the adult I totally am.

She smirked back at me. "That's my secret."

I studied her for a moment. Unlike me, who only had a farmers tan, Isa had skin the color of an Arizona dust storm. Her brown eyes were so dark sometimes I swore they were black when she got mad. Or red, depending on the time of the month and social issue at hand.

"Did you order?" I finally asked, not wanting to pry into her supposed secret. "Ugh, I would kill for a good quesadilla today." I almost drooled while opening the menu.

Isa kept that smirk going. "Well, nice to know, but let's give Jo some money."

I gave her a look over my menu.

"What? You said you'd kill for something. I'm merely suggesting an option with less jail time. You can still kill. Just make sure it's the right person."

I snorted a laugh. "Who should I track down this time?"

She stared past me, averting her dark gaze. "Mom was crying again." She sighed and stabbed at the table with her fork. "She always cries around my birthday."

I didn't know the entire story of why Jaime, Isa's mom, left Isa's dad, and neither did she. To this day even through her tears, she claims she did 'the right thing.' I guess I was allowed to want to punch her dad for that, at least.

"Ah, well," Isa said. "How was the drive up? What did your mom's doctor say?"

The guilt stabbed at me again and I suddenly realized why it existed. "I didn't go with them." I fought the urge to bite my tongue. "And then I didn't ask how it went after they brought in a walker."

Isa blew out her hair and tried to hide her worry with a smile. "Okay. Take it from the top," my younger than me, yet older than me friend instructed. "Leave nothing out."

I blurted out all of my screw-ups. The doe, lying, missing the appointment, and getting so absorbed in the garden that I forgot to ask questions.

Isa sighed. "Well, that's a shitty morning. I'm sorry I distracted you."

I rested my cheek in my hand, elbow on the table in such a way that moms everywhere would scold me. "Would not recommend. Don't worry about it. Something tells me the next thing I would have done was sit myself down in the garden and plan. I would have forgotten anyway."

Because I'm a horrible person.

I shook off that thought and replaced it, reframed it.

Because everyone makes mistakes.

I didn't believe it, but I believed something that a therapist told me before: Your thoughts sometimes lie to you.

"Sure," she said. "Are you okay? This is a lot on you, not that you can't handle it." She quickly backpedaled as I faced her. "You got a degree, for shit's sake! You didn't even think you'd graduate high school because you were in the hospital so much."

My mom, smiling, laughing, and sometimes lying in bed for the day because of the pain. I saw all of it in my mind and yet I knew I'd be seeing the last one in person much more. Would she still smile? Would she—

Isa tapped my hand. "Hey." I swallowed and met her eyes, my heart in my throat and tears at the ready. "You got this. Okay? I'll help, you know that."

Rapidly blinking back tears I had to remind myself: No crying, not in public. "Yeah. Hey, come on, let's figure out what we're getting."

An hour and too much food later, Isa and I left the restaurant and veered north and started our post Vallejo tradition: walking off Vallejo's.

I rubbed my stomach and groaned. I hadn't killed anyone for a quesadilla. Or the two tacos, either.

We started talking about this and that, her school, my old roommates. Then the topic that was bound to come up. "How's Marc?"

I lapsed into silence and sighed. I had no details. I felt pathetic. So what if I had always known he would go back to Belize someday? I guess in my mind I also thought I'd go with him.

"No!" Isa gasped, reading my silence well enough. She knew Marc. They followed each other's socials, but she must not have seen the news with her finals being this week, too. "He broke up with you? The asshole!"

I wiped away the tears that formed this time. There wasn't time before I left to really feel the pain, and my therapist told me it would be a process like losing anything or anyone else.

"I don't know why we couldn't have at least tried a long-distance relationship first," I said in a quick, angry burst.

Isa scoffed. "Is that what it was about? It's not the end of the world if someone moves, and who knows, Belize would probably have been perfect for a biology degree. I mean, not as useful as archeology, but it's useful. What a dumbass, not even wanting to consider it."

I had laid the foundation, and so I built on it. "He said that when he went home, he'd go back to his village. He claims they barely have regular mail delivery. They definitely don't have reliable internet. He said it would be 'impossible,'"—I held my hands up in quotes—"to have a relationship with no communication."

"What? He's got to be lying! How can you not have access to mail?"

We kept gabbing, taking those jabs at my ex-boyfriend that attempted to make me feel a little better, but in reality did nothing. My heart hurt as we kept talking, my thoughts ruminating. Had he known all along that this wouldn't be forever, and I had simply been naive?

"Come on," I said, changing the subject. "I want to get some custard."

"I don't think my girlish figure can take it," Isa said with a fake haughty voice.

Laughing, we hooked arms and changed directions. Instead of heading back to our cars, we were now going further downtown. It wasn't exactly a big downtown, but a lot of great restaurants were scattered through it, including a homemade custard shop. There were also several shops set up selling handmade items from jewelry to wallets. Most were locally owned, often by Natives or other generational shops. We passed by the chic shops and the palm readers, the homemade candies and chocolates, barely keeping track as our internal compasses took us on our way.

Isa made a disgruntled noise and shook her head.

"What?" I asked, turning around. I saw we were coming up on the edge of the path and would have to cross. "Oh."

"It's been like that for forever," she complained as we came upon the run-down end of the path. "I mean, why does no one do anything with it?"

They built downtown in the late 1800s in the same old style that you would normally find from that era: wood store fronts, large, open glass windows of the shops with some old-fashioned streetlamps thrown in for color. Though unlike Sedona, our founders chose stones instead of a wooden almost-boardwalk appearance. The downtown area was connected with these stone paths which eventually culminated in the city center and town square.

Well, except for this one small building. Someone had stuck a small, yellow shack at the end of the rows of wood and glass and put signs on it that read 'KEEP OUT' and 'PRIVATE PROPERTY'. According to Nana it had been there for over fifty years, never changing. Most people paid no attention after so many years, often passing by like it wasn't even there. It had never functioned as a proper building. Heck, it was one story when most of the others nearby were two.

We crossed the street when the light changed and instead started talking about what flavor custard we were going to get, and how many toppings.

That didn't stop me from glancing back when something moved out of the corner of my eye. For a moment the unmoving door to the shack was cracked open an inch or two before blinking closed again.

Chapter Four

I didn't want to get up.

The first night in a new place is always hell, but the bed felt familiar. Falling in it had been like meeting an old friend. Comfortable, warm, and dependable. With Carrie pressed to my side at night, contentment settled over me... once I got to sleep.

If I left this toasty bed, it would mean the day would start. If the day started, that would mean I had to look for work. That also meant yesterday actually happened.

Carrie purred against my back, seemingly as content as me. The cooler air bit my cheek, and the scent of morning hit me: dew and faint, sweet flowers. I inhaled deeply and knew that the war was already over. I pushed my covers off and stretched, shrugging off the night's kinks and stiffness.

This is where you might hate me.

I'm a morning person.

Don't get me wrong, I don't like every morning. Yesterday, for example, sucked. Until today, I'd always been in school, worked, or both. I had a laundry list of things to do most mornings. Days off happened, but even they were usually filled with schoolwork. That wasn't the case today, at least.

I grabbed my phone and checked the time and sure enough 5:30 flashed back at me.

Carrie made a noise somewhere between a squeak and a squawk as I pulled away from her and I gave her neck scritches in response. "That's a good girl," I cooed. "You stay here where it's warm." I pulled the blanket over her, and she snuggled in and started purring again as I gave her one more scratch before getting dressed.

I have a morning routine. People with bipolar disorder do better when they have routines to follow. That's probably the other reason my parents wanted me to get a job: it would be a routine so I wouldn't fall into a depression, or worse, a manic spending spree.

I sat on the edge of my bed and did my normal morning 'brain dump,' a practice that took about five or ten minutes for me to get started for the day. I won't bore you with the full page, but guilt seemed to be the prevailing theme. Then I made a schedule of what I wanted to do for the day. It wasn't much of a list today, but it would keep me busy most of the day with two tasks: gardening and job hunting. One of those I looked forward to and the other not so much.

When I got downstairs, the coffee pot was on, but less than half full. Dad had already been up. I studied the scattered newspaper while I waited for my milk to heat for the matcha and decided to go for my horoscope again. Two gut punches were unlikely, and it was usually some fun. After a moment of scanning, I came down to Aries and almost threw the paper in the garbage disposal.

'Some energy will be needed today. After rain there is a rainbow. When times have been less than ideal, there are signs but only if you can find them. Keep your eyes open.'

I crumpled the astrology section and tossed it into the recycling. Feeling better, I checked for a hint of movement from Mom and Dad's bedroom. I heard nothing as I stirred in my matcha powder, taking a delightfully earthy sip before going to peek in on Mom.

Padding to the door, I pushed it open slightly more. A sliver of light gleamed past the blackout curtains, scaring away enough of the dark that I saw her outline in bed. The thought that she wasn't breathing or moving at all hit me. With a taste of panic on my tongue, I about ran in to check on her, when she rolled over and started snoring.

Weird. That was just weird. She's okay, and you're okay. Take a deep breath yourself, Aspen.

I did as I told myself, took another look, and then went back to the kitchen and finished preparing my breakfast.

My matcha steamed through the lip of my sparkly purple travel mug, but my old muck boots made sticky sloshy noises as I trekked from the house to the garden. I listened as I passed Nana's suite, but I heard nothing except the chirping of the morning songbirds. Dad said he might have a meeting over dinner last night. I tried the door, but silence answered my calls.

Shrugging, I creaked my neck and loosened my shoulders before performing a mental checklist for a warming day of gardening. I wore a pair of faded jeans with a bright patch on the knees. I pulled my hoodie on over my t-shirt and put my hair up in a quick ponytail with a handkerchief at the ready. I managed to unearth my best gardening gloves from my bags and stuck them in my back pocket, along with a stolen pink cap from Mom. The mud-splattered boots rounded out the outfit, and I was prepared to do some seriously hard, but absolutely awesome work.

I inhaled the scent of morning so fresh and alive that the grass seemed cheerful. Birds soared above me. The quiet that I never had in all my years at university washed over me. Any bitterness I was holding onto about my parents selling our old home vanished. We use to live within the town limits before. We didn't see things like the family of quail that darted across my vision to the right in tandem with the chipmunks further up on the left.

The sunrise had long ago chased all color but blue out of the sky. I would have to wake up early tomorrow to catch it over the mountains and the forest that lined our property from all sides.

Upon closer inspection of the three sheds, the one with the least damage was actually a small greenhouse. It could use new shelves and needed a good scrub down, but it was doable. Much better than one of the actual sheds because I think a family of possums or raccoons had made it their breeding grounds.

I considered torching it rather than touching it.

Then I came upon the overgrown, broken, rotted beds, and reality crashed in like my car yesterday. The amount of work exceeded my expectations.

I assigned each bed a letter and each structure a number. There were columns in four random spots. They were different heights, but all low enough to put pots on them and easily tend the plants. I assigned those roman numerals. There was only one bench, and it needed to be scrubbed, too. I made notes of the things that I needed to do, such as which wood parts needed repair in bed A, while also checking the soil for bugs.

After about forty minutes of list making, my hand cramped up. My brain was swimming with enough information to make the average grad student throw their hands up in frustration. While I flexed my cramping fingers to rid them of the tension, I took a seat on the bench to survey the quiet morning.

The earth beneath my feet felt soft and moist from the morning dew. I shifted uncomfortably, realizing the bench was wet, too. I tightened my ponytail and stood up, patting my wet butt and glaring at the bench. Part of me wanted to kick it for making my ass so cold, but before I became violent, I caught movement from the corner of my vision.

It was too big to be another bird or squirrel. Had Mom had woken up? As I faced the trees, I gasped.

The doe from yesterday, the silver one in all her pristine, shimmery glory, was on the outskirts of the trees looking lost. If it weren't for her ethereal glow, she would be just visible instead of very Day-Glo.

I didn't want to startle her, but I sure as shit wanted proof of her existence. Holding my breath, I slowly reached for my phone. Just as I got my camera app open she turned and faced me. Neither of us moved and I fought to keep a stupid grin off my face. How often does something like this happen? I fumbled my phone and dropped it in the dirt. I cursed but didn't move to grab it.

The doe cocked her head. Sighing in relief, I slowly reached for the phone, never taking my own stare off of her. But I was too late and the doe galloped away... *above the trees and into the sky*. She stared at me and inclined her neck several times to the south, toward the road.

"Okay, okay," I said to myself, like any sane person would. "Calm down, Aspen. Take a breather. It's not real." I repeated the phrase several times, closing my eyes and rubbing them to get the image away. When I opened them, it was still there.

I slammed my eyelids back down, heart pounding as I tried soothing myself. "It's not going to hurt you. It's not real!"

The doe stubbornly remained. I wanted to say she was insulted, but somehow that would be even weirder.

I was pretty sure now that I needed to call my psychiatrist. I'll be honest, the few hallucinations I'd had were scary and dark. This feeling in my chest and stomach wasn't exactly the opposite, but it was a far cry from the terror and nausea I usually felt.

She galloped toward my house and back a few times and I had the brilliant, if also obvious, idea: *Maybe she's trying to tell you something, dummy.*

I took a step forward. And another.

She seemed to nod in agreement as she, in the sky, thundered down the driveway and out to the road that connected my home to the world and then back to me. She came so close that I threw my hands up before she ran back, repeating the elegant movement again.

I looked from my house to the road, wondering why I would need to go anywhere. I gulped down my fear and focused on the doe, my stomach twisted in so many knots. She enthusiastically, almost to the point of recklessness, ran up and back down the driveway again and again until I got the point.

"You're a hallucination, and I will not drive while I'm hallucinating," I told it. The doe paused, as if it understood me. "Go away, I don't want to see you," I told her. She ran up and down, but I stood firm, not even realizing how ridiculous I must have seemed, arguing at the air.

Finally, those red marbles met mine and I jumped back at the understanding, the intelligence and years that beheld her. She once again ran up the driveway, but this time she didn't stop and turn around. This time she kept running and veered off to the side of the house. She came running up on me and landed back on the ground. I flung my hands up to protect myself from the image.

Something fuzzy, soft, and warm brushed against my hands. Then a gentle lick. I forced myself to look up, half expecting to find a dog in front of me this whole time. The doe, however, insisted on existing, her stare intensely boring into me.

I cupped her chin as she pushed her muzzle into my palm. Holy shit, the doe was real, and she could *fly*.

She took off again, taking to the sky within seconds, and I ran into the house and grabbed my keys from the side table. My mind went blank as I tried to think what this meant. The door closed behind me and I ran to my car where the doe continued to ever so patiently wait for me.

Why me?

The 89A was a spiraling nightmare that made drivers tense and gave each other plenty of berth in case one of you went flying off into one of the tree-filled ravines on either side of the road. I hoped to avoid such a fate, but I felt the doe's impatience even in my car. She would run ahead of me, come back and go off again, as though my mere twenty-five miles per hour was insulting.

I followed her into town, keeping a look out for other animals and making sure she didn't take any weird turns.

Now, looking back, should I have followed the magical flying doe to her destination? I mean, probably not. Wouldn't you? I guess I could have run screaming into the house. This was magic, real magic, that I touched. Who wouldn't be curious?

I had so many questions. Questions I wouldn't know the answers to if I didn't follow her.

Most of the businesses in downtown Cora Alma were still closed with the occasional psychic or palm reader open. Though, all the restaurants and cafes were bursting with customers. Luckily, we weren't in peak travel season, so I was able to grab a parking spot (which the doe led me to).

She didn't make a sound when she landed on the stone sidewalk, taking a few steps forward as I held back. I had driven out here, but some part of my brain screamed at me that something was wrong. Something *had* to be wrong with me.

Jerking her head a few times, the doe pushed further into the middle of downtown. She lurched and passed through two people instead of beside them before continuing on. The people kept walking and talking. They apparently hadn't felt or seen the doe; they didn't pay me so much as a glance when they passed by. It was as though she wasn't there and hadn't just walked through them. But she had been so real to me back at the house.

We were almost halfway through downtown, but as she kept leading me further, my excitement grew. Was there something hidden? Something marvelous and wonderful? We kept pushing, until the two storied buildings stopped and the doe came to the legendary yellow shack.

She jerked her head to the door three times and then ran straight through it.

I blinked in astonishment and studied the door more than I had the night before. There were markings all over it, almost like graffiti, but they were painted on it a different transparent sparkly tan color than the red door.

The door handle itself was actually elegantly carved with similar characters, and I ran my fingers over the engraved markings. They flashed and then faded, warmth flowing over my hand. The handle turned of its own accord and I gasped softly as the door opened.

Chapter Five

M y day had been weird enough already—and it was way before noon. This was another moment where I probably could have—and should have—jumped ship.

But I didn't.

My dumb ass walked right through the door.

I cautiously stuck my head in, almost as though I expected there to be something odd about the room that a magical, mystical doe had run into. I know, not trusting at all.

The room was brightly lit and spacious, bigger than I had expected from the outside. Instead of a tiny, dark room filled with every horror imaginable, fluorescent lights buzzed softly overhead, illuminating a mediocre waiting room. Someone's back was to me as they worked at a desk stacked high with papers, folders, and magazines.

Their blue hair was shaved on one side and chin length on the other. I hesitated looking around before noting a nameplate right in front of me.

'Charlie.'

"Close the door already! What if some normie sees?" He snapped at me without turning around.

I jumped inside the building, not expecting him to have noticed me behind the stacks and with his back to me. I then let the door close behind me, sealing my fate with a soft 'click'.

A handful of squishy chairs surrounded a chipped and worn table strewn with more magazines. A watercooler and small stand with hot chocolate and coffee lined the opposite wall along with a box of cookies. There were two doors, one with a bathroom symbol on it, and the other said "Office" in crooked letters.

Biting my lip I glanced around, wondering where the doe had gone to.

Wait a second, how the hell did this place have power?

"Um, excuse me, sir?" I must not have been loud enough, so I cleared my throat and tried again. "Sir? Um, Mr. Charlie Person?" I winced at my childishness.

This time, I got his attention and wished I could shrink and die on the spot.

Her green eyes met mine, and for a moment, I considered bailing. They were brilliant, almost sparkling, but also lit with a fire that I'm surprised wasn't laser vision to burn me where I stood.

Yikes.

"'Mr. Charlie?'" she scoffed, her voice falsely high. "'Miss' would have worked fine." Her voice raised with each word and I shrunk back as her stare penetrated me, as though she could read my soul and everything laid witness there only existed in offense to her.

The non-bathroom door banged open and a woman—definitely a woman—about my mom's age, hurried out, her beautiful heart-shaped face full of worry. She was tall, easily towering over my 5'5", with hair so black it would have made Snow White jealous. I was envious, not jealous. She glided over to the assistant, her purple pants suit moving just as gracefully as she did against her sandy skin.

"Charlie? Charlie dear, why are you yelling?" she asked, her honeyed voice soothing even to me. She put a motherly arm around Charlie, cooing things.

Charlie fumed and pointed at me. The newcomer cocked her head to me and I felt the need to explain myself.

"I—I asked her—"

"She called me a guy!"

I winced and opened my mouth to apologize, but before I could the woman's gaze swept over me. Curious, but without judgment. "It's okay, she's just being dramatic. It's her thing." She swatted Charlie on the shoulder and then side-hugged her with a shake of her head.

Charlie tried to hide her smile and avoided both of our gazes, her green eyes on fire again, this time with mischief.

"I'll try better next time, Charlie." I continued to study her and wondered if she lived in Cora Alma. I think I would remember someone so color coordinated. Her hair was indeed shaved on one side and long on the other, covering her right eye. She wore little makeup, and her face appeared rather androgynous, with sharp angles and a pointed chin. Her colorful attire started with a jean jacket featuring patches from various social causes. It was over a yellow, baggy button-down shirt and a pair of baggy yet stylish black pants. I said colorful, and I meant it. Her boots were bedazzled in a rainbow. Her painted nails were an ocean blue that went well with her hair color.

Charlie let go of the woman and sat at her desk. She nodded to me and dramatically sniffed, clearly a sign that she was still upset, or dramatic, but I would be allowed to proceed.

If only I knew what to say.

"Can I help you?" the woman said, her tone still the soothing one that slid down my back and calmed me. Her voice did not match her face, which turned sharp and scrutinizing. "You seem lost, dear."

I hardly registering her words and pointed to the lights. "This place looks dark from outside."

"A simple bit of magic," she said with a wave of her hand.

Sure. I furrowed my brow and touched the door she came out of, trying to peer inside, or maybe outside? I didn't get far because the woman shut the door with a strained smile.

"Can I help you?" she repeated. This time without the honey.

"Um, the thing is, something weird led me here before running through the... That must sound so stupid."

The woman's face went from mildly curious to fascinated.

"I'm sorry. I've wasted your time."

Stupid. Who's going to believe this? Absolutely—

"Nonsense!" Her voice boomed a little and she swept to my side, linking her arm with mine. "All those who need Goddesses, Inc. can find us. But of course, *only* when they need us."

She said 'ink' instead of 'incorporated'. It sounded like they were trying to be 'hip' or 'in' with the kids.

I shifted my gaze back to Charlie, who ignored us by playing a game on her phone, and then at the woman, who had a soft, but expectant smile on her face.

Riiiight.

Now sure that some weird-ass TikToker was doing a reel, I cleared my throat. "Goddesses... Ink?" I looked around for equipment, business licenses, or even a magazine title that would hint at what this place did. I mean, it was supposed to be empty.

She spun us around and we were now heading toward the door, which changed when she threw it open. It definitely didn't lead outside. Somehow, there were more desks back there. "Goddesses, Incorporated of Cora Alma manages all the malignant maladies that plague humans in the American

Southwest, Mexico, and sometimes the Pacific coast when Portland is busy. Tell me, why have you sought us today? You have an air of magic about you, so of course you found us, no questions there. Come, we will discuss the details of your case."

My head swam with her words. Plague humans? Magic? Case? "I don't have a case." With some force, I untangled myself from her grip. She furrowed her brow and cast a glance at Charlie, who looked up from her phone long enough to shrug. "I think I'm going to go. This was a mistake. I don't know how I got here."

"Hey, Yurd!" Another woman, a little older than me appeared in the doorway, a thick manila file in her hand. If the first woman was considered beautiful, this woman would be found in the dictionary under stunning. Her thick curly black-brown hair, laced with ribbons, came past her shoulders. Her heavy eyelids held sparkling brown eyes awash in golden flecks, and she smiled at me. The single imperfection on her terra cotta skin sat in perfect position for a beauty mark. Her frilly Lolita-style orchid pink, gold, and black dress fell perfectly below her knees with matching bows and shoes.

The newcomer saw me for the first time and did a double take. "I thought I sensed unfamiliar magic, but I didn't think we had any appointments until this afternoon." She walked forward and stuck her hand out. "I'm Sif, it's a pleasure."

Something in me shouted they were talking nonsense and I should leave. No such thing as magic and all that. My curiosity took over.

"What is this, a coven or something?" There we go. The logical part of me grasped onto magic and tried to make it make sense.

The newcomer and older woman exchanged looks, but before either answered, someone else came out of the back-room clown car.

"Yurd? Sif?" Yurd must be a name, too. "What's going on?" The third one walked in, her auburn hair in a messy bun atop her head and her posture a little less sure. She was definitely rocking the goth look in all black, professional clothing. Her pale face was a perfect contrast to her scarlet stained lips. "Oh. Can we help you?"

"She asked if we are a coven," Yurd, I guess, said.

"A witch, huh?" Sif cocked her head and studied me again without the expected judgment that would come with that type of declaration. She shook her head. "No, you're not."

"I never claimed to be. What is this place?"

"I already explained it," Yurd said gently, her face now un-sure as she bit her lower lip and examined me.

"But what you said makes no sense." I took a step back, slowly easing myself toward the door. I hadn't seen things like that in almost two years, not since my last hospitaliza-tion. Now my hallucinations led to me being alone with some weirdos who were talking about magic. Great.

"You're the one who found us," Charlie announced from her seat. She had exchanged her phone for a bag of—popcorn? I knew right then that I wanted to get along with Charlie, if for no other reason than to not be the butt of jokes.

Everyone looked from me to the newcomer, who pushed her glasses up. "The spell says that only those who need us can open that door. Or those who are like us."

I felt a hard surface against my back and turned to fling the door open, only to splay my hand against the white wall.

The door was gone.

"Bring the door back!" I demanded, clamping down on my anxiety, because now was not the time. "You tricked me by showing me a-a hologram or something. I don't know how you did this but let me out!" I demanded. The wall felt solid where I touched it, banged on it, holding steady beneath my panic.

The newest goth woman, younger than the others, approached me and reached out. I tried to back away and sink into the wall as fear overtook me. Whoever these people were, they might be dangerous. I didn't know what they wanted. I had to—

Her warm hands, wrapped in typing gloves that only showed the tips of her fingers, clasped mine gently. The fear trickled away, traveling down my back and into my arms, where it pooled in my hands, as though it were being sucked out through my fingertips.

"Shhhh," she whispered. "It's okay. Now, come on in and tell us why you're here."

My mind suddenly became clear and the anxiety was back in its cage. My curiosity burned as I followed her and the other two into the back room.

Charlie waved at me as she vanished with the door. And then the room exploded into the cosmos.

Chapter Six

I gasped as I tried to take in the vastness of the stars burning in an unending sky. Swirling galaxies surrounded me with bright suns that beat life into other worlds. Wind whipped my shirt and hair, almost bringing me to the ground. The women stood before me, an unearthly glow upon them. The middle one, the one called Sif, now had a sword at her side. Her cutesy skirt transformed into old-style leather with leather bracers and a leather chest plate. Her windswept curls made her look more awe-inspiring.

The woman who zapped my anxiety wore matching armor to Sif's, but darker, almost black, with silver accents swirling and crisscrossing in runic patterns. Her weapons, two silver daggers—wait, maybe four daggers?—were strapped to her sides, her right shin, and her left upper arm. Her circlet held her braided red hair, with a rune carved in the front.

Yurd wore leather armor as well, carrying a staff instead of a sword. Her simple tawny outfit hugged her curves and gave the appearance of a down to earth robe. Her eyes, which laughed and sparkled earlier, were no longer so welcoming. Instead, they were flat, calculating, and wise. Her hair was up in a ponytail, ready for action.

I tore my gaze from them and took in the sky again. There were so many colors. Colors I'd only ever seen in oil paintings streaked across the galaxy, painting my reality too vividly. My senses were overloaded from the too real, but otherworldly, visions in front of me. I looked down at my feet and gasped, the sound echoing in the chamber, or wherever I was. Instead of stone or carpet under my feet, I felt wood. Living wood—*breathing wood.*

The was also so much else.

The tree twisted from the ground too far away for me to see. At the bottom, or as far as my mortal mind comprehended, were clouds and a tree so massive that redwoods and banyans could take lessons. Wisps of clouds clung to the nearest branches and ethereal energy moved slowly in the gaps in the sky. The wind that nearly blew me away before simply rustled the leaves in the branches, creating a melody that thrummed like a heart.

"We're losing her," someone said, their voice dim in the tree's song.

"Get the tea, Eir!" another voice said.

Warm liquid dribbled down my lips and I gasped, almost choking, but gulped it down. A hand to my neck, gentle and soothing, encouraged me to drink.

Brightness washed through me, a cleansing, a new understanding. I fell to the floor, or the tree or whatever. Under my hands, I felt it inhaling and exhaling. I heard and felt its heartbeat.

"Where am I?" I finally asked, glaring at the three women, who appeared as just women to me now. Their ethereal glow had faded. "What did you give me?"

"Strawberry and rose tea with lemon," Sif said, smacking her bubble gum, her hand on the hilt of her sword. "We felt you arrive yesterday, but thought we were wrong. It's been two hundred years since, well, since Eir, actually."

Felt? Two hundred years?

"As for where you are," Yurd said, "we brought you to Yggdrasil."

"Eddraseal?"

They exchanged amused looks. "Yggdrasil," the other, Air?—corrected gently. "It's the tree that holds the nine realms together."

"This is quite unexpected so, let's try this from the top. I'm Yurd. The one with the sword is Sif"—Sif waved at me, popping her gum—"and the one who calmed you down is Eir, our resident Valkyrie."

"Valkyrie? Like..." I thought for a moment. I didn't go to the movies often, but Marc always loved anything fantastic, like Marvel movies. We'd gone to see several together because, well, that's what you do when you love someone. He put up with my plant obsession in return. "Like in Thor?"

Eir, who had been looking proud of herself, made a face, and both Yurd and Sif laughed. "No," Sif said, "not like Marvel. Though I have to admit I like a lot of their newer portrayals of me... Anyway."

"Sif was like a warrior goddess or something, right?" I went to the movies, but I didn't say I paid a lot of attention to them.

"Try marriage and the harvest. The swords are a newer addition," Sif said, annoyance in her voice. At me or the labels, I wasn't sure.

"But you're right," the Yurd woman said. "She is a goddess. We are all goddesses. You have the same magic about you as us. We can feel it spilling off of you."

I gripped my hands. They didn't look or feel any different. I didn't feel different. I just felt alert, like I could reach out and--

"Wait a minute, what did you say?" I demanded, finally standing up. "Did you just say that I have the same magic as you? As goddesses?" I started pacing and a half-hysterical laugh escaped my mouth. "No, wait. This is, this can't be real."

I paced back and forth, touching the tree and finding it still solid and still breathing. I tried to match myself to its calm pace, though it didn't last for long and I burst out. "It's impossible. This... I shouldn't be able to breathe in space! And how is space in a run-down shack in the middle of freaking nowhere Cora Alma, Arizona of all places?" My hands whipped around wildly as I pointed at what I assumed was the sky, as though to demonstrate that Cora Alma wasn't worthy of something so amazing. "I mean... what?"

"Oops, I think we broke her, Yurd," Sif teased. She and Eir both grabbed my arms, and suddenly we were back in the shack. Charlie, now eating a breakfast sandwich, waved at us through the doorway.

"'elcome buck," she said with her mouth full of egg.

"Hold our calls, Charlie," Yurd said as she guided me into the back room, closing the door softly.

I slumped into the nearest chair and looked around. The room was big, too big to be the little shack in my hometown.

Were they warping space?

I had seen and heard things before. Everyone knows about the vortexes in the area; it's a big tourist draw. Right now, I still smelt the fresh air, so clean from around Yggdrasil. It hadn't been cold. No, the space was warm and full of light and life. I wrapped my arms around myself, trying to get that warmth back. I bet even sunlight wasn't so internally warm.

After several moments I said the words that probably sealed my fate. "Okay. You gotta tell me exactly what is going on here. Also, what was in that tea? It was pretty good."

Five minutes later, the four of us were in a circle of chairs, a tea tray filled with a teapot, cookies, and a few other necessities, like sugar, appeared with Charlie. She disappeared to answer the phone, but not without another unfathomable look in my direction.

"Goddesses, Inc.!" she snapped, closing the door. I internally shrugged. She must like the 'ink' pronunciation.

Jord—yo-u-rd —as she explained her name was pronounced, took a sip of her tea. "Sorry about that. I assumed you were a little more aware of your power when I changed scenery."

'Changed scenery' felt like a bland way of putting 'I teleported us to space,' but I went with it.

"Goddesses, Inc. is a front for tax purposes," Sif said, her hot pink and black dress brightly popping more than anything else in the room. "We're goddesses who ensure that threats from other realms don't cross paths with humans." She sounded like a bad actor reading from a script.

Jord picked up from there, sounding less robotic and more like a teacher. "When they do, it is our job to put them back on their plane of existence. Now and then, things get a little..." hesitated, as though unable to find her words. "Sometimes things are dangerous."

"If you're a goddess, why would it be dangerous?"

"We can die like anything else. If enough damage is inflicted." Another *pop* of bubble gum. "In fact, that's why we're here. Because of Ragnarök."

That was familiar enough again, thanks, Marvel, but I'm guessing it wasn't as dramatic as they made it out to be in the movies. Or maybe it was more so?

"Ragnarök means 'the fate of the gods.'" Eir pushed up her glasses, her intense gaze never moving from mine. "It foretold the time where the gods would die, the earth would sink into the sea, and the world would be born anew."

More so, I guess. "So, um, that means what, exactly?" My head swam, no, drowned, from the amount of information they had thrown at me already. Normally it took four classes, two tests, and six hours of homework to do that.

Don't give me that look. I just found out magic is real.

All three of them seemed to finally come to the same conclusion and exchanged worried looks.

"You don't know what Ragnarök is?" Eir asked.

"No? I'm a biologist. Mythology never interested me. Sorry."

"This is what happens when you do away with classical education," Jord said with a shake of her black curls. Wait, hadn't her hair been in braids? "It was well over 1000 years ago now. Ragnarök, 'the fate of the gods' occurred, exactly as prophesied. The gods—Odin, Thor, Frey, and so many, many more died. When we died, many had the choice to go on into the next realm or be reborn into this one. You, like us, chose rebirth."

"Yeah, we'll know better next time," Eir laughed.

Jord gave her a 'look' and continued. "If a human has magic and they aren't a witch, it awakens sometimes as early as ten winters."

"Why don't we have it our whole life?" I had never felt whatever now welled within me, this brightness, before.

"You have to come into contact with something or someone magical enough to awaken it. Witches will have magic most of their lives, especially since that kind of magic runs in families. You're a goddess, not a witch. Not like Freyja," Eir said with a wave of her hand. "She's both."

"Frey-ja?" I pronounced the name slowly, so I got the right sound.

Eir nodded at my correct pronunciation and then continued. "She's the only survivor of Ragnarök who wasn't foretold."

Sif took a pink cookie which matched her pink cup with the words 'Livin' Lolita Loca' on it. "She, well, I think that's a long story for another time," she laughed. "I think you're about ready to explode with what we've told you already."

"Well, maybe not explode," I drawled, "but I... this is so weird. Magic? Goddesses?"

I wasn't one of those scientists who wouldn't pick up a fantasy novel or anything—I'd punish you in the name of the moon for thinking that—but I liked to think I was otherwise grounded in reality.

All of them laughed. Eir grabbed my hands and I felt the confusion fall away. I raised our clasped hands, marveling as I felt the feelings drain out of me again.

"It's my power. I can heal almost anything." My heart leapt to my throat. Could she possibly heal Mom? Could a cure be a simple handshake away?

"What can't you heal?"

She smiled bitterly. "Enough."

Ouch. I wanted to ask but held back for now. "Like I was trying to say before I started freaking out again—sorry about that, by the way," I muttered sheepishly. All three of them waved me along and I continued. "Who am I exactly? You said we choose rebirth, and since I chose it, who am I? And why now?"

Jord tapped her cup thoughtfully. "Honestly, we don't know. You could be any number of people who haven't appeared yet."

"So how—"

"We'll know once you're able to access your powers." Jord cut me off, but in that way that we talked at the same time. I muttered another apology as she continued. "Like me, Sif is able to make any crop grow simply by touching it. You've experienced Eir's healing, and I guess I have some pretty powerful other kinds of magic." She winked. "We'll have to see what happens for you when you start to learn magic from us."

Ah, the part where the room changed. Got it. Do not piss Jord off or she might find a literal Hell to send me to.

We settled into silence and I ruminated on the information, both terrifying and amazing. Magic existed and I was, probably, magical myself. There was magic in the world and from what I've seen it was both beautiful and something that might easily swallow the world. Sif or Jord had power to bring ruin to crops, and I had no idea what Eir's true capabilities were as a real-life empath.

Though... I'm a freaking reborn goddess from Norse mythology. Not exactly something that'll get you a job, though.

"Well, it could, with the right freaking people."

I winced. "I didn't realize I said that aloud."

Eir continued. "I mean," she looked at Jord and Sif meaningly, "there's usually some of us around Earth these days, like us. I know we always need more help here."

Sif brightened. "Hey, yeah! We'll train you. It's been so long since I've made a newbie cry!"

I froze, but all of them laughed. Jord waved her hand at me. "She's just kidding. Though she made Thor cry one time..."

"Once? Ha!" Sif sniffed back.

That sounded like fun drama.

"Listen... um, what's your name?" Sif asked.

"Aspen."

"Listen, Aspen. It's been over two hundred years since a new god arrived. We can't see anyone coming, so it was only a matter of time before they seek us out. And you have."

"So now," Jord continued for her, "it's time for you to learn."

My head swirled with thoughts and I studied my hands. They weren't any different from yesterday or last week. Now

I knew someone used their hands to calm others, so in reality, what would mine do? Wonder bloomed through me as the thoughts of what I might do. Have super strength? Run really fast? Have x-ray vision?

"But you don't even know who I am," I said. My elation faded. "How can you grow power when it obviously doesn't exist?"

Eir got up and went to a mini fridge jammed behind one desk and came back with a small container the size of a baby food jar. She placed it on the table between us, pride radiating from her. Inside were small black things that might have passed for bumpy boba in some sort of a thick syrup.

I glanced between all three of them, hoping someone would explain.

Sif pulled Eir back into her seat and Jord gave me a look that clearly said 'They're hopeless' before going on.

"These are the fruit of Idunn," she said. "Idunn had many orchards of fruit that she tended. Whenever a god became tired or felt the advancing years, they would ask her for some fruit and their vitality would be restored."

While I had a newfound appreciation for the boba, it still looked like something someone spat up, not ate. I was going to lose my lunch if the goop burped like a swamp.

"Freyja saved as many as she could after Ragnarök and preserved them. That's how she's been alive all this time. When Frey was reborn, she had him eat them and the line of gods was restored."

Oh. Oh, no. With growing horror, I realized what they wanted. "I have to—"

"Eat those, yep." Sif pursed her lips and tried to contain her laughter. "We all did, and still do now and then." The laughter died and she glanced at the jar with a spark of worry but before I had the chance to dwell on it, she kept going. "You don't need to sit down and eat a bunch of them at once. That would probably kill you, having all that power rush back. It's a slow process."

I took the jar and weighed it in my hand. There were several types of fruits in there, including pieces of tiny strawberries... or something. They all appeared dark and glopped together. Honestly, I couldn't be sure what they were unless I put them under a microscope or did a taste test.

"What do I need to do?" I asked.

Jord smiled serenely at me, a happy, content smile as pure as the life of Yggdrasil had been beneath my feet.

"Well, first, you'll have to file the new hire paperwork. If you get injured on a job, we need to have our asses covered," Sif said while getting up, cutting Jord off before she spoke. She wandered to a desk clean enough to eat off. The other two desks were laden with folders, papers, and heck, I think a clod of dirt on one. The desk drawer clattered open and then she pushed her hip against the drawer to close it.

"So... I'm hired? And you'll teach me magic?" My jaw dropped. "Holy shit, I'm going to be a magical detective goddess."

"Well, more like a magical office goddess until we know who you are and what powers you've got."

"Holy shit!" Charlie yelled from behind the door. "You're going to be a magical paper pusher!"

Eir groaned and turned to Sif and Jord, her eyes narrowing. "We really need to put a muffling spell on that door."

Chapter Seven

A magical paper pusher.

Charlie might have been trying to get me back for misgendering her? I mean, I guess it can be upsetting, but... Anyway, I'm saying Charlie was right.

I left shortly after the proclamation. The girls—women?—goddesses?—my overcooked brain settled on goddesses. The goddesses told me to come back tomorrow with more questions and to start my brand-new job, if that's what I wanted. They were going to pay me—hell, they were going to pay me well!—and all the forms I filled out were similar to any other job. They were going to help me discover my powers. In exchange, I would occasionally back them up when they needed what Sif referred to as 'collateral help.'

Yeah.

They hadn't answered all my questions, but to be fair, it was only now after leaving that so many more popped in, along with the thought of—

WHAT ARE YOU DOING, ASPEN?

Big, bold, highlighted words flashed through my mind. Maybe they slipped me something and caused me to hallucinate everything. What if...

Ugh. My mind had trouble stopping the negative 'what ifs' sometimes. I kind of wanted to hit my head to get them out.

I saw the doe, I rubbed its soft fur... and then I felt all their power and mine while I stood in literal space on a tree that connected nine worlds across the cosmos.

This was real. Really real.

For now, I didn't push for answers on the doe. It felt like something I should keep to myself for the time being. If they hadn't done it, who had? I picked up my purse and pulled out the plastic bag which contained a single wrinkled fruit. The tea had been the start. It had the dried fruit in it, but when I hesitated to eat the fruit, Sif suggested I think it over. That's when we settled on me coming back the next day.

"Hey, you going to sit out here all day?"

I jumped and palmed the fruit back into my purse for safekeeping. Dad grinned at me from the front porch where he sat, covered in sweat and paint. His grin dropped. "What's wrong?"

Putting on my most winning smile, I climbed out of the car. "Nothing, nothing. I was just following up on a lead for a new job." He looked skeptical. Cursing, I realized I'd spent the whole day in my gardening clothes from this morning, dirt on my pink patched knees and all. Damn. I pulled out the new hire paperwork, ran my fingers through my hair, and put on my best 'innocent daughter' smile.

I stumbled and basically thrust it under his nose like some sort of overdramatic Hollywood scene. "See!"

"Goddesses, Inc.?" He almost tripped up his speech at the end. "What is this, some kind of... club?"

A club? What kind of club would he be talking about? There's no clubs here, there's just the— Oh, dear God.

"It's not a strip joint! It's a detective agency!" I protested so loudly the nearest neighbor probably heard me. Dad laughed at my overreaction and waved at me to calm down. I grabbed the papers and huffed into the house, my cheeks burning.

I stopped short, almost running over Nana on her way outside. I held the door open, but she glanced outside, said something to Dad I couldn't hear, and then closed it behind her.

"Aspen! I hoped that was you." She grabbed my hand and pulled me into the living room to sit on the couch. "Come, come," she instructed, pulling out her phone. "I was just telling Flo that I had to see you."

Mom casually took a sip from a mug from her spot on the couch, trying not to laugh. I smelled something sweet and wonderful wafting from the kitchen and started toward that when Nana continued talking.

"The Cards said you needed a message."

The Cards. Right.

Except...

I stood up a little straighter, realization and wonder flowing through me once again. Like I was back with the goddesses.

If magic was real, could fortune telling be real, too? Or was it a hoax, like it seemed? What about the vortexes? And palm reading? Telepathy? UFOs? Probably not those. Suddenly I felt like a small child in a world that had never seemed so vast.

I did what I always did when Nana brought up her psychic and tarot cards: I smiled at her and said, "What else did it say today?"

Okay, so maybe I usually said, 'Oh, yeah?' and listened half-heartedly. I'm genuinely happy that she gets whatever it is she gets from these readings, but that doesn't mean I understood any of it. This time, maybe the first time since my young nature and science-driven mind rejected the notion of 'real' magic, I meant what I said.

Nana brightened, smiling. I blanched, my smile faltering. I kicked myself for seeming too eager. She whipped her phone out faster than most teens managed and pushed it under my nose. So I guess it wasn't suspicious to her.

Mom, on the other hand...

"My daily reading was all about you." She said it in such a way that I had to ask.

"Are they usually not about anyone in particular?"

She waved her hand as we sat at the table together. "It's not that. I pull a card to see who or what is on my mind. Today I pulled you for my subject. See?" I took her phone and took in the picture she shoved under my nose. The card was stamped 'The Empress' with the Roman numeral 'III' at the top.

"That's the Empress," Nana explained. "She's always represented with a crown and things like flowers and nature." Around her head, below the crown were wheat stalks, like rays of light on a Catholic saint. "That's why she reminds me of you. When I pull her, you are always on my mind."

I nodded again; my mouth dry. "What does it say about me?"

She swiped to the next picture. I quickly counted ten cards arranged in a cross pattern of six with four to the right of those in a straight line. "This is called the Celtic Cross spread—there's a lot of information"—she must have caught my wince—"but we'll just cover the basics!"

I sighed in relief. I would ask more questions later. Maybe I would pick up a book on tarot later. If much more got real to me today, I might implode from the overload.

Nana enlarged the picture, giving me a better image of the cards. "This one in the middle is the inverted Two of Swords. It means you're letting the opinions of others weigh on you. The one on top of it is the Page of Wands—the messenger to tell you good things are coming if you allow them. Which means not letting the opinions of others weigh on you." I couldn't see the first card as the second covered it along the horizontal, showing only its designation. The Page of Wands portrayed a bird in flight, carrying a message in both its beak and claws. The good news, I guess.

"This one," she pointed to the one below the first cards with four discs being clutched by a disembodied hand, "is the Four of Coins, or Pentacles. I like Coins better. It signifies holding on, or a rut while upside down, or inverted. Three of Cups," she moved to the one above the middle with three silver chalices stacked on top of each other, "points to tension in relationships."

"What relationships?"

"Well, any really. I heard about that boy..." My stomach tightened. So far, I had to admit it did sound like how I'd felt the last couple of days, right down to every relationship in my life being in some sort of turmoil. Nana excitedly moved on.

"The Emperor signifies coming into power, but it's in the past, which I found odd," she mused, zooming in on the crowned head of a handsome man.

So did I. Technically I was coming into power now. Unless it meant way, way past? Come to think of it, the goddesses hadn't said how old we were when we died in Ragnarök. Just that we were otherwise immortal. Who knows how far back my spirit, my soul, really went?

"Maybe it means my graduation?" I glanced around, and noticed I was wringing my hands. I shook them out and tried to look natural.

"Yes!" She hit her palm to her forehead and I felt relief washing through me. "Of course, your graduation. Which I am bragging about to everyone at the recovery center." Being Nana, she focused on The Cards™ so we kept at them.

The next one held the classic symbol for a lock with two spiraling and curled keys crossed in front of it. "The inverted Hierophant, the next card after the Empress and Emperor. You're on a path, but there's a block to it. Something is blocking your spirituality, maybe?" She touched my shoulder again, this time even more gently than before. "Maybe you're unblocking it now," she whispered in my ear.

I forced a smile, the knots in my stomach tightening even more. This was no longer a coincidence; this was officially scary. Luckily, she interpreted it about me moving home. Getting my ducks in a row. I could see it. This reading was about my newfound goddesshood. She moved the picture over to the row of cards and I gasped as she focused on the bottom card. The Death card.

"Don't panic." Nana's voice held a teasing ring.

"Don't panic?" I tried to keep my voice under control and not let my new knowledge of magic bother me. "About death?"

Maybe you make peace with death as you got older, maybe you didn't. Personally, I almost hyperventilated at the thought that this was real. If my grandmother predicted my death in her morning reading—

Luckily, Nana broke into my thoughts. "Death in your reading means there's a transformation coming up. A rebirth, a new awakening. It can mean a lot of things. Like a new job, for example."

Relief flooded me before the feeling of ice set in. I thought she had my attention before, but now I hung on every word, wishing I'd been recording this.

"It's not a bad card. There are no bad cards," Nana babbled. "You can see it's a butterfly, flying away from its cocoon." The muted colors of the deck made me think of a moth at first, but she was right. The more I studied the art, the more I saw the overlaps of the symbol of death and others for life. Scythes curved around the border, the sun and moon hid in the background, and even a skull pattern emerged in the spots on the butterfly's back.

Maybe it wasn't a bad card, but it wouldn't have made any sense to me yesterday.

"Next," she changed to the card above Death, "is the inverted Ten of Coins—there are challenges with your loved ones, either real or perceived. Well, that's always true, isn't it?" She winked at me and then touched my arm. Sure, we all have our problems, nothing out of the ordinary there. Not even Mom's progressing MS was a 'challenge' so much as quicker than expected.

The ten coins arranged in a spiral told me nothing, and if it wasn't about my current loved ones, this had to be about the past. So, who?

"The Seven of Cups says you have choices in front of you. Many choices." The laughter then died out of her voice. "Make sure you're using your best judgment, Aspen. So many face cards. This is an important reading for you." She dramatically put her hand to her heart. "I have always worried that you wouldn't take a serious look at what's around you."

"There's always choices." I kept my voice as innocent as possible. I even blinked a few times to add to the cuteness.

"Hmmm... I wonder. Anyway," she waved us on, "the last card is a puzzle."

I sat up straighter and she dramatically pushed the picture to reveal the last card. Instead of a beautiful or haunting drawing, I stared at nothing. A card without color or even a border or number. Simply white. "What is it?" I finally asked. "It's blank." Nana nodded curtly and didn't say anything else. Her expression was strangely pinched. "What does that mean?"

"You're not meant to know at this time."

I scoffed and resisted the urge to either strangle her or bash my head on the table. "Come on, Nana. If you're showing it to me, I think I can know."

She plucked her phone out of my hands. I tried to grab it again, only to have her dance away. "What does it mean?" My play whining morphed into real and somehow, I didn't care. But I did rein it in with a look from Mom.

Nana took her seat at the table again, her finger tapping her cheek. "That's what it means. You're not meant to know yet. The blank is in the spot that signifies your future. And with so many choices before you—the Seven of Cups—and coming into power at some point behind—The Emperor—it means your future is what you choose."

Oh. I deflated and had to restrain myself from hitting my head on the table "It's what you've told me my whole life. I control my own destiny. Awesome."

"It's not that, though." Nana shook her head, up from her seat again and pacing in thought. My stomach tightened. She would always go on about her different mystical avenues, but this was the first time I saw her so worked up over it.

"In all my time divining tarot, I've never pulled the blank card."

There weren't even a hundred tarot cards. She'd been into them for longer than my mom had been alive. I found that very hard to believe. "Never? Not even once?"

"No." She tapped the screen with a perfect pink nail. "I can't draw it because I always take it out of the deck. In fact, I thought I threw this one away since it was so plain. I don't know how it got shuffled in there this time." She shook her head again. "I think whatever choices you have before you, it's going to be life changing."

"Mother," Mom huffed, breaking into the conversation. Her mug made a dull thud as she set it on the table heavily. "She's feigning interest; the least you could do is not scare her."

I flashed my mom a grateful look, but that didn't stop the thundering of blood in my ears. There were choices to make.

In that moment, there was only be one choice. The job that would pay me and teach me magic... Or I could put my head in the sand and forget any of it ever happened.

The sound of the oven dinging gave me the excuse I needed to help Mom finish whatever she was baking. I tried to force The Cards out of my mind, but it made too much sense and caused a chill to run down my back.

Thank God(s) that Nana assumed it was about school, Marc, and typical family drama.

My mouth watered at the sight of the already complete cookies and bread Mom had baked this morning. I wanted to pump my fist. Baking meant she could move, and that meant she had less pain. It meant she was having a good day, but I restrained myself. She must have gotten started soon after I woke up... and left. Without a note, or so much as a glance back at my house.

In my defense, the deer dancing in the sky had been important. Life changing, even.

Um... let's just get back to the cookies.

I reached for the biggest, most chocolate-filled one I could find when Mom tsked at me and I hesitated.

"No lunch? Just going for dessert?"

"I could die before dessert," I reminded her. I grabbed a cookie and broke it in half. Gooey chocolate chips dribbled down the sides and the still warm interior melted in my mouth immediately, the taste of extra brown sugar to make it chewier exploding right with the chips.

Heaven. I had died in that car crash, gone to heaven, and now I got to eat Mom's goodies forever. Or something else entirely. Maybe it was Elysium. That thought brought me back to the brand-new magic that I seemingly inherited.

"Indeed. So where did you go so early this morning?" Mom asked, stirring the pot on the stove. Ooh, it was a double boiler. She must be making fudge.

"I was out applying for a job," I told her, not yet ready to let her know that I'd filled out the paperwork. I wanted to tell everyone at once, especially Dad.

"You already applied for a job?" Mom opened the nearest window and set the loaf of bread, hopefully pumpkin, on the sill to cool.

Wait, cookies and bread? I took in the sights around me. The kitchen, while beautiful, had become a disaster. Every surface showed the typical signs of Godzilla storming Tokyo when it came to making said delicious treats.

"Yeah, Isa had a good lead," I lied, averting my gaze. I bit my lip to suppress a groan from escaping as I realized the extent of my task. I rolled up my sleeves and got to work since I was going to enjoy everything she baked as she and Nana grilled me on my new 'possible' job.

"What is it?" Mom began slicing the cooled bread.

"Filing at a detective agency."

"A detective agency!" Nana exclaimed before her face screwed up in thought. "Anyone hot work there?"

Oh, dear God. I did not even wanting to know why she asked. "I mean, I guess. There are no men on staff."

"Well, you don't play on that team. I guess you'll have to look for new love elsewhere."

"If you try and set me up on a date again, Nana—"

"How much? For filing it won't be much, will it?" Mom asked, cutting me off and derailing the conversation.

"It's over minimum," I quipped back, scrubbing at a crusty piece of burned on batter.

Mom had the 'calculator' look when I turned around to get the cutting board. "How often?" she asked.

"We didn't get that far. But they said they were flexible."

I felt like I was dancing on pins and needles. I wanted to scream the truth. Tell them I saw magic and more. I felt it under my skin, wanting out so badly. They hadn't said not to tell anyone, but I also know what this would sound like, at least to Mom. Logic-brained Mom would call the doctor. Maybe I should talk to Nana about it? That is, if I could get her to not go and blab about it to her psychic.

Nana and Mom started chatting about the prospects and how it might work better for me, and I kept piling dishes into the sink and wiping counters as I went along.

Eir said... wait, what about Eir? My mind went back to her grasping my hands, explaining her powers, but also noting there were limits. I felt my heart soar with possibility and a hope I hadn't had since Mom's diagnosis. She was holding a bowl against the counter and testing something in her current batter. Could Eir help Mom? I mean, she said she had the ability to do just about anything and she drained my fear and anxiety.

Tomorrow I would talk to Eir.

I concentrated on the cleaning up for the next few minutes until I heard a bang from the other side of the house. I jumped, but Nana laughed. "I wonder if he put something through the wall!"

That's right, Dad was working on Nana's suite. "How long until it's done, Nana?"

"About a month!" She beamed. It was kinda cute to hear her go on about how amazing Dad is. She treated him like her own son. A refreshing change from what I remembered of my dad's parents. They were... not the most supportive.

They were assholes, to be fair.

Instead of relying on my family, who were deep in conversation about what they were going to do when Nana moved in,

I dried my hands and walked out to the back porch. Taking a few moments to relax in a chair before pulling out my phone, I checked the time. It was after eleven. I had been at Goddesses, Inc. for hours.

Before putting it away, I sighed and dropped my head. I'd been so shocked. Thinking in a crisis had never been my strong suit. Frowning at myself for only now thinking it, I typed 'Norse mythology' into the search bar and started reading. The first website that popped up was a Wiki article from "Norsewikia" and I shrugged before tapping on it and reading.

'Norse mythology stems from a set of beliefs c. 500AD to c. 1000AD but probably are from an even further back belief system. The Æsier gods and the Vanir gods, the two races of gods attested to in the Eddas, are possible proof of a merger of beliefs from even earlier times, though the stories of the supposed war that they fought before exchanging hostages are lost.'

Wow, there was so much to unpack there, I wasn't sure where to start. With links to many of the different names and dates, it would take me forever to figure these things out. Before long, I fell down the rabbit hole of Norse mythology, clicking link after link to learn more.

Nana came out with a plate of cookies, muffins, fresh bread and butter, and I ate, attempting to digest as much information—and as much food—as I could. I quickly found the story for Ragnarök. It was the first of this guy named Snorri Sturluson's tales. I scanned the introduction and frowned. In fact, he was the only person to write down any Norse mythology in the 13th century, long after Europe's heathen ways had been burned away.

I read on, honestly believing that if there was any truth in this myth, any part of it would be horrifying to see. I don't just

mean the death of the gods. It started off with Odin raising a
seer called a 'volva' from the dead and then she divined the
story of Ragnarök and told him the gods' fate. Loki and his
children slaughtered the gods, who slaughtered them in return. There was no mention of the goddesses, but that wasn't
too shocking.

Shivering in the warm May air, I kept reading.

My phone beeped at three o'clock before I realized I should
probably take a break. The battery was now down to 20%
and my neck and back had cramped from sitting too long and
looking down. I'd been following links in the Norsewikia, and
while I knew little about mythology, I knew they were all filled
with weird shit.

Norse myths were no different. From half-dead girls who
ruled the underworld to a god with nine mothers and even
some interesting gender/sex swaps, Norse myths were weird.
How much was real, though? Was there really a squirrel who
carried messages between two enemies on Yggdrasil? Or was
that a tall tale?

I cracked my neck and sighed, letting the thoughts go and
trying to relax with some breathing techniques.

Not three seconds had passed when my mind did the thing
all minds do: it realized I'd forgotten something. With a rush
of undue panic, I jumped up and stumbled into the kitchen,
only to find it perfectly clean and the room silent. I pushed
open the kitchen door and the sound of two people snoring,
one high and wheezing, the other an occasional snort, met my
ears. The blinds were closed and in the low light I saw both
Mom and Nana crashed on the couch. Mom had fallen asleep
sitting up, a paperback book resting on her chest, while Nana

had a blanket tucked up to her chin, curled up on the other side.

They didn't move as I studied them and took what an old therapist called a 'mindful moment' and enjoyed the sound of their snores and the lingering smell of baked sweet breads.

About a minute later I closed the door to the back porch, deciding a walk was in order to clear my head. It gave time for my mind to wander.

From the stories I'd read the gods did age, and they could die if they were maimed. Loki had seen to that with the whole Ragnarök thing. So the fruit would have limits.

To quote my dad here: cheezus.

Who was I, though? A Valkyrie like Eir? Or a goddess like Sif and Jord?

Or would I just be plain Aspen?

I sighed and continued my walk around the house, going from the front to the back, passing flower beds along the front and into the sides. Normally I'd be checking each bed's soil, making plans for colors and species, but my head was full of mystery and ideas. What else was true?

Why couldn't life be easier?

"Surveying your land?" Dad asked from behind me, his voice mildly amused. I let out a squeak, stopping in my tracks. I had walked around the house and stopped close to the entrance of the suite. Dad carried a rolled-up carpet on his shoulder, amusement clear on his face. I yelped and hurried out of his way to give him entrance. He grunted a thank you and kept going toward the closed door of the suite.

Kicking myself, if only mentally, I trotted ahead of him and pushed the door open. He smiled and hefted the carpet in with no obvious strain. I slipped in after him, but only got a quick look at a half-finished kitchen with no cabinets before he turned on me, holding up his hands with a smile, pushing me back toward the door without touching me.

I tried to protest, but he kept walking forward until he closed the door behind him, the unfinished room still unseen.

"Dad!" I whined, only half-joking. "Why'd you do that? I know how to walk in a construction zone."

It wasn't an exaggeration. Dad had been bringing me to his job since I could hold my head up. Taking me to his Take Your Child to Work Day was infinitely better than Mom the schoolteacher. It didn't interest me for work, but I liked to blow people's minds by fixing little things in houses, like a dripping sink or patching holes in walls. It came in handy in the dorms.

"Your Nana wants to shock and awe us all once she's moved in and decorated. Until then, only I'm allowed in there."

I must have looked as disappointed as I felt because he shook his head at me, a grin still on his face. "Come on, it's a room with a kitchen. It's nothing you've never seen before."

"But it's a new something I've not never seen before."

He chucked, turned me around, and steered me off the stoop and down the length of the house, where I didn't try and look in the windows at all.

"You have so much more to do here than try and defy your Nana's few wishes." We got to the end of the wall and I playfully dug my heels in and tried to prolong my leaving. He obliged my game and 'pushed' me harder before he pointed my limp and disappointed form to the grove of trees.

"Mom and Nana are taking care of getting the house in order. I've been working on this. The garden needs a lot of work."

The rotten boards, bad soil, and the overgrown trees danced in my head. I promised my parents a year, so I would give it to them. It would give me enough time to get that garden into the best shape possible.

I slipped my hand in my pocket and rolled the small nugget of fruit in my fingers. Fruit that I would later throw into a corner of the icebox with last year's fruitcake as I made my mind up for now. I could only work with what I knew.

"Tell Nana to leave some flower pots open for me."

Chapter Eight

The next day I woke up and did what I always did: took my meds, made a list of things to do, and then I started doing them. I planned for an extra hour of gardening today before I would shower and go accept the job at Goddesses, Inc. Then I'd come home, tell the family, and everyone would applaud my skills. I didn't need an emergency job, or worse, one of pity. I wanted to be somewhere with purpose.

The list for repairs for the garden was growing painfully fast. I also did some weeding, pulling the worst and biggest of the overgrown weeds off the flowerpots. I checked my watch. It was almost ten and I was as sweaty as a virgin at a Satanic ritual.

I dashed upstairs, running my hand up my cat's soft back and tail along the way—*so fluffy!*—got showered and changed into nicer clothes than yesterday. Honestly, I didn't know what to wear as a goddess or Valkyrie or whatever. I went with chic casual and wore a pair of khaki pants with a pale purple button-down shirt. I left my hair down. I could do just about anything in this outfit.

By the time Bessie and I pulled up to Goddesses, Inc. my nerves had taken over. The puke your guts up or pretend you went into witness protection type of nervous. Did I want to do this? I could change as a person. I knew I would change. Change is good! Immortality, I wasn't so sure of.

Did I want to become magical, see magic, and know something as strange as all that?

Hell yes, I did.

I stepped up to the rune-inscribed door of the yellow shack. I stood there for several moments, and for possibly one last time, the moment to turn around arrived and flew right by me. I grasped the handle and swiftly closed the door before a 'normie' could possibly see me.

Charlie sat at the receptionist's desk on the phone. Her blue hair was pulled back with sparkly pink barrettes today. She had on a sparkly pink vest over a black shirt, with a skirt that was obviously hand lined with rhinestones on the bottom. Her shoes were a pair of sparkly pink Sketchers. On her nameplate, or rather right below it, was a new addition. A simple pink sticky note with the words: 'Pronouns: Bite/Me'

I wasn't sure if I should laugh or be offended and I opted for a cough to hide the laugh.

She gave me the stink eye anyway. "Yeah, hold on Detective Daniels, I'll get Linda for you." Charlie touched a button and a moment later her voice changed to a more causal tone. "Hey Sif, it's the detective. Yeah. Okay." She hung up and saw me. I had made it only a foot or two inside the door; my lead shoes unable to take another step. My face must have betrayed me because she shrugged. "Sif's mortal name is Deolinda." Ah, that made more sense. "They all have aliases. You should learn them."

The last part was said in such a sweetly patronizing tone that I almost didn't feel stupid at all.

No one had told me that, but it made sense. There weren't many people running around named "Eir" and "Jord" these days. Plus, they were all hundreds of years old, so they needed some kind of cover story.

"Since you're here, who are you?" I asked, feeling brave.

Charlie shrugged. "I'm just here for the paycheck. Benefits aren't bad either. But I'm not a goddess, if that's what you're asking. I'm a witch."

"Like *Har—*"

She cringed. "Uh, no. Real witches; sage, Samhain, the Great Goddess—who honestly might be Jord with what I know now."

"It could be Frigg for all you know," Sif said as she poked her head out of the back room. She smiled at me and waved. "We've been wondering if we scared you off. Charlie, please try not to burn anything down."

"I'll try!" She called while the door closed.

"Which one?" Sif muttered under her breath before quickly smiling at me. "Good morning, Aspen."

"Come in, dear, come in." Jord appeared beside Sif and hooked arms with me, ushering me to the tiny sitting area of the crammed room. I took the same seat as the day before and Eir came over to join the three of us as we sat in a circle. "Last night we called Freyja and performed seeing sedir on you."

"Okay," I said noncommittally. I tried to think if I felt weird or different last night. Nothing stood out. I spent most of the night obsessing over the fruit in the freezer or the weirdness of the myths I had read. Despite my answer, I tried not to let the clawing feeling in the back of my head take over that the sedir... wait.

"Sedir is magic, right?" I had to make sure I was remembering things right.

"Ritualistic magic," Sif answered from the kitchenette. "It's not your garden variety magic."

"How is it different?"

"Ritual magic takes time, energy, and the addition of something from the practitioner, like blood or hair." I made a face in disgust, but Eir kept going. "Those three things make it extremely powerful even if the caster isn't," she answered, her cat-eye glasses sliding down her nose.

"And regular magic?"

"You can have all of that, but you also need power to cast without the ritual."

"Oh," I said softly, hoping there wasn't a test.

Jord thankfully spared me. "The good news is she confirmed you are from the Norse pantheon. So we weren't wrong."

Okay, so I'd joked about Greek gods, but I hadn't thought they were also real. "There are others?"

I snapped my mouth open and shut a few times as I restrained myself from blurting out, 'Wow, that's so cool!'

"More than you'd think have survived. But we don't need to talk about that right now." Jord sat across from me. "Right now, we're going to start with the basics."

Yeah, speaking of those. "What's your real name? Your alias?"

"We didn't give our aliases?" Jord laughed and shook her head, tsking herself. "Well, it's proper for us to call each other by our alias in front of mortals. We all have unnecessarily complicated fake backstories that will completely check out if needed. My name is Demi, like Demi Moore." I knew the name and the pronunciation but did not know who that was. "Sif is Deolinda, and Eir is Erin."

"Erin? Eir is... Erin." I fought back a laugh, but it escaped, sounding something like a strangled cough.

"Hey, it's easy to remember!" Eir snapped at me, her cheeks burning from what I assumed was deep shame at her choices and not anger.

Yeah. Not the first to laugh at that.

Jord coughed and I snapped back to attention. "But as I was saying, you're one of us. Magic can't tell us exactly who you are though; only you can do that. Freyja said if she divined anything else, she would let me know. We have some theories."

Sif came around and set cups and a teapot on the small table jammed between the chairs. Jord delicately lifted the pot and poured two cups.

"Cream? Sugar?" Her face never changed from a pleasant, soft smile. "We couldn't ask last time. I think you should have a say."

"I liked it plain." Picking up the cup, I examined the liquid through the clear, delicate china. The brown liquid looked like any other tea, but it smelled faintly of a flower I couldn't place. Small amounts of vapor wafted up, and I tasted it lightly on my tongue. A perfect, delicate mix beyond compare.

"You said I only needed to have the fruit once a week?"

"Consider the tea like a micro dose. It won't do much, but as you saw yesterday when you didn't have any in your system at all, it's enough. So please, drink. We think it's going to help you develop your magic faster."

"You think?" I paused mid-sip, holding it steadily in my hands. "Don't you know?"

Jord sipped her tea. "No, we don't, actually. This tea wasn't made until the late 1800s, after we found Eir. It slows our aging down to give us more time in one backstory. But," she continued, "it works as well as any balm. It accelerates our healing after getting injured. It's not a cure-all, and it doesn't hurt. So do drink up."

I think she assumed I had already eaten the fruit. I stirred in a sugar cube to keep my gaze down. The opaque liquid shimmered unassumingly in the light. If this was a micro dose, then it might still have a potent effect.

I sipped my tea, this time savoring the mixed fruity and floral taste on my palate. Never in my life had I tasted such a perfect tea. The sugar made the cooling bitterness fade. I wanted to keep drinking, but I forced myself to ask my burning question.

"You said it has healing properties?" All three of them nodded affirmations. "Can it heal neurological, physical, or mental disorders?"

Jord set her teacup down and offered me a cookie from the tray. "You mean chronic illness?"

"Yeah. I mean," I bit my lip. I didn't want to advertise my condition, but I would never get the answer if I didn't say it. "I have bipolar disorder. And anxiety. It's better controlled than it has been but..."

She blinked, but other than that, her face didn't change. Jord wasn't shocked by what I said, or at least she didn't look it. Most people would throw out something like, 'But you're so normal!' or my favorite, 'You're not like others who have that!'

"That must be a difficult disease to live with. I'm sorry to hear it."

She said something so normal it shocked me into silence. Before I could thank her for not being a jerk, Eir continued the explanation, and I saw neither pity nor fear in her, either.

"From what I can tell, the fruits make healing quicker and bring us from advanced age to youth. If a limb is cut, it will not regrow it any more than it will change how your neuropathways work."

I expected that. The tightness in my chest and how close I suddenly was to tears, were a bit of a surprise. What was there to be upset about? I'd been living with my disease for almost a decade, even if it didn't have a name until I turned seventeen. Mom said... oh.

The tears weren't for me.

"We've talked," Jord said, changing the subject, "and we think there's a good chance you could be Gurd. She was the wife of Frey. Or Fulla, who was Frigg's handmaiden and a Valkyrie. There are a few others, of course."

Fulla. Gurd. I tested the names on my tongue but felt nothing. They didn't ring a bell, didn't invoke an emotion. I guess expecting it to would be too much.

"So, what are my powers? When will I get them?"

"Over time, the more fruit you eat, the more power will come to you. Yesterday the tea awakened your mind to magic. Both Fulla and Gurd were nature goddesses, like Sif and I are."

Nature goddesses. If that was true, a lot of things made sense.

"I guess that's why I like to garden," I said, almost laughing.

Sif poured herself a cup of tea after she sat down with us. She put some forms for the state on the table. "Ya in?" Her bubbly cheerfulness spilled over in waves.

"We all show some signs of our past," Jord said, ignoring Sif's question and shooting her a look that caused her to purse her lips in return. "I used to climb trees and back in the 1300s, that was somewhat unusual for a girl."

My head snapped up and I gaped at Jord. She might be the oldest looking in the room, but on her worst day she couldn't be over forty.

"We know it's a lot to believe," Sif said, her voice low with a heaviness I hadn't heard before.

"I mean, I knew you were immortal, but when you put a number on it, it's a lot."

All three of them laughed and Sif put her hands together in a prayer position like a saint statue. A smothered flash of golden light made little spots appear in my vision. When it passed, she held her hands toward me, opening them like a book.

I peered and did a double take. Seeds. There were dozens of seeds in her cupped palms. Small ones, pits, even a few with green curlicues growing out of them. She poured them into my palms, some falling to the floor when I wasn't ready. I rolled them, seeing that they were all real, and all of them ready and perfect for planting.

"Nothing is immortal."

"I have a warning for you." Jord's voice lost some of its carefree sound. She had my attention as I poured the seeds into a cup that Eir produced. "Not every god or goddess, even ones of kinship, are going to be good. Some are good beyond measure, others are interested in only their own gains. More than our fair share are vain and cruel." She frowned, disappointment and anger marring her face. "Never promise something you aren't willing to lose."

Wow, that was way more ominous than I liked. The stories I'd read the night before—of Loki and Thor and even Freyja—all but said that none of them could be trusted, while also showing a kinship between them that ran so deep it created mortal enemies when tested. "Is there anyone I should run from if I see them?"

Trouble clouded Jord's gaze. Her lips pursed and her eyes went flat as she perched herself on the edge of her seat. I thought I crossed a line until she nodded curtly. "Be careful of Loki. He's a trickster through and through. He only pops up every few decades. Since his rebirth all Freyja has known is trouble from him."

"Oh, I thought Odin was in charge? The All Father?"

Jord shook her head and even Eir's amused expression wasn't hidden. Sif waved her hand as though swatting away a pest. "Freyja's the oldest, and probably one of the wisest, of the gods. Odin wasn't reborn until the 1750s. I'm older than him. It was hard for him to make a case that he should rule beyond 'I did it before and got us all killed.'" She tucked her chin in both hands and beamed at me like a schoolgirl. "She kicked his ass."

I couldn't help laughing. I had an image of a twenty-year-old trying to lord himself over a goddess who had survived the end of her race. I choked back more laughter and Jord smiled at me, confirming it was exactly as silly as I pictured it.

After our giggles died down, I came back to the topic. "Do I get to meet Freyja? I mean..." I stuttered as I realized how forward I sounded. "I guess she's pretty busy as the ruler of the gods now."

"If you want to meet her, I'm sure it will happen," Jord said. "Odr isn't reborn, not yet at least. She sometimes travels the Earth, crying, trying to meet him again. Poor woman." She heaved a great sigh. "So much information! Let's stop there for today. If you have questions, write them down and let me know next time you're in. We'll try to answer them."

I started at the sudden cut off, but a wave of gratitude washed over me. People, no *gods*, had been alive for centuries, maybe even millennia and they watched over humanity. It felt like studying a semester's worth of philosophy all in one night and my head pulsated from the overload.

"Sure," I managed out, my voice cracking.

Sif winked at me before sauntering back to her desk. Eir, not giving me a second glance, retreated to a darker corner of the room. Well, fine. There's always that one that you don't get along with. Jord touched my shoulder and gently helped me to my feet with a steady, perfectly soft hand, almost as though she'd never even held a pen.

We walked past the others. "Originally, we had the entire office to ourselves, front and back. When we hired Charlie, we rearranged things to give her room to work and take clients." We made it to her desk which smelled like damp earth and rain, a scent that would always relax and invigorate me. The dozen or so plants lining her desk blocked the organized chaos from view. And I had to admit, I wasn't expecting her to be the one with the dirt clod on her desk.

She gestured for me to sit, which I did, and then handed me the new hire paperwork Sif had procured. Biting her lip, Jord looked around the office, a finger to her cheek. "I think with you, we can ask for an extension of our office. Yes." She nodded her head confidently and then smiled at me. "You being here is most fortuitous."

"It... is?" I asked, letting my confusion leak into my words.

"Yes. Freyja said there was no need to increase the size of the pocket because Charlie doesn't count as added magic, being only a witch. You are definitely added magic, so I can easily make a case to add space to our little dimension we've created in here."

Ah, so that's what caused it. Another dimension. Holy crap, I was sitting in another dimension?

She smiled at me. "I'll have to wait for the two full moons to finish the spell, but it's a cinch once it's started."

"You can't wiggle your nose or snap or something?" I joked.

"Samantha was a witch," she intoned, "not a goddess. And it's not that easy. Our powers are limited by the surrounding forces. I must ask for the power from the elements and others, such as the moon itself, for this expansion to work correctly. If anything goes wrong, it would be terrible."

"So, is that how magic works? Asking outside things for help?"

"All magic is different." Eir joined the conversation, a stack of manila folders in her hands. "It's all the same while being different at the same time."

Sometimes I take a second to get things, but even that made no sense. "Huh?"

"Here, like this." She held up her wrist, showing an intricate beaded black and white bracelet that made up a Celtic cross. "This is a protection amulet that was made for me by a Catholic monk from Europe. Jord"—she gestured to the older woman who held a simple white quartz wrapped in leather around her neck—"has that. It's a New World protection spell. Different people made them, from different eras on continents that had little interaction, but they do the same thing. All magic is like that. Basically the same, but always tailored to someone's personal history and environment."

"That doesn't mean you don't have power," Sif called from her desk. "It means that certain magic comes from outside of you."

She continued as I soaked in every word, fascinated. "So to answer your question, magic works like Jord said, with the moon, the stars, and the elements all working together with someone bringing them together in a certain way."

Eir jumped back in. "Magic types are as personal as family and blood. And like DNA, there are never two magics that have been created the same. It's always changing."

"What about the marks on the door?" I thought back to how they briefly warmed, almost a flash under my hand.

A look of pride, for me or another I didn't know, flashed across her delicate features. "Odin's work. He is gifted in crafting and rune magic."

"Can I trust him?"

"Hey!" Charlie's muffled yell broke us out of conversation. "You can't—"

With a loud crack, the door flew open, breaking the frame. A large man with a thick mustache and a beard neatly tucked into his white shirt front and a worn black leather jacket pushed through the door. He wore a bandana around his head, and I was sure from the tattoos to the leather to the beard that he was in a biker gang.

"I'm sorry, Ms. Linda," Charlie said, trying to get the nice hulking man to go back into the other room. "I'll have him wait."

"I can't wait!" the man thundered. "I have a real haunting to report, and this shit can't wait."

The looks on Sif, Eir, and Jord's faces clearly said it could, but they went from 'What the hell?' to business so fast my neck cracked.

"It's okay, Charlie. This is perfect for our new recruit to see how we work," Jord soothed.

Eir was beside Hulking Motorcycle Guy before he started complaining again. She put her hand on his arm and then as she had done to me, the tension melted away from him. She led him to the cozy sitting area where I had previously been, sitting him in a chair, which I half expected to buckle under him.

Sif took the tea from in front of them and bustled about, making a new pot from a box of store-bought tea. She also produced a box of cookies and a bowl of fruit.

"Tell me about your emergency, Mr...?" Jord prodded.

"Egert. Just call me Egert." His head spun from one side to the other, taking in the entirety of the small office. "Huh? I thought this was a supernatural detectives sorta place. You're just regular people."

Jord continued to talk to him in a soothing, calm voice that made me long to be at home in my mother's lap. Eir rushed past me, and dishes clattered in the tiny kitchenette as Sif got plates and cups.

"Even humans can end up with other than human problems," Jord's serene voice continued.

"Tell me about it," Egert sighed with a mighty shake of his head. "This is nuts. I went to the Rock Cathedral, ya know, in Sedona, a few days ago. Friend of the family's funeral and all. Well, I was the last one in the church, and I thought I heard laughing, so I hung back to see if some kid had been left behind, ya know, doing my part." Jord gave an encouraging nod and he kept going. "Anyway, next thing I know there's this huge wind, and the laugh is now a roar and, well, ma'am, I roared out of there, I tell you what.

"Next thing I know, things are falling off shelves at home. The doors are being flung open. I can see this trail, like it's right out of the corner of sight." He hesitated. "I got all manners of people to look into it, and finally my mama brought her psychic out to us. Woman said it was a spirit from the church. She sent me here."

"Mr. Egert," Jord started again. "Do you mind if we keep asking you questions? Or that our esteemed... in-training clerk takes notes? She needs some actual case experience." Jord looked specifically at me when she said this. Next thing I knew, I was sitting in the circle with a pen and pad of recycled paper in my hands, noting dates and times and how often the 'spirit' was around his home.

Jord and Eir completed the circle, but Sif remained standing and took over the conversation, her stern voice a mismatch from her pink puffy sleeves.

"Mr. Egert, I need you to explain exactly what is happening in your house," she instructed. "Don't spare any details."

And boy, he did not. My fingers ached for relief as I struggled to keep up with him. But after an hour, a strange tale emerged. One of mystery, intrigue, and strange sounds at night. A tale of a supernatural entity that over-enjoyed salty snacks and *Pretty Little Liars*.

After taking Egert's information, Sif instructed him to go home and that the goddesses would respond to the situation with a plan in less than forty-eight hours.

Then he was gone, whisked away back to Charlie so fast his beard almost got caught in the door.

"Why Charlie?" I asked after the door closed.

"Because Charlie's better than even Sif at getting money out of people," Jord said. She sighed. "That child is wasting all her talent."

Sif snort laughed and slapped me on the back. "Welcome to Goddesses, Inc., Aspen. It's going to be a bumpy ride."

"How can I learn more about magic? How will I find out who I am?" They had given me names, Fulla and Gurd. "Should I read the myths? Are they even real?"

"Even though they might have changed a little, the basic stories are correct," Eir said from her desk. She pushed her glasses up and stared up at me, and I shivered. "The situations may be correct, but not everything said is. Some things, like Idunn growing apples, were downright wrong."

"As for your magic," Jord steered the conversation around, "that will all come out in the months and years while your body gets accustomed to godhood. Here." She handed me another preserved fruit. "I know it's too early for you to eat it, but this way you don't get behind. You should eat one a week," she reminded me.

I had no intention of eating this one either, at least not yet. I wanted to know what they were, and more importantly, I wanted to know how they worked.

Chapter Nine

I pulled up to my house with a schedule for the next two weeks. Four days a week, six hours a day. It had been all up to me, and I could change them any time as long as I gave them at least a day's notice.

Freyja had only seen my pantheon, not who I was, or why my soul took so long to be reborn. I could be a goddess, or a Valkyrie, or—holy shit, a goddess!

Mindboggling, weird, surreal even.

But it felt right. It was right. A hum inside me, one that hadn't been there before, wrapped me in all the comfort I needed. I knew, as I listened to the hum, that I didn't want it to go. I only wanted to know more. I didn't have to go to work at the café and I would be getting paid way more to explore my magic.

Both of my parents' cars were in the driveway, so I shouldered forward, getting my story straight in my head.

Detective agency, clerk and filing...

I put my keys and bag on the table inside the front door and kicked off my shoes. "Mom?" I called. The house was dark and all the curtains drawn. Scraping sounds came from the kitchen. "Dad?"

The door swung open and Dad, armed with a tray laden with sandwiches and soup, popped through. "Aspen, you're home." He then hefted the tray into my arms, causing me to almost drop it. "I have to go to an emergency. Burst pipe at your mom's school, actually. I was afraid I'd have to send someone else."

Yeah, like that would be the worst thing.

I didn't say it, but it must have shown on my face, because he sighed. "Look, just take this to your mom. She's having a rough day. The pain pills have red caps on them. She can have one in forty-five minutes."

I nodded dumbly.

"Great, see you in a few hours, honey." He patted me on the head and then he was gone.

I swallowed down my heart and instead focused on the task ahead of me. Anxiety gripped my stomach and throat, clawing at me, scratching and scraping against my chest, threatening to burst out in hysterical sobs.

Though I didn't know why.

"Hey, Mom," I called, balancing the tray and knocking on her door gently. I'd deal with the feelings later and continued to squash them down. "Dad went out. I have your lunch."

I didn't know what to expect when Dad said it was 'a bad day'. Maybe more fluffy pillows? She laid back against three in a sitting position. But from her shallow breathing and the trembling of her hands I saw her normal glow being replaced with a pale, ashen shade of grey. She radiated her pain. Her red hair had gone at least three days without washing and now stuck up in multiple ways while also being plastered to one side of her head.

She looked—actually looked—sick. Her eyes were smiling and kind but every inch of her screamed pain, suffering, and hopelessness in a disease that would only get worse as time went on. It had been a long time since I'd been home during a bad flare, but I know she didn't look like that last time I saw her during one.

"Aspen," she whispered. Even her voice seemed to shake from effort. "I'm sorry. You've never seen me like this." She tried to sit up and adjust herself so she could hold herself up, and now the pillows actually made sense. "Don't worry, it only hurts when I exist."

"Come on, your dad was going to share with me." She motioned to me, and I went around to Dad's side of the bed and climbed in next to her. There were no pillows left for me, so I sat against the wall and took one of the sandwich halves from the tray. Turkey. I didn't eat tons of meat, but I did like turkey and cheese.

We ate in silence; the TV providing background noise. I reached for my second sandwich but mom handed me the bowl of soup so I could take a sip. Corn chowder wasn't my favorite, but it melted down.

"So," she said just as Nanny Fine began to shave Mr. Sheffield, "you said you were going to talk to them about that job offer. How did it go?"

I grinned, the anxiety about Mom's illness momentarily gone. I might not be able to tell her about the magic, but I could tell her that the job was fun and challenging. More than that, I was actually excited to start.

"Oh, my God, it's great! I'm going to work four six-hour shifts a week, and I can choose my days. Plus, I get all major holidays off, and apparently some minor ones, too." The goddesses had been pretty vague there.

"You're only going to be doing their filing and clerk work, right?" she asked hesitantly. "You're not going to be doing anything stupid like taking pictures of cheating spouses?"

I giggled at the thought of Hera hiring the goddesses to finally catch Zeus in the act. "No," I said. "Nothing crazy like that."

Sure, nothing crazy like that. Other crazy shit, though, that was game. Apparently, in forty-eight hours, I'd know how to trap ghosts or something.

"You should do what your heart tells you about this job, even if it is a little crazy."

"Ooh, permission to go crazy. I can do all sorts of stuff with that," I teased.

"Except live here rent free, missy," she teased right back. She reached for her juice on the tray and as she brought it up to her lips, it slipped from her hands and spilled everywhere on the bedspread and sheets.

Mom swore and I jumped out of the bed to avoid the offending sticky orange liquid. Only one of us should have to take a shower.

"It's okay." I picked up the cup and sorted the sheets and napkins out. Mom, soaked down to her lap, carefully took off her shirt and dumped it on the bed to avoid dripping on the floor. She then shimmied out of her pants and skirted into the bathroom faster than even Carrie would have.

I sighed and massaged the back of my neck. This was technically day one. On day one, she had to take a shower in the middle of the day. I hadn't been able to prevent it. I didn't see it coming. Sure, it was only juice. As I heard my mom's cries fading when the shower turned on, the prick in the back of my head told me I could never do this.

How could I possibly give her as good of care as she had given me when I was the one crying in the shower, all hope for my future gone?

The rest of the afternoon and early evening went with no other incident. I pretended I hadn't heard Mom cry, and she pretended she hadn't cried.

After Dad got home and took over, I went upstairs, determined to keep myself busy until dinner. Carrie, fast asleep on my pillow, stretched and turned her belly upwards, demanding pets. I slowly stroked her, earning a purr, and surveyed my kingdom. I didn't enjoy living out of boxes. Somewhere in this mess I'd brought home was the lab microscope I'd been required to buy.

Tiny seeds, or maybe achenes if they were strawberries, were still visible with the fruits the goddesses had given me. Before I ingested it, I was going to do what I spent way too much money to learn to do: I was going to study it.

Maybe, in its current form, it became stunted. Fresh fruit might have been different. Maybe the types of fruit would make a difference. I might know if I just ate the stupid thing.

Normally I'd have been rocking out to P!nk or maybe some Billie Eilish, but a quick search of YouTube brought up something that I needed: a version of Snorri's Eddas, the only surviving Norse myths, on audiobook. I played it at 1.7x because I needed this information *fast*.

Four minutes later, I found a book written by a contemporary author that did a much better job at that speed than a textbook. That cost me money, but alas, I was a supporter of the arts.

I opened one of my favorite notebooks—a cute one with the words "You Don't Have to Try" printed on it—and began to put things in their place. I made a list of questions.

'Who are the Norns?' was first on the list. I planned on googling as much as possible, but if I knew my history, I would have to go to the sources to clear most things up.

Other than Freyja, I don't think they remembered any-thing.

I stayed up late listening to the author read the book and set up my room, making notes of questions each time one came to mind. I finally unearthed my microscope, and more plans took root for it. Eventually I went to bed listening to the story of how Loki became bound to a rock with venom dripping on his face. The Vikings believed that any time the earth shook, it was because Loki's wife, Sigyn, emptied the bowl she held over his head and the venom actually dripped on him.

Knowing this was real in some form caused my stomach to turn and I switched off the audiobook.

Chapter Ten

Armed with my list, some very basic knowledge of Norse mythology, and a box of Kristie's Krispie Donuts, I eyed the graffitied door from my parking spot twenty feet away. The doe could have helped me park much closer the other day, but I'd run through downtown chasing it like some lunatic.

But it led me to Goddesses Inc., where my shift started in five minutes. I'd gotten half the donuts filled with chocolate cream and the rest were Boston cream. Suck up doesn't even begin to describe it when it came to these donuts.

I put on my most confident smile, one with too many teeth, and waited for the doorknob to warm before pushing the door open. Inside sat Charlie, as always, on guard and ready to help until she noticed it was only me. Then she went back to reading a bodybuilding magazine.

Today's sticky note was yellow and read: Pronouns: 'Not/Today/Satan'

The goddesses weren't the only ones I planned to suck up to.

"Good morning, Charlie," I took a step forward, noting with appreciation she was dressed in slacks, a sweater vest with platform boots, and blue lipstick. "Have you ever had these? I got two kinds, chocolate filled and Boston cream." She looked from my face to the box I held and back again. I had her attention. "I got a dozen. I don't know if you've ever been to Kristie's, but—"

"Heaven," she interrupted. "Heaven in a fluffy dough, lightly glazed, because inside is so sweet you need milk to save you."

I grinned and opened the box, letting her take one of each, as she watched me wearily.

With only a few minutes to do this, I pressed forward with my questions. "I've already asked Jord and the others, but what else is there to really know about the fruit? Anything?"

"You mean the one the world would probably go to war over because it's going to give you immortality? You mean that stuff?"

I hadn't thought about that. "I, uh, yeah. That's what I mean."

Charlie studied the donuts, realizing the bribe. "I mean, I know stuff..."

I sighed. This would not be easy, or cheap, I guessed.

"What do you want?"

"You get the coffee for the next month. I like mine iced no matter what the weather is." She stuck her hand out, a little old fashioned, but I returned the handshake.

"Done."

Charlie stuffed one of the chocolate cream in her mouth, moaning dramatically. "I don't know much," she said through a mouthful. "Except what everyone knows: In the myths, they were said to be apples, but that's probably Christian influence. Berries make more sense when you think about the cold climate. Apples don't grow well in cold weather. Freyja preserved them. They have magical properties from Idunn herself."

"Did they give the gods their magical properties?"

"Some of them, I think," she agreed, taking another bite. "Anyone with Earth powers gets them from the earth because they're usually born from it. That means Vanir gods like Frey and Freyja always had their power. Only a few Æsier were born with magic."

"What were they before they had their magic? Were they mortal?"

"Ooh, this is so good," Charlie moaned, having finally given into temptation and enjoyed the shop's specialty: the Boston cream.

Oh well, I'd lost her. Next time I'd try the coffee with some bagels.

I opened the door to the other room and deliberately stopped at each desk to say good morning to the goddesses. Eir fascinated me most—she lit up at the sight of the donut box but then clouded over with suspicion when she saw me. I shrugged it off and put on my gloom-blasting smile before continuing to the dining cart that served as the kitchen and plopped the box down on the top counter next to the teapot.

Package delivered, I saw the three desks and the sitting area but... nothing else. I bit my lip and shyly eyed Jord and then Sif, but both were busy working. In fact, Eir was the only one unsuccessfully trying to look busy. I took a deep breath, put on my big girl pants, and walked back to Eir's desk.

"Can I help you?" she asked without looking up. Her voice held a slight edge to it and I shrank back, my self-esteem leaking out through my feet.

"Where am I supposed to work?" My timid voice shocked me. Eir looked up, and my shoulders drooped even more at the dark look she gave me through her wire-rimmed frames.

She glared at the back of Jord and Sif's heads and when they didn't move she pursed her lips. "The spell won't be ready for weeks, I guess for now you can do paperwork in the sitting area. But that might be cramped for you."

"The sitting area is fine," I assured her. "I also need to know what I'm doing. Like, what kind of paperwork, how to file it, the general job."

Sif suddenly laughed and I jumped at the sound. Eir even smirked at me. "What?"

Sif stood in a lightly ruffled purple dress with long frilly sleeves, and the smile on her face didn't falter or mock me. "For the first few weeks it'll be training. Mostly in magic, a little in our filing system."

Eir snorted.

"Okay, we don't have a system. Or a computer system for them."

My stomach cramped and I wanted to swallow the next words, but they came out anyway. "Am I going to be doing anything other than filing?"

"Of course," Jord assured me, joining the conversation. "It's just that we haven't had time to do a system, so each of us keeps some files here and there and..." She trailed off and coughed. "We contacted the N-o-r-n-s last night." She changed the subject and I tried to remember if there had been anything about forbidden words in the myths. "The only thing they would tell us is that we should be, and I quote, 'abundantly happy' that you are here. Then they vanished."

"Who exactly are the Nor—"

"NO!"

The yell from all three of them was so powerful that I backed up into the desk behind me.

"Don't say their names." Sif's voice held a sharp edge. "If you say their names, they will come. And when they come and there's nothing for them to do, it's possibly the worst mistake ever."

I noted that all three of them had gone from somewhat happy and mirthful to dead serious. Okay. Do not speak 'Norn' out loud.

"Erm, what are the, um, N-o-r-n's?" I tried again. "I haven't had a lot of time to catch up."

"They're the embodiment of fate," Sif said, abandoning all pretenses and going for the box of donuts. I did a dance on the inside. "There are three that are concerned with the gods and their lives, and only three, the others are for mortals. They don't mind helping us, but it always comes at a price. Whether or not you meant to call them, you will pay."

I swallowed hard. "So, they're like the Fates from Greece myths?" I was learning a lot, and not just about the Norse myths.

"More like they *are* the Fates of Greek myths." Eir picked up a donut and set it on a napkin on her desk. "We all have different names, but they do the same thing. Those gods have Clotho and the others to watch over them. The Ns are jerks compared to those guys."

"Is anything not dangerous?" I gave in and took one of the Boston cream. Talk about a joyous experience glazed in chocolate. Sweetness exploded in my mouth as the dough and cream met and I suppressed a groan of pleasure.

"There's nothing in any world that isn't dangerous in the wrong hands," Jord said.

I shuddered at the warning but pressed on. "You called them. What does that mean?"

"That's all they said when we asked." Sif threw her hands in the air, lobbing a blob of cream up to the ceiling. "'Abundantly happy.' Best we could figure is Fulla, who was already a contender. Fulla is the goddess of abundance, and they used the word with purpose."

"Fulla?" I tried the name out, not for the first time, hoping something would change with this new knowledge. I closed my eyes and whispered again. "Fulla." Nothing stirred, no memories came bursting forward and though I felt the magic inside me, the brightness, it didn't stir.

"I think it's a better chance than Gurd. Though you could be one of a dozen goddesses." Jord picked up a chocolate cream and sighed. "Shame you weren't here for the chocolate-covered strawberry cream ones on Valentine's Day."

I made a note about the holiday specials. Never let it be said that I don't suck up properly.

I brightened up. "Okay, well some possibilities, and wording that points to one? I'm okay with that. Fulla... Full... a?" I groaned. Abundant, full. Got it. "Goddess of abundance. Did she have any special powers?"

"A silver tongue," Eir said.

Sif elbowed her and Jord frowned. "Fulla was Frigg's handmaiden, trusted friend, and advisor. Not even Odin had Frigg's confidence like Fulla."

The Queen of the gods? Wow! But... "Does that mean I have to be her handmaiden now? I mean, the old days—"

"Are gone," Eir finished for me. Her pale face was tinged pink, dark lips standing out. "They're gone."

"Yeah." Sif grinned. "If things were still like then, I'd be miserable. You don't have to be anything you don't want to be. You don't have to meet Frigg if you don't want to. It's up to you if you even want to be here."

"I want to be here," I insisted. "I want to know, to learn." I had to. If I didn't, there was no hope for Mom.

"Curiosity isn't a good reason to do anything," Eir said, still not eating my deliciously yeasted bribes.

"Seemed a good enough reason for Odin to hang himself for knowledge," I argued.

Three sets of raised eyebrows. Good. They should know I was learning on my own.

"Tell me about me!" I put on my best grin and grabbed another donut. I wasn't going to let these go to waste. "What kind of powers will I develop?"

"Fulla was always in negotiations because her power was within her voice." Jord stood and paced, a far-off look resting on her elegant face. "She had the ability to turn negotiations in someone's favor and was the voice of reason in a conflict. Apparently, she and Eir were often called together for medical problems. And abundant can mean anything from money to people in your family, so she had a long reach."

My sponge-like brain threatened to revolt. I imagined someone stomping on it to keep it in there, but that only gave me a headache.

Turning to Eir, I once again offered the donuts, this time with them directly given to her. She took one, but she didn't eat it. "You worked with Fulla? Do you remember her?"

Eir shrugged. "That doesn't matter, does it?"

Jord shot a glare at her. "All she means is that you can't look at the past to look at the future."

Ah, mindfulness. In the now, I could do that. Eir's brush off didn't hurt me at all because I didn't know her. I couldn't judge that action as—shut up, Aspen. She probably hates your guts, and lying to yourself isn't going to do you any good.

I slumped slightly and turned my face down to the floor. My shoes, nice little pink and blue ones, were my most comfortable and cutest pair of tennis shoes.

I hated feeling insecure. It was like someone put a vice on my heart, or worse, like I wasn't good enough to do something with a vice on my heart.

"Here." Eir stood in front of me, holding a pickled fruit in a small jar. "Eat this tonight. You'll get a new fruit every week until your powers come back, then we'll slow it down."

I took the jar and studied it like the others. Another berry, this one smaller than the others, and definitely rounder. A cranberry? More likely a lingonberry, but I wouldn't know unless I tasted it. I slipped it into my purse, glad for another specimen to study. "Is that a lot of fruit? How much do you eat?"

"We only have to eat it when we feel age," Sif said, twisting her hair around and around in a bored way. "When we were discovered, we all went through the Fruit Fattening as Loki called it. Stupid prick." The last part I don't think I was supposed to hear, but I caught it.

Loki seemed like a jerk in the myths. After all, he caused Ragnarök and everything. I wondered where he was and if he was half as bad as the myths said.

Or possibly worse.

Chapter Eleven

u okay?

The message blinked across my phone screen with a scream, and I cringed, cold guilt flooding me.

The past couple of days had been weird. Really weird. And I had no ideas how I was going to tell Isa about all of it.

For now, I turned my ringer down and stared out the passenger side window. Eir and I were on our way to The Chapel of the Holy Cross in a 1969 pale blue convertible. We had the top down and didn't talk during the twenty-minute drive to the church. Instead, I sat with a stupid grin on my face as we took turns a little fast and sped past every trucker on the freeway from Cora Alma to Sedona.

The chapel came into view and as always, it took my breath away. The entire red-rock colored church appeared to sprout from the boulders, supported by a cross with stained glass at the center. The stained glass that made up the one visible wall glimmered hopefully in the light and with a small smile, I relaxed. There was both natural and unnatural beauty in this.

She parked in the furthest spot from the steps, even though there were only two other cars in the lot. The tourists weren't here yet. Probably for the best if we were looking for a mystical creature.

Eir cut the engine, and in the morning's silence I heard a humming. In my chest, something thumped through me, on the edge of anxiety. It sounded like we were too close to electrical lines or something, but there were no huge lines that would make that sound around us.

"What are you doing?" Amusement laced Eir voice instead of boredom or hostility. She saw me lean over the side of the door. How could she not? My ass was up in the air.

"I hear electrical humming," I said, more worried as I couldn't find a source. "It's around here, but I can't find it."

"Is your hair standing on end?"

My skin prickled as the humming intensified. "Yeah?"

"That's not electricity, that's the vortex." I gave her a dis-believing look, and she gave me a knowing one back. "You're going to tell me you're a skeptic about vortexes when you were taken to Yggdrasil a few days ago?"

I avoided her gaze, feeling like I'd been pushed down and laughed at. After all, if prophecies and goddesses were real, why not the energy points that gave people's healing powers or something?

"Vortexes are well known." Eir got out of the car and shield-ed her eyes as she stared up at the Chapel. "They baffle scientists. But the energy is magic leaking out of Yggdrasil. It's linking worlds. It's why we're here in a sleepy town and not a big city. Big cities rarely have vortexes because the energy makes people feel weird. So, humans generally stay away." She kept her focus on where the Chapel of the Holy Cross overlooked us. "Generally."

We climbed the levels up, bit by frustrating bit. The climb twisted around the rocks until we eventually got to the top of the mesa and could see the church properly. Normally it was a few minutes, and maybe a little steep, but it was Eir who made it frustrating. Every few feet, she would stop and check the surrounding bushes, looking for what, she didn't say. That didn't help since I thought I had come to learn things. I seethed on that, my clenched jaw giving me a headache, and continued to speculate on what her problem was as we climbed the stairs to go inside.

We finally got to the top, but the back wasn't nearly as cool the cross growing out of the red rocks. The front wasn't any different than any other Catholic church out there. All glass doors and clean-cut lines.

"We're going inside," Eir said, removing her sunglasses and putting on her regular ones. "Have you ever been to a Catholic church?" I responded that I had and she turned her attention back to the church. "Then act like we're here to pray. Don't touch anything."

I followed Eir inside. She dipped her fingers into the stoup of holy water at the entrance and I have to be honest, I wasn't expecting that. I followed her example but before we went in further, I tapped her shoulder and motioned for her to lean over so I could whisper as softly as my voice would allow.

"Holy water is okay?"

"Why wouldn't it be?" She also kept her voice at a whisper.

"Because you're a literal heathen?"

She threw a hand over her mouth to muffle her laughter, but then swallowed it. Still radiating amusement, she whispered back. "The Christian God isn't wrathful." I did a double take, and she explained hurriedly. "No, really. I have to admit, whoever they are, they are pretty elusive. No one has seen them in eons and even the gods we only have stories."

"Huh."

Dark shrouded over me and it took some time to adjust to the lighting. The flames of prayer candles, off to each side and in the front, provided more light than the obscured sun. Only a single parishioner knelt in the front praying. Eir walked quickly and silently, and I could barely keep up. First, she went to the candles and stuffed money in the jar before lighting one. It took her almost a full minute to decide which candle to light. Then she was off to the other side of the church to apparently study the walls.

I checked the person at the front. They were still bent over in prayer, not noticing that my companion was now touching the walls and—oh, dear God. She moved again and was now looking under the seats on her hands and knees.

I crouched down beside her and hissed, "What are you doing?"

"Looking for a sign," she muttered, sweeping her phone flashlight under the seats. "There's always a sign."

The parishioner hadn't noticed us, but I continued to keep my voice down. "Do I get to know what the sign is? Or are you going to do all the work and then complain that I didn't help?"

She sat back on her heels and glared at me. "Do you under-stand that there are fairies in literally every type of mythology and they all have different tells?"

I pushed my lips into a thin line, trying to come up with something besides outright admitting that I didn't know what to look for.

She went back to searching.

Anger flooded my veins, flushing my cheeks hot, and re-leasing me of my usual good humor. I grabbed my phone and turned on the flashlight, joining her on the ground. "Well," I bit back, "I won't know unless you teach me."

Her annoyed stare met mine from under the pew but she turned away just as fast, keeping her opinions and knowledge to herself. I'd been nothing but nice and amenable since this whole... *thing* started. I like to think I would have understood a little hostility, but her tight-lipped approach was starting to piss me off.

She peeked in everything. Under the pews, around the candles. She even sat down on the pews to make sure there was nothing actually in them.

Then she came to the first row where the person, an older man with graying hair, still prayed. She sat down on the edge and made room for me before folding her hands and lowering her head.

I followed her example, continuing to glance over at the man piously bowing his head. It seemed like forever that we sat in the dim light, stale air being returned through the over-worked air conditioner, but it was over when Eir whispered, "Showtime."

I snapped to attention and glanced around. With the old man gone, we were alone in the church. Definitely a good thing since Eir began climbing up the steps, making a direct beeline for the altar.

"Eir... n. Erin!" I hissed, monitoring the doors. "You can't go up there."

"It's just an altar. They don't even have it roped off." She lifted the white cloth that covered the raised altar and smirked. "Come look at this, noob."

I sent a quick prayer to the completely real deity I might piss off, and peered into where Eir had disappeared. I leaned over and then did a double take. Under the altar was a place that was, well, alive. Green moss coated every surface in its spongy texture, causing a wet, earthy smell. There were three not so small rocks also covered in moss, five empty bags of chips, and bottles of water. Either a small child was performing extremely strange rituals, or we'd found Mr. Egert's elusive fae.

"A pixie, probably," Eir muttered. She shined her phone in the different crevices, revealing a few mushrooms and, strangely enough, some alyssum on the 'ground.' "They have shit senses of direction and end up everywhere, and I mean everywhere. I once found one living in a garbage bin of a movie theater." She paused. "Ya know, I think that one liked the movies more than anything."

I snorted. "You'd have to. Come on, let's get down before—"

"Excuse me, young ladies?" a calm, priestly voice interrupted.

"Were you going to say, 'before we get caught?'"

"Yup."

One stern lecture from a priest later and Eir and I were back in her convertible, this time with the top up so we could talk easily. Honestly, it was a relief after the way she had not talked to me in the church. What came next wasn't an apology or even strategy, it was a lesson in fae.

"Pixies are lesser fae, and not just because they're smaller than most," Eir began, her voice taking on the quality of a professor at a lecture. "Usually, they're as small as a few inches to a couple of feet tall. They get pulled in directions of strong magic and will generally do the bidding of any greater fae when asked. But like I said, they have no sense of direction and can end up anywhere when they're lost. This one found the vortex and wanted to stay as close to it as possible."

I absorbed the information, taking in every last bit before asking my question. "So why did it leave and follow Egert around?"

Eir mulled it over and then shrugged. "We can ask it. It might tell us, but more than likely it's going to deny it's lost. Fae, even small fae, are proud."

Twenty minutes later, we pulled up to one of those types of mansions that made you mad money existed. But there was no point getting bitter and angering Mr. Egert on accident. Even I knew a pissed-off client didn't pay.

When he opened the door, loud, strangely rhythmic music blasted out. Eir missed her footing and slipped off the stoop in surprise. She righted herself quickly and had the decency to blush when she did so.

Mr. Egert came outside, slamming the door behind him. I'd never seen someone puce before. The beard made it a real treat, too.

"What kept you?" His voice was sharper, slightly higher, and definitely panicked. "You said first thing this morning!"

Eir didn't budge and it took everything in me to fight the urge to throw up my hands in defeat.

"Yes, Mr. Egert." Her voice soothed him, coated in the honey of someone who was about to lie their ass off. "I've been working on your case diligently for the past twelve hours."

Hours, minutes. Who's counting?

"You could have come and looked at it!"

"It's visible?" Eir's honey voice evaporated. "Come on, Aspen!" She pushed past the man and I followed, glad I thought to leave my purse in the car. "That thing I did with my voice is something Fulla would be able to do, too, only stronger. Her words were always laced with power and intent." She glanced behind her. "Concentrate. Will what you feel—the power that is under you—and put it into everything you do and say. That is how Fulla would talk this pixie into leaving."

"Wait, I'm doing what?"

"You'll do fine," she reassured me, but the flip-flop in my stomach said otherwise. I tried to stammer out a denial. Any denial. I couldn't use magic; I'd only just found out what it was!

"Eir!" I finally found my voice, but she continued to push me forward. I dug my heels in and grabbed the nearest thing I could—a doorframe—which finally brought her to a stubborn halt.

She huffed and put her hands on her hips. "What? You need to speak, that's all. Tell it to leave. It's fae. Earth goddesses have some dominion over them."

Well, that sounded creepy. "Sure, but how? If I talk, what happens then?"

"No one told you how to use your magic?"

"No one told me anything." I threw my hands up in the air. "I know nothing. I understand nothing. Pretend I'm five and explain things to me."

I half expected her to patronize me further. Instead she launched into a hasty and probably oversimplified explanation. "You know how you used to just wish things were true as a kid? Wish and wish so hard in your mind and your heart and with all your soul?" I nodded slowly, not quite catching on. "That's the closest thing there is in the mortal world to magic. Asking, willing it into happening. Your powers are only limited by the strength of your heart and mind."

Wishing? Okay, I could do that. I had a lot of practice in wishing in fact. So many nights in the hospital, shared with strangers because we couldn't afford the places with single rooms. Also so alone that I couldn't feel anything but the pain of loneliness. Talking and laughing with my roommate after lights out, but still feeling that emptiness.

You never wish harder to be 'normal' than when you're in a mental health facility.

Right now, I wished to be more than normal.

The music had stopped at some point during our conversation, and we proceeded at a cautious pace. Crooked pictures lined the walls with cracked spider webbing over the faces and expensive artwork. We peeked into the first room—the office—and found a toppled over monitor, a roller chair on its side, and several volumes of books lying about with torn pages. There was going to be one hell of a cleanup after this pixie.

A bang sounded, followed by canned laughter. We listened as voices floated around us and she put a finger to her lips. I bit my lip to silence any questions and followed her down the hall to the open living area where I stopped to take it in.

What had been a pristine white leather couch was covered in dirty feet and handprints, about the size of a toddler. The remaining wood furnishings were now all the size of my shoe or smaller. Some of it had been used as kindling for a failed fire, according to the soot stains on the ceiling and the charred wood in the middle of the room.

The TV and everything connected to it were all that sat mostly untouched. In front of the TV, a small childlike creature laughed along with it. It probably would have passed for a child in most circumstances, but in the bright light its strange proportions were easy to see. Its arms were too long and its skin was pale blue with darker tips on its sharp fingernails. Mud and leaves made a crude outfit, while its long black hair hung in a ponytail down its back. Despite the dirt, its appearance was ethereal and not of this world.

The TV had it entrapped with an 80s sitcom, if the clothes and hair were anything to judge by. Eir craned her neck toward the pixie and jerked a couple of times like she was having a stroke. It took me way too long to realize she was telling me to do my thing.

It was about power and wishing. Right then, I wished I was more prepared.

"Pixie? Um, excuse me, pixie?"

Eir put her hand over her eyes in what I guessed was frustration and/or embarrassment. She wasn't alone.

"Give me more to work with," I said to her, racking my brain for what I knew about fae. I knew they liked to bargain. Maybe that would work for me?

"Such a lovely television," I drew out the words on purpose, speaking loudly and clearly. I walked up so the pixie saw me, putting myself right next to the TV.

The pixie turned overly large sky-blue eyes to me. I kept my poker face, but seeing myself reflected back in those pupilless irises disturbed me.

"Sure is beautiful. I'd like to bargain for it."

Yep, that other look must have been embarrassment because now Eir's face held pure abject horror. She went so pale I almost bailed on the plan to stop her from fainting. Luckily, she either trusted me or wanted to see me fail, so she let this go on.

The pixie's face didn't change, but its high-pitched voice was laced with amusement. "A witch? A witch who would test a fae?"

"I'm not a witch! I'm a—" Goddess? Valkyrie? College graduate? "—detective."

Go, Aspen, go.

It—I refused to determine the gender—smirked at me, its tiny wings flittering. "Does 'detective' now mean 'foolish' in the mortal tongue?"

I touched my hand to my mouth and tried to appear shocked. "Aren't fae supposed to be polite?"

The pixie's child-like laugh held a musical quality. "All mortals are different, and so are we, detective." Its pointed teeth gleamed. "You would not let the will of others bind you?"

"As much as the courts allow, anyway. Good point, mighty fae." A slight flutter of its wings again as it regarded me suspiciously. "Everyone's different. Thank you, kind fae, for teaching me a lesson."

Somehow its eyes got rounder, and it blinked twice, wings still. "I—I accept your kindness?"

"Wonderful!" I clapped my hands together and continued to study its new den, trying not to sneeze from the soot smell. "You know, I said I wanted to bargain for this television."

"NO!" The pixie went from sly and small to doubling in size, its blue irises tinged with orange around the edges. "It's mine! I want it, I have it! It's mine!" The magic wore off within a few seconds and the pixie was back to the size of a toddler.

A toddler?

"Well, if it's yours, then for you leaving this house and returning to your own home, you may take the television."

I sneaked a glance over to Eir, whose face hadn't regained color. She had covered her mouth with one hand and was looking at me through her fingers, apparently horrified.

"It won't fit in my old home. I decline."

Oh, oh damn. Didn't fae prefer the outdoors?

A small bead of sweat trickled down my back. "You absolutely can if you move things around, I'm sure. Wouldn't a faerie like you rather be somewhere in nature?"

The pixie scrutinized me, and in an instant, its eyes blazed red. Its child-sized hands grew into claws, and I fell backwards out of fear and shock, ready for those claws to rip and tear me before I could protect myself.

Eir shouted something incomprehensible behind me, and air blew up from the ground and cushioned me as I fell, gently letting me regain my composure as I gawked at the windstorm surrounding the pixie. It became even smaller in the storm, pushing and clawing at an invisible barrier. I turned around and saw Eir calmly holding a piece of wood the size of her palm with runes inscribed on it.

"You're a witch?"

"Anyone with magic can make spells. Jord said witches as an example. And what in the absolute hell were you doing?"

I gasped at her tone and took a step back. "I was—"

"Bargaining with a fae? Calling it a faerie? You might have lost your life. You might have lost your soul!" The air whooshed out of my lungs as Eir continued to read me the riot act. "I couldn't step in once you started. You're lucky he declined to take the deal. Do you know what kind of damage you could have done?" She snapped her fingers and the pixie, still fighting, floated to her. She rooted around in her purse and pulled out another smaller piece of wood with cuttings on it, this one painted purple. Again, it was illegible to me, but I suspected they were runes. She murmured a few words, turning the sphere opaque, and I couldn't see or hear the little guy anymore.

"Hey, what did you just—"

"He's fine. This disguises the magic." She grabbed the now stable ball, which looked like a volleyball without stitches, and tossed it from hand to hand. "It's so stable in there he can't even feel that."

I followed her out to the car, sphere in hand, as she dealt with getting payment from our client.

Well, I may be stupid, but I doubt she'd have been able to get that spell off without me distracting that little bastard.

Chapter Twelve

I thought my faux pas with the pixie was going to be the end of my career, but Eir didn't mention it when we got back to the office. She put the pixie on her desk and made a phone call while Sif led me to her area. She pulled up a seat and waved me into it with an enthusiastic grin.

"I'm the office manager." Sif shuffled my paperwork in her hands and tapped it on the desk in front of her. "Did you really survive two years at that cafe down the street? Ugh. So many tourists. We deal with tourists all the time. People get followed home by ghosts from this area so often, but if you're local, they leave you alone and sorry... I've been rambling."

Thank God she stopped. Uh, gods? Goddesses? Whatever. My brain throbbed, about to implode from how fast that conversation with herself had gone. She talked faster than a teenager with Mountain Dew in their breakfast cereal.

"Maybe a little." I laughed and cleared my throat. After this morning, I had more questions than ever before. "Is the pixie pretty normal? And ghosts?"

"Yeah, pretty much. We deal with a lot because everything is drawn to the vortexes, but they're mostly harmless pests. We get one about every other week."

That was another mention of the vortex.

"What's so special about the vortexes anyway?" I almost wanted to take notes. This was only scratching the surface of this world. So far, the taste of it was more delightful than the sweetest of desserts. And maybe a little dangerous.

Sif took a moment to think about her answer. "Vortexes attract magical beings, like the pixie and other fae-like creatures. When we set up on Midgard—ya know, Earth," she said at my blank expression, "we go where there's a lot of magic. We moved from Sedona to Cora Alma about sixty years ago. Since humans are put off by our spells, the building gets mostly left alone."

My phone vibrated with a new text message. "What else is magical that's real?"

"You know," Sif grinned at me, bobbing her head back and forth, making a choice, "there was a time where I wouldn't have to explain what magic is. People used to know about it."

My phone went off again, but I ignored it. I was getting so much information, I reached deep into my brain to keep her going. "What caused them to stop? The Spanish Inquisition?"

Sif's mouth twisted in displeasure. She looked away, confirming my theory with a nod. "There's so much out there these days, you know, in the media." Her bubbly personality was back as she changed the subject. "So, telling someone vampires are an old cult, not a group of sparkly or goth, hot bad asses—See? You didn't know!" She snapped her gum and laughed, spinning delightfully in her chair.

I nearly fell over. "All those myths, the stories, none of them are real?" Another buzz in my pocket.

"Well, they are about the blood thing. But everything else is most assuredly false."

"Sif, just do her paperwork," Jord said.

"But—"

"Paperwork, Sif. Stories later."

Sif frowned and stuck her tongue out at Jord before turning her attention back to my paperwork. "You're definitely hired. We've already checked your background. One question about your sister. She's Wiccan? In a small coven in Flagstaff?"

"Yes?" Was that bad? My phone went off again and I bit the inside of my cheek, annoyed and worried at the same time. Who was messaging me over and over and not calling? The family rule was to call in an emergency.

"That's so nice of her. Do you know who her patron is?"

"Uh, no. No idea. Cypress and I aren't really close," I admitted. Sif

Another buzz. Shit. My stomach twisted, and I gave in. Checking my phone this time, I tried not let my worry and guilt show on my face while I scrolled through my DMs.

hi

hellooo

hey

what r u doing??

haven't seen u in days text me...

Isa. My stomach cramped with guilt. I'd lost myself so far in this new world so quickly that I left her hanging. It was three now and I knew that she'd be working. I resolved that once I was done for the day, I'd go see her.

"Aspen. Aspen?" Sif waved her bangled hand in front of my face.

I blinked back awake from my thoughts. "Sorry."

"No, no, this is on me. Why don't you go home for the day? It's been almost four hours. We'll pay for the whole day."

I checked my watch and realized Isa's work was less than ten minutes away. I hopped up and stretched out. "It's been an interesting day. Oh." I turned back to Sif. "Why wouldn't you want to call a pixie a faerie?"

Another pop of Sif's gum. "Uh, yeah—that would be bad. They barely tolerate being referred to as 'fae,' but 'faerie' is how they refer to their babies. So, when we call them that—"

"—It's like we're calling them children. Gotcha." It might not have been my poor communication skills and non-existent magic. The pixie just didn't like being insulted.

I bid the goddesses and Charlie goodnight. My mind swam with new knowledge and, as before, so many more questions. Why were they afraid of the Norns? Is there a proper way to negotiate with fae? Speaking of fae, my nightmares were going to be haunted by images of weird toddlers.

I sighed and stuffed my hands in my pockets. The sun shone brilliantly on a painted blue sky. I passed by a large window that held crystals, tarot card decks, and even crystal balls. Just days ago, I'd cackled over how ludicrous these things were and now I had the urge to find out what would protect me better: black jade as advertised by the shop, or a large dog.

What was charlatan and what was true?

"Ya gonna stand in the window all day, or are ya gonna come in and say 'hi?'"

I had made it to the cafe without even realizing it and Isa was sticking her head out of the pie pickup window and calling me over.

I scuttled in, shuffled around the tiny squares that David called tables, and took a seat at the booth with 'Reserved' printed in Isa's handwriting. She came by, snatched it off the table, and put it on another. I went to move, but she shot me a Look and I sat right back down.

That Look haunted my dreams because whenever I got it, it meant I was in trouble. We'd been friends for nearly a decade and not once had that Look been wrong.

Isa dropped the coffee in her hands at the only other occupied table. Wiping her hands on her pressed blue apron, she headed to the back.

I waited. And waited. After a while, my phone was too boring, and I couldn't figure out what was taking Isa so long. The cafe wasn't busy—there were only three other customers there—and they were all being waited on by someone else now. In fact, I hadn't seen Isa since The Look.

Worry clawed at me, but I bit it down. Isa and I had been friends since high school, and she'd seen everything my mind could offer. When I went off the rails and she transferred up three grades to be a freshman, we'd both been alone. Despite my illness, she stuck by me and I did by her when she would rage about life at home.

So why would I worry now?

I waved at David as I stepped behind the counter, then pushed the door open into the back room. Small towns are wonderful sometimes. I didn't have to go three steps before I found Isa sitting at the employee break table, stone faced with her hands folded in front of her.

"Doesn't feel nice to be forgotten, does it?" she said a little coolly. My blood went hot at her accusation, but before I opened my mouth, she continued. "Three days." The heat melted away and I almost kicked myself as she continued. "You've been here for three days and then you stopped reading my texts. I called Mama Flower and she said nothing is wrong, so here we are."

"Okay, point taken. I got a job, Isa." She didn't move. "And that's not an excuse. But this job, it's... I can't describe how important it is for my future. I got so caught up that... I left you on read. I'm sorry."

Her stance softened. "I get it, girl, I do." She hummed in frustration. "But what is so important about this new job that you left me on read, and haven't gardened since you got here? What, you lose yourself in one of these spiritualist traps or something?"

I winced and her jaw dropped. "No shit. How did they get you?"

I sat across from her. There was no one else back here, but it still wasn't safe to talk about the fact that I had 1,000-year-old fruit in my pocket that was going to make me immortal.

"Aspen?"

"I'm sorry I forgot, well, not forgot... but I guess I forgot? I promise it won't happen again. It's just that I got caught up in the wild world of detectives."

She tapped her fabulously polished nails against her cheek before turning back to me with a full grin. "Ah, hell. Sisters gotta fight sometimes."

I snorted and when she stuck her tongue out at me, I did it right back before we started giggling.

"You made your point, Isabela." Even though we were alone, that could change at any moment. "I don't know if I should talk about this here."

"Aspen." She dropped her voice. "Are you in trouble? I mean, did some cult get you for real?"

I shook my head. "No, but I..." My stomach was in knots and my feet didn't feel like they were on the floor. I couldn't lie to her.

"Oh, come on!"

One quick shouting match ended with David throwing his hands up in exasperation, and Isa was off for the day. She threw on her sweater and followed me to the streetlight and the old, dilapidated shed, where I stopped and tried not to let my nerves overtake me.

"The shack?" She put her hand on her hip and pursed her lips together. "Are we on someone's reel or something?"

The runes warmed to my touch, and I opened the door into the office. Charlie, whose expression went from boredom to horror as I fully opened the barrier between the mortal and immortal realms, grabbed the phone and dialed.

"It's bigger on the inside." Isa's tone was somewhere between awe and disbelief as I ushered her into the waiting area. She immediately noticed the magic that I took for granted in the beginning. Her face was alternating between child-like wonder and adult skepticism the more she took in the larger interior.

Charlie spoke in hushed tones on the phone before hanging up quickly. I let Isa take in the longer and taller interior.

The back door burst open and Jord, Eir, Sif and a man I didn't recognize rumbled into the room, answering the question of who Charlie was talking to. Isa jumped and her jaw dropped.

"It's even bigger than this?" Her statement was now a high-pitched question.

Eir shook her head and the man, a ginger with a smattering of freckles, laughed. He was wearing boots, jeans, and a nice button-down shirt. His boots were a little mud splattered, and he had a five o'clock shadow, but his face could have been carved from a block of graphite with its sharp angles.

"Thanks for the help as always, my ladies." He sauntered, his back almost as pleasing as his front, to the door leading outside. "I, uh, wish you luck with your new... sister."

I forgot him just as quickly after his exit, because Eir stormed forward, her face a raging inferno. I backed up, almost into the wall. Was Eir a war goddess and the world had forgotten about it?

"Why did you bring her here?" she demanded, her flushed cheeks showing through her makeup.

"I—"

"Mortals have no place here, Aspen!"

"Bu—"

"It's not like books or movies, there's only us! There's no shadow government to clean up messes like this. We could have to relocate!"

"If you would just—"

"The rules are—"

"No one told me any rules!" I shouted over her. She jumped back as though I'd taken a swing at her. "I had no idea how fae work, and no one told me that this is a big secret."

"What did you think it was, public knowledge?" Eir's exasperated tone did nothing to placate me.

"No." I kept my creeping anger out of my voice. "But I sure didn't think you'd lose your collective shit just because I told my friend."

"Best friend and sister," Isa hissed in my ear.

"My best friend and sister."

Jord and Sif exchanged a look. Eir sighed and deflated. Charlie laughed and popped a piece of popcorn—how does she do that?—and crunched loudly while watching with animated interest.

It was going to be a long explanation.

"Huh. So your grandma isn't full of shit?" Isa brushed the walls and reached up on her tiptoes to touch the ceiling, missing by an arm's length.

It was not a long explanation.

Jord's piercing gaze bore into me. "Did you tell anyone else?"

Trembling, I shook my head, and that seemed to relax the goddesses.

Isa turned back to me in awe as she pushed herself into the back office. "It's real. It's all real."

I grinned, the guilt already fading. This girl got me. "Yeah... Nana might know way more than previously believed. Jord—uh, this lady right here is Jord." Jord finger waved to Isa. "She says that crystals, palmistry, tarot readings are all real."

"So is TARDIS magic," she said, touching the bigger on the inside walls.

"Can be real," Jord corrected me. "Most people in this town are only out to make a profit on others. True magic practitioners are understated. You should really vet your grandmother's psychic, dear."

I hadn't thought about that.

"Well, cat's out of the bag. Come, come, Isa, was it?" Jord held her hand out and Isa let the older woman lead her.

"Uh, yeah. Isabela Maria Hernandez Soto." We took seats in the multiplying comfy chairs and within minutes, Sif had produced a traditional tea set with sugar, cream, and a tray of goodies.

"How do you do that?" I asked her.

"You'd never ask Bastet that question, would you?" Sif winked at me, though I had no idea who Bastet was.

"Bastet is in Egyptian mythology," Isa said, not reaching for tea or the stacked cookies. "Jord is the embodiment of Earth in Norse mythology, right?"

All three goddesses perked up. "You know your myths," Eir observed.

Isa gave me a side-eyed glance. "I loved taking mythology courses in high school and college. Lots of stories to memorize."

"A simple thing for you?" Jord asked, offering her the tray of cookies.

"Sometimes." She refused to budge.

Why was Isa being so curt with them? Somehow, the temperature in the room dropped to frosty. Isa's posture was rigid, her back straight and eyes darting back and forth as she observed the three of them like trapped prey.

"They're not fae," I assured her. Her look turned from frightened and questioning to wary. "No, really. They're uh, we're, uh, well..."

"Well what, Aspen? What is going on here? What does this have to do with your new job?"

I had come this far, may as well go all the way.

"This place is a supernatural detective agency called Goddesses, Inc., and I'm their newest reborn goddess and/or filing clerk?"

"Holy hell," Isa whispered. Then she swore much more colorfully. "Reborn?"

Eir sipped her tea casually. "Ragnarök already happened."

"The Voluspa prophecy?"

"Bless you?" I said, looking between Isa and the goddesses.

"She *is* good," Sif squealed.

"This is insane. This is so weird. Who are you all, then?"

Jord introduced everyone, including Charlie the witch, and then she stopped at me. "And Aspen is... we aren't sure. Though now we are fairly sure she isn't Fulla. She couldn't talk a pixie into leaving a house."

"She tried to bargain with it," Eir reminded everyone and my face burned. Sif tried to hide a snigger in her tea.

"No," Isa gasped, her face begging me to deny it. I shrugged and stirred my tea. "But everything's fine?"

I shrank into the chair as they went on. She engaged so easily in conversation about things I barely knew about. I caught Sif's eye and she smiled kindly at me, holding her tea up in a salute.

It was past dinnertime before the goddesses, Isa, and I said goodnight. I dropped Isa at her car and then continued on north to my house. There were no streetlights after I left and without a moon, I put the brights on.

I loved to drive and mull over events, but night in Cora Alma was not the time to do this. I took the mountain path slowly but fast enough so no one would run me off the road. Tonight, a fog lingered low on the ground, hindering my view. This time of year was typically too warm for fog.

Damn, it was so hard to see.

That's why when the elk came into view, I had no time to brake. Cold horror flooding my veins, I gasped loudly and waited for the impact. I still slammed on the brakes by instinct, because this was going to be horrible.

It didn't come.

Bessie came to a screeching halt on the side of the road, but the elk wasn't in front of me, or anywhere nearby. I glanced around frantically to find a man sitting next to me.

Screaming, I then cried out, "Who are you?" while reaching for my seat belt.

I hadn't heard the door. Hell, as I opened mine, I heard a click of the door unlocking. But there was no time to wonder about my hearing, because the door suddenly shut and my seatbelt came around me again, clicking into place.

Magic.

I stared, slack-jawed, at my 'visitor,' who calmly, patiently stared back at me.

He was tall, lean, and easily over six foot. His blond hair curled along the nape of his neck, perfectly long and well-groomed. His hazel eyes were haunted, but there was a dangerous sort of mirth in them. Something I did not want to test.

"Hello, Aspen." His voice slithered around me and I shivered. "It's so nice to meet you at last. I'm Loki."

Chapter Thirteen

M aybe he thought telling me who he was would calm me down.

Though he *had* unleashed his children on Asgard killing them, the gods, and himself at the same time.

So, I screamed.

"Well, you've heard of me," he said as I took in a breath for the next round. "Ah, stop stop stop!" he yelled while simultaneously putting his hand over my mouth to muffle me. When I stopped for a moment, he pulled his hand back, a look of relief washing over his face.

I put my gut into screaming, desperately trying to think of an actual plan. Once again, his hand clapped over my mouth. I tried to bite him and he pulled back, which only made me keep screaming. Trying my door again, I found it jammed.

It was dark. No one was passing by and no one would know I was missing until the morning. What did he want? To kill me? To torture me for information I didn't have? Or something I couldn't even fathom?

"If you stop screaming, I'll tell you why I'm here!" The pleading in his voice wasn't lost on me and I will admit to taking some pleasure in that now. How often does a girl get a god to plead with her?

Listening, or pretending to would give me more time to cultivate a plan of escape. The picture the goddesses painted of him didn't give me much hope. After all, he was holding a stranger captive. I had been willing to give him a chance.

Congratulations on blowing that, Loki.

"You're feisty." He chortled, far more amused than I think a killer god should be. I continued glaring at him and opened my mouth.

"You said you'd tell me—"

"I will. Drive."

Excuse me? I puffed up, trying to look taller than him. Because we all know supreme beings are like bears.

"Why would I—"

"Drive, or I will drive for you," Loki threatened. There was an edge to his voice that caused the hair on my arms to stand up. My legs shook, but I planted my feet firmly on the mat below me and crossed my arms.

"Who do you think you are?" I ignored his question and stared daggers at him, using my anger and terror to keep up my bravado. He changed the question. "What goddess do you think you used to be?"

My back hurt from the tension, but I sealed my lips, barely able to stop myself from trembling visibly. I don't think it fully worked, but I was determined to not give him even a iota of information after he frightened me and ordered me around.

He smirked, which pulled slightly more at his right than his left, giving him a slanted look. "Obviously not Fulla."

I jerked my head slightly in shock, trying to recover quickly. How did he know? "Obviously." I kept my tone clipped.

"Are you going to drive?"

I swallowed and didn't let my voice squeak or shake. "I will once you get out."

Chuckling at my defiance, Loki flicked his fingers, purple lightning dancing off of them. The car lurched forward. I grabbed the purple-glowing steering wheel, trying to take control back, but it glided perfectly back into the lane.

I continued to gape at the steering wheel as it turned, before turning back at the smirking jerk, then back at the wheel. It straightened and then turned a bit. A perfect curve.

"What kind of magic is that?"

He snapped his fingers and a small sprout of purple fire ignited. "A location spell mixed with a bit of telekinesis. I don't need an object or rune to cast it."

"Why not? The others have used runes." I remembered the carved wood that Eir had used to trap the fae and save my ass.

"Maybe I'm stronger than them."

"I take it humbleness wasn't an Asgardian trait. Hey!" I yelled as we passed the turnoff to my home. "That's my house!"

"I know," the ever-so-humble god said, continuing to drive the car north.

In this time, I came up with exactly zero escape plans. Jumping out wasn't an option, and the creep also knew where I lived. I could try to smash a window, but he would be able to stop me before I did it.

"Then who, dear, who?"

"Are you also an owl in your spare time?"

Oooh, good burn there, Aspen. You really showed him your wit and strength. Say something about his mother next.

"Birds are more of Freyja's thing than mine. I suppose you don't remember that."

Trees whipped past us as he took us further north.

"Your family moved recently, isn't that right? Were you born here?" Loki kept his voice neutral.

"You're pushy," I grumbled, all the while my brain tried to wrap itself around a way to escape. It always went so much smoother in my mind than this. I was magically buckled into the driver's seat and the doors were magically shut. Vague purple light glowed over the locks, just like the steering wheel.

He wielded many spells at once. Without runes. Maybe he *was* more powerful than the goddesses.

"Pushy isn't the worst thing I've been called."

"I didn't want to lead with 'murderer.'"

Loki laughed and I relaxed a little when he didn't lash out. If nothing else, he didn't seem to want to hurt me. "The goddesses rarely did battle in our times, but even Sif was trained to use a sword."

"Did Sif fight in Ragnarök?" I remembered how she laughed at some of the 'modern portrayals'.

Taking on a far off look, I was shocked when he replied. "It's been so long; a lot of the details are lost to us. Memories fade." He laughed in a humorless, dry way. "Most do, anyway. Everyone fought, even Freyja. She survived. Every pacifist threw away their ideals to stand up and yell, 'No, Loki, you will not kill us. You will not take our home.'" He paused in the middle of his dramatic speech, and I decided the best thing to do would be to give him the attention he wanted. He had to be here for a reason.

"In the end, we just killed each other."

"That's all public knowledge. What do you want, a repeat of your greatest hits?"

Jord said I'd need to judge for myself to know who to trust. So far, Loki was very, very far down on my list.

Very.

"Have I offended you, Goddess?"

"Well, you have kidnapped me." I gave him a Look. The one mothers give small children who have been warned twenty times. The one that every mother—and somehow Isa—is so good at.

I was not a mother, so I guess it was futile.

Loki pushed himself close to me. He needed a shave. A thin scar ran from the edge of his mouth on the left side almost up to his left temple. His calloused palm cupped my cheek, and he pushed so close that our noses were millimeters apart. I tried to yank my face from his grasp, but he held firm.

Was he going to kiss me? I felt his breath on my lips and for a moment I completely panicked, unable to do anything but pull frantically at his arm and try to get away. He turned my head and put his lips by my ear.

"You haven't been ensnared by the spider," he whispered. My panic melted into confusion. I pulled away and his face contorted as though he was in pain. He grabbed his chest, gasping, trying to force out the words. Why couldn't he talk? "The spider—the spider—"

"Are you alright?" I reached for him but stopped myself just as quickly. This was probably a trap.

"I'm fine," he panted, still gripping his chest. His heart. The smile returned, but this time as he looked into my eyes something flashed, almost as though he was looking through me. He wiped his face—had he been crying? —and then hissed, "Asshole."

For a moment we just sat there, both of us breathing hard, but not from exertion or even anything fun you might do in a car. The car continued to steer us around the mountains, never faltering through his apparent pain.

After an eternity that lasted only seconds he cut through the silence. "You'll have to figure out the rest, Aspen. And don't count on any detectives helping you." He lifted his hand and then said, "Oh, and just so you know: the last mile marker we passed was 392."

Then he snapped his fingers, disappearing from my sight, leaving a distinct smell of charred wood behind.

I grabbed the steering wheel just in time to watch the purple magic fade away from my seat belt, the locks, and the rest of the car.

"Shit!" I grit my teeth and slammed on the brakes as my heart pounded so fast I thought my ribcage would burst. Bessie sputtered, lurched, and then died, rolling a bit before she stopped.

I looked down in disbelief at my dashboard and banged my hand several times on my steering wheel, anger rolling through me.

I was out of gas.

Chapter Fourteen

M ile marker 392 was between Cora Alma and Flagstaff, too far from either for cell service to be reliable. It took almost ten minutes of walking around the dark forest before I found a spot the text would send. I sent a text to Isa with '912' (non-life-threatening emergency), the mile marker, and the simple message:

BRING GAS

And then, I waited. Thanks to Dad, I kept an emergency kit in my car. And thanks to Mom, that kit included dried fruit, three liters of water, and a book to read.

Normally I might have pulled that book out and read it by car light while I waited for Isa. Even though I hadn't gotten a response, I knew she would be here soon. So while I waited, I climbed up on the hood of my car and I did something I hadn't done in a long time. I stared at the stars.

I know that most of the stars were named after Greek mythology, or at least the most famous ones. Sirius, the horoscope constellations, Orion. I now had to wonder, what other names did the stars have? What had I—whoever I had been—called those stars? I closed my eyes and let the cool wind of the night whip over my skin, chilling my flesh. I shivered and rubbed my hands over my arms. I'd forgotten that it got chilly well into what Phoenix considered summer.

In the distance, I heard the song of wildlife, the rustle of the wind in the trees. The planet felt so alive as I sat there with my head against the windshield, staring up at the stars. I swear I felt the heartbeat of the planet beneath me, like Yggdrasil. Just as I was dozing off the sound of an approaching vehicle tore me from my thoughts.

Out of the dark, twin beams of light came into view. I sighed with relief and waved Isa down in her old Pontiac POS. She parked behind me but left the headlights on as she approached.

"Are you alright?" She demanded, her long hair giving her that near 'halo' effect from the light. "What happened? Why the hell are you all the way out here?"

"Grab the gas can. It's been a long night." While we filled my car up, I filled her in on my encounter with the Norse god of mischief and my opinion of him.

I finished my tale and the anger bubbled in me like I had been set on an open flame to stew. "If I see that sneaky little jerk again, I'll—I'll..."

Isa snorted. "What? Ask him for more information and maybe his phone number?" I glared at her and she shrugged. "You said he was hot."

"I said he was easy on the eyes."

"For you, that means hot." I resisted the urge to make a face at her and instead climbed into my car and took a long drink from the water bottle.

The gas canister scraped against my car as Isa finished with it. "So, the god of mischief. What exactly did he say?"

I handed her a water bottle, which she took with a grateful smile. "I don't know. Something about me not being ensnared? It seemed like he was in pain. He couldn't talk once he mentioned it."

Isa mulled that one over, taking a swig of water. "I think there's more going on with the goddesses than they're letting on."

Nodding grimly, I turned to the stars again, but they gave no answer. They simply twinkled and glittered, mocking me. They had seen it all. I'm sure if they could speak, they would answer my questions.

I led Isa into the house, pressing a finger to my lips. It was late, way late, and all but the family room light was off. I couldn't even hear Carrie's collar jangle as we crept through the dim light.

"Go on up, I'll get a snack and be right there," I said in a hushed tone.

"Which one is yours?" Her voice was a whisper-hiss. "I've never been here."

"Up the stairs, take a right, second bedroom."

I pushed the door open to the kitchen and easily found Mom's baked goods from the other day. It didn't take me long to gather banana and pumpkin breads, cookies, and two cans of cola. All the things growing girls like us need. Not a sigh or a rustle escaped from my parents' room. Still, I held my breath as I climbed the stairs with my tray.

Isa sat cross-legged on my bed, playing with her hair in one hand, writing things down with the other. She kept muttering to herself and I had to resist the urge to roll my eyes. She never stopped thinking, which was probably why she'd graduated three years early. It was a wonder the girl even slept.

Her glasses slipped off her nose as I came in.

"Oooh," I teased. "The glasses are out. This must be serious!"

"It is. Mom been baking?"

"Just a little. Help me hide it."

She helped herself to the breads first. I did the same. The cookies would be our dessert. It wasn't until now that I realized I was starving, and before Isa got a word in, I'd eaten two pieces of pumpkin bread.

"Damn, girl."

I shrugged and then swallowed. "Today I have bargained with a fae, endangered my job, possibly my soul, had to convince you magic was real, and have been stranded in the forest by a god. I've earned this."

"That was all yesterday. It's now Monday."

I groaned. This time I reached for a cookie.

"Now, again, what exactly did Loki say?"

She was poised with a pen. I shrugged and started again. "The gist—"

"Not the gist." She tapped her pen against the pad. "I need to know, word for word, from the beginning. He's a trickster. Deceptive by nature. Every word is probably a clue." I groaned loudly. Isa smirked in response. "You should have taken the mythology course with me in school."

It took nearly an hour, but we had almost all of his words out of me by then. There were still some that I'd not remembered, but like I said before, we got the gist.

"Ensnared by the spider... that has to mean something. Because nothing else means anything; it's just head games."

"Maybe that was his goal. To play games. He did desert me."

She grimaced. "He also told you how to get help. No, tricksters are supposed to represent the upending of the status quo. They show what could happen if everything was out of order or if people behaved however they liked." She rubbed her hands over her face. "We'll look at it later. Can you make coffee without waking your parents up? Ugh, sorry, matcha."

"Matcha for me, instant coffee for you?" She perked up. "We've got some cafe for you. Vanilla cappuccino."

"Your parents are the best."

"Hey, I might have bought it."

"Aspy, I know you'd forget. Your mom remembers these things."

I stuck my tongue out and went back downstairs and made us our cups. I was walking by the fridge, trying to remember if Isa took milk in her coffee, when I blinked in remembrance.

The fruits. I'd barely had time to study them though I'd pulled out my lab microscope. Between my knowledge and Isa's brain, we might be able to figure something out, to see something. I snatched the fruits out of the back of the freezer and headed up the stairs with the mugs and the frozen fruit.

"What's that?" Isa asked as I handed her the mug of coffee.

"The Fruit of Idunn," I said, handing her the plastic bag.

"Wow, really?" she muttered while squinting up close with her glasses both on and off. "That seems... I thought it would have been a metaphor." She looked at my desk, a slow grin spreading on her face. "I see your microscope is out." She shimmied off the bed, mug and fruit in hand. "This I have to see."

"Hey, not before me."

"Bite me."

"Taste better and I might."

She cleaned the butter knife I'd brought up with the bread and cut a tiny piece of the fruit away to fit it under the slide. When she was done, she stood and adjusted the knobs and eyepiece, taking a full minute to study the fruit. I tapped my foot and even heaved a too loud sigh. "I'm waiting."

"It looks like your run of the mill blackberry. Check it out."

I copied her movements and frowned. She separated a seed from the fruit and put both on the slide. Sure enough, she was right. It appeared to be your everyday blackberry. A little discolored from the pickling process, but otherwise it didn't look like anything I hadn't seen before. If Marc got some tests run on—oh, right.

"I could do some base tests on it," Isa offered. "I'm sure you can do those, too." She squinted at me. "You haven't eaten one of these yet, have you?"

"I've drunk tea with it in it. That was because apparently mortal minds can't comprehend Yggdrasil and I was going insane, so Eir poured it down my throat."

Isa's face shifted from curious to horrified and then back to curious with a little exasperation mixed in.

I shrugged in response. It did sound bad when I said it. I couldn't change what Eir had done, and a rather large part of me didn't want to. The path to immortality had begun, whether I liked it or not.

"They said it would take months, maybe years, before I'm immortal. The fruit works slowly, but it speeds up when you keep eating it. Or so they said." I babbled, trying to soften the blow.

"They're probably not lying about that. Just about something else." Her tone turned dark and she frowned at me, worry etching her face.

"You think so, too?" I blew my bangs out in front of me. Moving over to my bed, I grabbed a pillow and held it close. Carrie came into the room, winding around Isa's legs. "Damn."

Trying not to trip, she joined me on the bed, leaving room for Carrie. "Loki showed up for a reason. He told you a lot more than you think."

"Like what?" Carrie jumped up and pawed at me a couple of times before rubbing against me.

"Like his pain," she said, also grabbing a pillow to hug, her face scrunched in thought. "He had to know he would be in pain, because if he wasn't, he wouldn't have talked in code. It hurt even though he was talking in code. What about how he left you right after that? He couldn't tell you more." She smiled faintly. "He told you a lot more than I could."

The hair on the back of my neck stood up. The ladies had warned me that some gods were not to be trusted, but they hadn't said which ones. In fact, unless I specifically asked, they hadn't given me much of anything.

"Maybe they can't say things about other gods?" I suggested.

"Maybe."

They probably wouldn't be able to tell me about Freyja. Just like Loki. I dropped my hands to my lap and sighed. "I wish Marc was here. He'd know what to do."

Isa started. "He's into magic?"

He wasn't, but he loved fantasy. That wasn't the reason I wanted him here. I wanted him here for me. To tell me I was thinking too hard, or that none of this was even real. My heart still ached from the scar he left on it. I had to wonder if I would ever feel whole again.

"No, he was just great at thinking on his feet," I lied.

"That ungrateful ass." Isa launched into a variety of insults against Marc that I think were supposed to make me feel better, but I only missed him more.

Chapter Fifteen

It was almost six in the morning by the time it hit Isa and I that we'd been awake all night catching up and puzzling over the world of the gods.

"No," I moaned, drawing it out with a deep yawn. "I am going to be so anxious later today." If I didn't take care, I'd be jittery like I'd had too much caffeine while also being so tired I could barely see straight.

Isa stretched. She had unearthed her spare pajamas and toothbrush from a box in one of the other rooms labeled 'Why Does Isa Have So Much Stuff At Our House?' Thanks, Dad.

We decided early into our gossiping session she would stay the night. She'd left a note for her mom saying that when she came to my rescue. We just hadn't done the actual sleeping part of the plan.

"You'll be okay." Isa stifled her own yawn and pushed my curtains aside for a good look at the sunrise. "You can nap."

"Can't nap. Too much to do today. Come on, let's go hit the garden."

"Yes!" Isa pumped her fist in the air partway. "I'm looking forward to getting some fresh fruit." I gave her an exasperated look and she shrugged. "What? You always give me your extras."

We were dressed in record time for people who hadn't slept. I think adrenaline from the night before kept me up. Who knows?

The sky was still tinged pink on the horizon when we made our way out. Insects buzzed around the tall grass that gently nipped at me as we stomped through it. Isa inhaled sharply as we got closer.

My grandfather had had excellent taste.

I let her wander the mist-filled garden as I picked up where I had left off yesterday. Today I wanted to carefully remove some of the overgrown alyssum, so I got to work with my trowel and cultivator to loosen the soil and gently remove the plants. It surprised me that the alyssum hadn't spread so much outside of the planters, but because of how hearty it was, I couldn't replant it nearby or in the forest. It might overrun local wildlife and completely ruin the ecosystem.

"Can't have you getting out," I teased the plant as though it would answer me. While part of me always felt bad for doing things like this, the anxiety I felt about killing them fell away, because the plants almost seemed to be okay with it.

It's okay, they whispered and giggled. *We know, we know.*

I liked to tell myself it was them, at least. It made me feel better. When I pulled that first one out, I only winced a little.

"Geeze," Isa huffed, "can you at least do it without crying now?"

I was ready to give her the best glare I could manage after sleep deprivation but stopped. She leaned over, delicately inspecting the flowers as though she heard their whispers, too. The look on her face held a little bit of mischief and a lot of understanding.

I smiled at the tiny buds in my hand, inhaling their strong honey fragrance deeply. "It doesn't feel right to kill something, I guess."

"You eat vegetables." She pointed out. I glared at her. "Yeah, yeah, you apologize to them, too."

I set the flowers to the side and started working on the other ones. "Just like our lives have horrible truths, so do plants," I said. "You need to prune them to keep them growing correctly, just like we need to be told that nuclear weapons exist. It's a necessary evil of being alive."

Isa smirked at my philosophical musing and changed the subject. "It looks like you're going to have a hell of a citrus harvest next year. Most of those trees look great." She paused. "Right?"

I laughed and sat back on the heels of my muck boots. "Yeah, because they were more inside the grove, they got less direct sunlight. Less chance of rotting. I'll have to get in those branches and do some pruning work for the next season."

I was already planning a second harvest? Way to go, brain. Who wouldn't? Who couldn't? There was so much potential in this land. I could feed the family off this land, but I didn't want to cut down any more trees to make room. Also, I didn't want to grind my own flour.

I continued my work and Isa continued her gentle explorations of the grounds. After about a half hour, her phone went off.

"Uuuuugh." She drew out the sound as she came back toward me. "That's my wake-up alarm. I'd better get home so I can shower and get to my shift. Call me if you run over any more gods, but please, don't run over Odin or talk to any birds without me. That would really suck."

She waved and jogged back toward the house. My phone rang and I grabbed it from my back pocket, slowing down my journey to the house as I did.

Blocked? At this time of day? I was prepared to let a telemarketer have it.

"Hello?"

"Aspen? It's Jord."

I deflated my false bravado just as quickly.

"Hi, Jord!"

I winced at my volume, but apparently it wasn't loud enough as Isa continued retreating. "What can I do for you?" I continued in a more normal voice, praying she wasn't calling me in.

"Can you come in tomorrow? We've gotten two more possible fae cases in this morning and a lead on another one."

I inwardly sighed in relief. Not today. "That's unusual, isn't it? I mean, I thought you only got those types of cases every couple of weeks." I had to give myself a little pat on the back for remembering that. Always good to show your boss that you're listening.

"It is unusual." Bewilderment leaked into her words, but her voice mellowed. "I'm not worried about it."

If she wasn't worried, I wasn't going to waste my brain space either. "What's the other case about?" I switched gears and continued walking back to the house.

"We should talk about that in the office."

I stopped again, my gut tightening. "What's that mean? And why?" Silence met me on the other end. "Does it have anything to do with that guy at the office yesterday? Or any of the other gods?"

"Guy...oh! You mean the detective. No, not him. And no, no other gods. There are things you can do to help us, so you can come with us. Can you be in by ten tomorrow? Charlie can scare anyone away until later."

That hadn't been my aim. If this was a chance to see them in action, I wasn't going to say no.

"Yeah, yeah, I can."

I went inside after getting more information and recomposing myself, dirty and more tired than ever. Wiping my heated brow, I downed a glass of water as soon as I got inside. It felt so good I filled up a second time and sat down, feeling relief return to my back and legs as I got off my feet. I took slower, longer gulps and waited until the heat had passed and my body temperature was more regulated.

The scent of coffee filled the air. Mom was either up or would be soon. I put together my second cup of matcha, stirring the pre-mixed powder I made into the warm milk. It had a bit of cane sugar in it to take away from the extreme bitterness. I loved the earthiness of it and savored the warm cup for a moment.

Mom pushed the swinging door to the kitchen open. Blurry-eyed with her hair a fuzzy mess, which matched her fuzzy emerald-green robe. She mumbled hello and shuffled right to the coffeepot. I hid my smile. Mom was not and never had been a morning person. She resented—but not really—both Cypress and me for being way too chipper for her in the mornings. So had Dougie, until he'd hit puberty. Then he'd joined the Night Birds as we called our parents.

"Wendy geddin las' nigh?" Mom mumbled while pouring her coffee.

"Huh?"

She took a quick swig and then said in a much clearer voice, "When did you get in last night?"

Isa and I got our stories straight this morning. We had years of practice.

"A little after midnight." I took a sip of my matcha and relaxed into the chair. Nothing off, nothing at all suspicious.

"I thought you were working?" She was done with her first cup already and was up back at the coffee pot.

"Yep. Then I ran into Isa, and we hung around her work until they closed." Most of downtown closed at five pm, the rest by nine. The cafe and a couple of bars were the only places open later. Luckily, Mom has never been a 'prove it' type of person.

Her curiosity seemed to be satisfied. "Are you having a good time at the new job?"

"It's really interesting with all the different things they do. I've already sat in on some meetings," I answered, hoping she wouldn't press.

She considered that and seem to accept it. Mom and I sat in silence, only the sounds of the morning wafting into the kitchen through the open window. A quiet, picture-perfect morning.

"Helloooo!"

Mom choked on her coffee as Nana's voice rang through the halls. I jumped up fast and smacked her on the back, the sudden movement causing pain to cripple me as I got a cramp in my left thigh. I made a face and silently moved my lips in swears and prayers for relief, rubbing it enthusiastically.

"Hi, Mama!" Mom yelled, still coughing. The look she sent me said 'she never calls ahead,' and I giggled. "We're in the kitchen."

Nana came in the swinging door, her hips sashaying in that way that meant she had some kind of news, or possibly a new theory on the origin of life. Huh, I wonder if the goddesses knew the real origin of life in the universe. I'd have to ask them.

"Ladies, ladies, ladies," she squealed. "I have... crystals, crystals, crystals!"

We both looked at her like she had grown another head. Mom snapped out of it before I did. She'd been doing this for fifty years, not me.

"Oh, Mama, you know we don't—"

"Nonsense, nonsense, nonsense," Nana said the three words as she began reaching into the bag on her arm and piling rocks onto the table.

"Is there a reason you're repeating yourself, Nana?"

"Three is the number who do holy work," she said matter-of-factly. "All religions have a significance in three."

I knew that couldn't be true, but I let her roll with it.

"Angie was reading my palm this morning when she said that I had to protect those close to me. Danger is coming."

A chill ran down my back and I found myself sitting up straighter only to come back down when my leg cramp protested. "What kind of danger?" Yes, I know Nana was probably full of it with some things, like the power of three in regular conversations, but now I knew too much to discount everything.

Mom pressed her lips together and tilted her head to the sky before addressing Nana. "Mother, you cannot tell those things from a palm reading."

"Angie is very psychic, I'll have you know."

"Angie is a cafeteria worker in your building, not a psychic."

Nana sat between us and squared her shoulders, her face pinched in an unusual show of stress over her beliefs being challenged. "People can be two things."

While they were going back and forth, I noticed a pure black crystal smoothed into a cut crystal shaft among all the colorful ones. It looked like volcanic ash. I closed my palm around it, feeling the crystal vibrate softly. I jumped and looked it over again, but it lay perfectly still in my hand.

"Nana, what's this?" I asked, breaking up the fight as I held the black crystal up to the light. Mom threw her hands up as Nana turned her attention to me.

"That's obsidian, dear. Protection." She raised a manicured brow at me. "Do you like it?"

Protection didn't seem like a bad thing to have right now. "It looks like it could have been a falling star." I marveled at the crystal.

Nana closed my hand around it. "Keep that one. If it speaks to you, you should have it. This crystal also provides positivity. I know you haven't been so depressed these days, but everyone could do with a little extra positivity."

I smiled softly and closed my hand around the crystal, feeling it warm in my palm. "I guess so."

"How are you feeling today, Flo?" Nana asked Mom as she poured herself a cup of coffee. "I can tell just by looking at you that today's a bad day."

Was it? Mom blanched at Nana's words. Oh, dear God, it was true! She was fine. I mean, she looked a little tired, but she had just woken up.

"I'm fine—"

"Don't you dare lie to me. I can tell."

Mom stared into her coffee cup and I sipped my matcha. The battle of wills hung in the air. I got up and busied myself with making the three of us some toast and eggs, trying to shrug off the feeling of unease in the room. They didn't want to leave, but they didn't want to talk about it, either. I took some slow, deep breaths to calm the fluttering in my stomach. I get it, they don't want to fight in front of me, but I'm twenty-three. I can take it!

Mom started talking, but kept her voice low even though she had to have known I could hear her.

"It's just the trigeminal neuralgia today, Mama."

"'Just? Just? *Just?*' It's 'just' more painful than giving birth?"

I swallowed hard. Mothers have long joked with children and fathers about how painful birth and postpartum were. The seriousness in Nana's voice meant that this was not something we were going to be joking about around the dinner table anytime soon. I flipped the eggs quickly, so they didn't burn. Nana and Mom liked theirs over easy, which... ew. Scrambled, please.

"It's not that bad today," Mom insisted, her voice lower than Nana's.

"I don't like it. Daily physical therapy, pain worse than heart attacks and birth and nothing is working. I can't stand seeing you in so much pain, honey."

"I understand, Mama."

Despite myself, I kept facing forward, making the food. In my pocket the little crystal seemed to vibrate again. Protection and positivity. Something we all needed more of.

Chapter Sixteen

When I arrived at Goddesses, Inc. the next day, I carried with me the fruit of my labors: coffees and donuts balanced precariously in my hands while I considered the yellow building on this grey day. The coffee carrier was pressed against my side and the donuts at my front as I tried to turn the handle to the front door, only to have it keep slipping out of my grasp. I had to set my spoils down before it would let me in, and even though it was too early for tourists to be out, by that time I was surely attracting attention.

I scuttled inside and plunked the treats down on Charlie's (Pronouns: Try/Me) desk. Her eyes lazily lifted from her baking magazine and then bulged in what I hoped was shock and happiness. She grabbed for the only iced coffee of the bunch and took a sip.

"Too perfect to be real," Charlie said in her alto voice, with a hint of wistfulness at the peppermint mocha. "How'd you know? Where's yours?"

"In my travel mug." I jerked my head to the mug clipped on my purse. "No way am I revealing my secrets," I said over my shoulder.

Charlie looked shocked again, but her laughter caught the goddesses' attention when I opened the back door holding my prizes.

Like Charlie, Sif lit up as she pawed through the cups. "Flattery gets you nowhere, but bribery will absolutely get you everywhere," she said. She sipped her hot chocolate and nodded vigorously. "Every now and then I like peppermint hot chocolate."

"Who doesn't?" I parried.

Jord drank matcha like I did and seemed pleased with that. Eir read the side of her cup where the phrase 'large caramel macchiato' was printed. "Did you figure out everyone's drinks?" No one said anything. They were too focused on their own early-morning happiness. "How?"

I jutted my chin forward and stood my ground. "You're the magical detective."

Sif smirked and Jord coughed right that moment before tactfully changing the subject. "Have you been paying attention to the dry drownings recently?"

I was mid-sip in my matcha and quickly swallowed, trying not to think too hard on what a dry drowning was. "I don't follow the news too closely. Is dry drowning as bad as it sounds?"

Eir was at the little coffee station in the back, pouring what looked to be more caramel into her macchiato. "Worse." Her voice was grim. "Like the word says, they're drowning on land. Five people have died in the last three weeks."

"That's not something we would look into. Is it?" Each goddess wore a similar look on their face. "Okay, so we look into it. Why?"

"We recently got information that all the people who have dry drowned visited Slide Rock in the days leading up to their death."

Now that was a lot more than a coincidence. "All of them?"

"Within three days, max."

I shivered. Too much to be a coincidence. They still hadn't answered my question. "Why are we investigating this? If people are dying, shouldn't the police look into it?"

Jord and Sif exchanged looks, but Eir laughed. My cheeks warmed. Stupid, stupid. If it's magic, of course the police can't help.

"Magic isn't real," I said in a whisper. "Police won't investigate things that aren't real."

Eir took a sip from her over-sugared caffeine hit and sighed. "Sorry. It's just, the idea of the police acknowledging magic is real and beyond their capacity is funnier than Will Ferrell trying to be funny."

Slide Rock was nestled between Cora Alma and Sedona, only a ten-minute drive if you drove like ninety percent of Arizonans. Luckily—or not—Eir was apparently an adopted Arizonan, and we were there in nine minutes flat. When we arrived, I almost had to peel myself out of the SUV.

We shielded our eyes from the sun and searched for the best spot to sit and observe while still having access to the water. Jord pointed to a nearby Joshua tree and we piled under it, towels, blanket, food and water in tow. As soon as we sat down, I slathered sunblock on my too-fair-to-be-out-here-without-it skin.

A kid screamed and I jumped before then sighing in realization. Ugh, I hated places like this sometimes. Especially when I'm already super anxious.

I kept a watch on the splashing and laughing, but I saw nothing out of the ordinary. Lots of kids and families, and all of them splashing. After several minutes, I looked to Sif, who stayed near me while the others fanned out. "What are we looking for?"

"We don't know." She sat down on the chair next to the cooler. "A shapeshifter, kappa, djinn, another pixie. We rarely get things that are deadly, and when we do, it's usually much bigger."

I had to check to make sure my heart was still beating. She had said bigger in such a blasé, tired voice that it made it almost sound boring. When did these wonders get that routine?

"Bigger? When have you ever gotten anything bigger?"

Sif bit her lip and lowered her voice. "We've covered up our share of problems with fire."

Fire? I recoiled away in shock and she laughed nervously. I wouldn't have put an earth goddess as the instigators of destruction. If my guessing was right, if they had bodies to hide, it wasn't something that happened in the city. "How often do you have to do that? And to what?"

"Mom! Mom!" Someone screamed as they splashed frantically. "Mom!"

Sif and I both reacted immediately, ready to jump into action to help anyone if needed, but quickly sat back when we realized the child just wanted his towel.

"Like what?" I prompted again, bringing her back. "What is so big that you would burn it down?"

"A Jotun." At my blank look, she cleared her throat, checking from side to side to see if anyone was listening. "Uh, giants."

I tried to wrap my mind around this new bit of information. "Giants?" Sif stood up and grabbed a soda out of the cooler, cool and casual, as though we were talking books or sports or even our evil mothers-in-law. "Giants. Giants are real? Fe fi fo fum, I smell an English bum?"

Sif snorted into her soda. She coughed and I took a cola from the cooler for myself.

"No, no, that's... not it." She coughed again and rubbed her nose. "Most of it's real. You just haven't seen it yet. Hell, neither have we," she added the last part with a growl.

"What haven't you seen?"

Sif blushed and screwed her face up in a childlike manner. "I've never been to another realm," she admitted.

Screwing my face up in a similar fashion, I racked my brain for the word she was using. "Realm? Oh." I snapped my fingers in realization. "Those are planets, right?"

"Right." Sif sat down next to me and took stock of the water and people before her. She rested her hands on her knees and sighed. "It's hard to explain how Yggdrasil connects the worlds together, and it's almost embarrassing to say I've only been to Midgard and Alfheim."

"Why is that embarrassing?" I asked. "Two planets is double what I've been."

She smiled wanly, bitterness creeping into her voice. "Except I'm 350 years old, and there's nine realms."

I'd hit a sore spot, and while I wanted to press it—and learn more about the other realms—I wasn't going to push and possibly ruin this new friendship that was happening on its own. I didn't make friends easily, and usually once they knew I had bipolar they ghosted me anyway.

"So... what am I looking for?" I asked, changing the subject ever-so-smoothly.

Slide Rock's sheer size, the canyon it was naturally carved into was not a singular space. In fact the name was a bit of a misnomer as the slide was several cascading rocks that eventually landed the rider into a deep pool on the other side. You could go down a very short way or a longer one depending on how brave you were.

The history of the area was well known to locals, and anyone who did a quick read up of the area. Until the 1980s the park was home to a farm, apple orchards mostly, which helped create the ecosystem that was still supporting Slide Rock today. The canyon was in levels that allowed people to climb up and stake their claim for the day in haphazard, yet picturesque, spots.

Don't ask me who decided that sliding down rocks was a good idea, because if you weren't careful, you'd tear up your clothes. I watched a woman, who obviously hadn't been there before, learn that with only her swimsuit and a long shirt on. Sure enough, when she stood up, her shirt was ruined, and she had a large hole in the right cheek of her swimsuit.

"We're going to spread out more, I think." Sif glanced at Jord, who jerked her head once, then did the same to Eir. "What you can do is sit here and make sure no one steals our stuff." I wanted to protest. "We don't know what we're looking for, and we've been doing this for lifetimes. Watch what we do."

Sif waved as she headed toward the banks and stuck her feet in. I grabbed a baseball cap that read "Natural Goddess" and shoved it on my head. I didn't need to be sunburnt, and even though it wasn't officially summer, temperatures were warming up. Today was supposed to be hotter than the last few days had been, with temperatures climbing into the low nineties. Hot enough to send some of our more spoiled residents into their air conditioners.

Not the families and small clusters of people my age, though.

Sif was the only one who looked like she was having fun, blending in more in her long shirtdress and jeans. Eir wore a wide brimmed dark purple hat and her usual dark clothes, making her stand out. Jord, while also appropriately dressed, seemed too willowy to do something as harsh as sliding down a large rock in near freezing water. I glanced down at my jeans and t-shirt combo. I looked just about right.

A quick look and I decided that there wasn't much to steal. Most people were leaving their belongings and splashing in the water anyway. I left my stuff and self-respect behind and scrambled up the bank, shivering in the icy water. I started by shoving my hands in as deep as I could to know what I was going to feel in a few seconds. Wading into the water, I abandoned all hope of this not being horrible and walked up the 'steps' to the top and threw myself down the slide.

The water might have been in the forties, maybe, and it sloshed over my legs and soaked my shirt, sending gooseflesh up my arms. I squealed and landed in the pool with some people laughing at my carefree attempt at going down the rockslide. I laughed and got up so the next person could go down. My hair was wet and stringy in front of my face, and I didn't realize at the time how big my grin was as I went up and rode the slide again.

For a few minutes I threw caution to the wind and forgot my shivering as I waited in line. No stress, no thought of why we were here. The third time I waded further downstream, careful of the rocks so I didn't fall or cut my feet open. After a few times, it wasn't so bad. My teeth weren't chattering as much when I sat down, and the current gently pushed against me as I kept observing others going down the slide. The same few kids and college students were the ones to ride down, laughing and smiling each time. I had to admit it was fun; and something I hadn't done since graduating high school.

Despite what we were there for, I was enjoying myself here with the cold water and the laughing and splashing. The others still roamed around but never entered the water beyond a quick wade to their calves. Maybe I needed to be more cautious like them, but they had seen me go in and hadn't pulled me out of the creek.

It wasn't long before the water bit against my skin and I started shivering. Some kids had been in since before I got there, and I marveled at their ability to face this kind of cold. I had one foot out of the water when I heard someone cry out.

One teenager was underwater and instead of breaking from the creek, he jerked as though fighting off... nothing, actually. For a moment I thought I saw a small whirlpool pushed against the teen. I sloshed forward, unsure of what I would do. I had seen weirder things already this week, but water holding someone down was high on the list. As soon as I changed my movement, the teen was up, gasping for breath and coughing. He sloshed to the side of the creek bank and then he was out and running.

"Something grabbed me!" he yelped. "I felt something!"

A couple of people reacted with confusion more than anything else. Two of his friends came up to him, but you could see from their faces they didn't believe him.

"Come on buddy, you just slipped." One of the friends assured him.

"No, really." The boy wiped his braids out of his face and pointed, his voice rising. "Something was holding me under. I could feel it!"

Nope. Nope, nope, nope.

I hopped out of the creek, my need to survive much more important than magic or a paycheck.

The goddesses surrounded the spot where he had been dragged under. Jord touched the water and Eir scanned the banks.

Sif waded over to me. "Are you okay?"

I wanted to shake my head but instead just nodded once, not taking my eyes off where the boy had been underwater.

"What did you see?"

I hesitated, unsure if I saw anything at all. "I saw something, but I don't know what. He couldn't move. It was like he was fighting something off."

Sif pat my shoulder and went to report back to the others. I studied the near-drowning victim and he was drinking a bottle of water while glaring at the river. The others were talking and packing things up around him, but the look on his face said something else.

"Hey," I approached him, wringing out my shirt as I did, hoping it wasn't nipple city down below. "You okay?"

The kid looked at me, his expression puzzled and pale. He shook his head. "I don't get it. I just don't get it. You saw, right? I wasn't trying to screw with anyone. I was stuck."

I let him rant. He had almost drowned after all.

"And now they won't listen to me. My girlfriend says I'm trying to mess with them, but I ain't messing. Whatever it was, it held me down with these skinny fingers." He pulled his towel tighter around him. "All I could hear was... music? It was weird. There ain't no amount of money worth going back into that water."

Chapter Seventeen

T he next morning, I wrote my morning list, sipped my matcha, and went out to the garden. Things had gotten weird, but that didn't change the fact that I needed to keep my mental health balanced. Routine is important for people with bipolar disorder, and I'd spent five years making mine. I wasn't about to break it. When I came back in from my detailed list making and soil checking, Mom was already dressed and on her second cup of coffee.

"Good morning." She turned the page of her paper and gave me a weak smile. "You're a little dirty for Pain and Torture."

"Pain and Torture?" We had one thing to do today and as far as I knew there wouldn't be torture.

She laughed and set down her coffee mug. "It's what some of us call physical therapy. PT: Pain and Torture."

I faked a laugh and winced when she turned back to her paper. I hurried to wash up, trying not to think too hard about torture, but did a double take at the back of the newspaper Mom was reading. I had to marvel at how quickly the goddesses worked.

"'Slide Rock Closed Due to Algae Bloom,'" I read aloud.

"Yeah." She flipped to the back page. "I saw it on the news last night. Happens now and then. Some idiot probably put something in there they weren't supposed to." She tsked and then turned back to her page.

Like an earth goddess's spell, perhaps?

Staff at the office had apparently taken the time to get to know Mom. The receptionist asked about the baking she did the other day, and she showed him a picture of our completed kitchen. As she flipped through pictures, a therapist came over and called her back.

The receptionist flashed a smile at me. He was in his late twenties and wearing scrubs that brought out the blue in his hazel eyes. "I'm Luke," he said. "It's Aspen, right? Your mom said we'd get to actually meet you soon."

Oh, boy. My mother didn't just talk about herself. "Is that so?"

He held his hands up, and I noticed he had a woven ring tattooed around his left ring finger. "All good things." His voice held a note of teasing. I relaxed, sending him a smile, trying not to stare too closely at that pattern, which wasn't a pattern. Something about it kept catching my eye.

"It's asymmetrical," Luke explained, folding back the rest of his fingers and 'flashing' me his ring finger. I flushed in embarrassment and took a step to the side. Some parts of the tattoo were pushing past the circle and each overlay contained different hues of blue and black. Asymmetrical in both pattern and color.

"I know the signs of someone with sharp eyes." He flexed his hand and grinned at me. "It doesn't happen as often as you would think." I nodded dumbly, unsure of what to say and he decided to spare me, pointing to the table next to where he stood. "There's a Keurig over on the counter. I think it's got some coffee, hot chocolate, and tea."

Mechanically, I walked up to the pot and poked around. There actually wasn't any hot chocolate or tea. Not even decaf. Instead, I pulled up the browser on my phone and found my search from yesterday for 'trigeminal neuralgia', reading while monitoring my mother's progress.

She did little things like riding an exercise bike, using a yoga ball, and some weights. I mean, it didn't seem like much, but as the appointment wore on, she moved between exercises slower. Sometimes she'd wince while she pulled on the bands or moved slightly too far over.

'Trigeminal neuralgia is also known as tic douloureux. It is a type of chronic pain disorder that involves severe pain in the forehead, neck, lower or upper jaw, and cheek. It can be activated by trauma to the nerves, dental work, or other chronic diseases.'

Chronic pain. Severe chronic pain. My head snapped up and I stared at Mom with new appreciation. She was still on the yoga ball, moving her legs back and forth with the ball, getting checked on by the tech. She wasn't moving too fast, and her face was contorted in concentration.

I googled 'how bad is trigeminal neuralgia pain?'

The first highlighted result was enough to drop my heart to my knees.

'Trigeminal neuralgia pain can be so severe that it can bring an otherwise healthy person's life to a standstill. You may be unable to think or talk during an attack. Some describe it as worse pain than childbirth or a heart attack.'

I scrolled down, feeling cold in my stomach spreading through my body.

'severe pain'

'worst pain I ever experienced'

'incurable'

'lifelong'

I swallowed and dared a glance back at Mom, now using some small weights to build up her arm strength. How? How had she sat there the other morning? Like nothing was wrong, drinking her coffee. She even admitted she hid the pain.

I stood and put a pod of Italiano roast into the Keurig, then chose some sweetener packets to add. I needed something to do with my hands. I needed to not think about it. I couldn't help it. I realized things were bad, but why hadn't I realized how bad they truly were?

My coffee finished brewing and I stirred in some powdered creamer, barely tasting the boiling liquid on the way down.

After an hour of pain and torture the therapist led Mom back out on unsteady legs. I know they asked for the car, and I remember parking in the handicapped spot—disabled placard on display—but I don't remember how we pulled out of the lot. She'd gotten into the car on her own, but my mind swam with more information than ever before. I'd gone down a rabbit hole, I admit, but I felt more empowered because of it.

Though also less qualified than ever.

We were maybe fifty feet away from the parking lot when Mom, looking out the window, knocked me out of my stupor. "Aspen, I need the trashiest of trashy food."

I grinned. For now, we could indulge in things like this. "The trashiest of trashy? We don't have a Taco Bell," I joked.

"Ha!" She flipped her visor down and applied some lip gloss. "No, I want a burger worth 10,000 calories. With a Diet Coke."

"Sure. You always ruin it with Diet Coke. Fannie's?" I suggested. It's the only burger place that wasn't a huge chain that still existed in the city.

"Only if you'll split the onion rings with me."

"What? Why are there conditions? You're the one who wants a huge gross burger."

Not that I wouldn't eat one of those. I tried not to as often as when I was a kid. But bacon was a thing and until the fake was as delicious as the real thing, I would get it from one of the local stalls at the farmers' market.

My stomach grumbled. The bacon did sound good on top of a gross, greasy burger with cheese and jalapenos. I flipped on my blinker and Mom pumped her fist in response, dancing in her chair the way only someone in their fifties can. We took the next turn off and got in line at Fannie's. There was only one person ahead of us and we were there before the real lunch rush hit.

Perfect.

Someone pulled in behind us and I pushed forward, already knowing exactly what I wanted.

"Welcome to Fannie's Fried Food!" The way, way too chipper voice crackled from the speaker, taking away my ability to hear properly on the left. "Would you like to try our onion ring basket today?"

Oooh, a basket?

"Yeah, one of those," I said, scanning the menu since there had been changes. Nothing else I saw seemed important, so I kept going. "A number three with a Dr. Pepper." I lowered my voice. "Mom?"

"The usual."

I turned back to the box. "A number four, Diet Coke."

"Is Pepsi okay?" the voice chattered again.

Cardinal sin there. "No!" Mom snapped. "Since when do you not have Coke?"

"I'm sorry, Mrs. Sommers," the box squawked, and I saw the tiny camera sitting on the brand-new menu. "It's Candy Q. by the way. We have a new owner. So some things have changed."

"You still have Dr. Pepper though, right?" When I got an affirmative, I thanked her and rolled forward, but not before changing Mom's drink to 7-Up. "Well, at least I get my caffeine hit, so the crisis was partially averted."

Candy Q turned out to be Candy Queen, the mayor's nineteen-year-old niece. The rumor mill suggested she wasn't being hired by her aunt because of some family strife that no gossip dared to confirm.

"Hello, Candy," Mom gushed upon seeing the girl. "Gosh, has it been two years already?" She reached across me and gripped Candy's outstretched hand in hers. "You're a manager!"

Candy squeezed my mom's hand and gave me a half-hearted smile. She knew about Mom. Hard to live in such a small town sometimes. As they continued to chat, I realized they had a rapport, a connection. Mom had bonded with this girl at school. That caused my heart to swell and tears to flood at the thought that she would never have that experience again.

"Five months now, Mrs. Sommers," Candy Q beamed, which was more than I'd ever done. Except now I knew something I wasn't allowed to share with anyone. That brought my mood down even more. The two of them chatted for the three minutes it took for our food to arrive.

"Good luck, Mrs. Sommers." Candy's perfect red lips turned up in a kind smile. "I hope you can go back to working at the school soon. I heard it's not the same without you."

Mom's face almost remained the same and I sighed at her palpable change in demeanor. "Thank you, Candy Q," I muttered, put the car into drive, and got out of there as fast as Bessie would let me.

The rest of the drive home was so quiet I heard the sizzling of the onion basket. Even though my mouth watered for them as their crispy, oily, aroma filled the car, I was suddenly not hungry.

"No one gets it. Why does no one get it? The MS isn't going to go away like magic," Mom blurted out. "It's not going to just give up and stop attacking my body! It's not like... I had a choice but to do this. I couldn't... I couldn't..." Her breaths came in harsh bursts, and tears ran down her cheeks.

I wanted to do something, to say something about how it would feel better, things would get better. To point out the therapies she was now trying, both physical and medicinal. It was all changing, and that was good, right? I wanted to say it, but I knew that there was no point. While my illness waxed and waned, hers was a progressive spiral downwards. I might lose myself, but she felt she had already lost the things that mattered to her most.

I let her cry quietly, moving my right hand over to her left and letting her grip it as tears dripped down her cheeks.

How did you tell someone their life wasn't over when so much of what they enjoyed out of life was taken away from them?

I pushed that anxiety back. I had to get home and then we would have lunch together. After that, I would go upstairs and cry. Not before then.

It clawed at me. It tried to rip out of my skin and grab control of my life. I stamped it down.

Not yet. Not until we get home.

It still fought me, but I held firm.

We're almost home.

The house came into view. The pushing increased in my chest, as though my heart would leap out and run off. Maybe it would take my anxiety with it if it did that.

"I'm going to go lay down," Mom announced as we pulled up. "Put my food in the fridge, okay? Have as many of the onion rings as you can while they're hot."

I grabbed the food and gave her a grin from across the hood of the car, afraid that if I opened my mouth, I would beg her to stay. Or worse, I would say something that would make her want to go cry over me and my words. So I watched her as she slowly limped out of the car and made her way back to the house.

As the door closed, I threw the bags of food back into the car and bolted, running from the front yard to the back.

The tall grass whipped against my legs, occasionally stinging. My chest was caving in, pressure building up as I tried to do my exercises to stop the sobs from coming uncontrollably. Tears burned down my cheeks and when I stopped, I was past the garden into the thick grove of trees.

I collapsed under one of the more gnarled cherry tree. I tried to breathe out calmly, but then I burst into sobs. All I could see was Mom's face, crushed, haunted. So alone even though I was right there.

She had wanted to be alone. She knew there was nothing to say to make her feel better. Which was good because my mouth was sandpaper.

The berries.

Jord said they couldn't 'cure' the bipolar, but MS was a visible illness, or at least a much more tangible disease.

The sky opened. The cold drops would have been refreshing this morning, but instead they continued to sour my mood. I sat there as it pattered around me, occasionally splashing on me through the foliage. Listening to the rain, my heart slowed. My sobs turned to simple crying, which then turned to sniffles as the anxiety attack passed.

I lifted my face to the cool rain and opened my eyes to the bright sunshine.

Wait, what?

Tears still leaked down my cheeks, but I furiously wiped them and turned my face to the sky. It was raining, but there wasn't a single cloud in the sky. I stood and craned my neck to look for the broken sprinkler or even Isa holding a hose, but it was still raining. I walked. It was still raining, but the sky was still clear blue.

"Who's there?" I demanded, hoping it wasn't Loki again. "Come on, is this magic? Because if I'm having a mental breakdown right this second, I will be seriously pissed off."

Light, masculine laughter filled my ears, and I turned my head up towards the sound. A handsome man with blond hair and a mirth-filled smile sat on the lowest branch of the cherry tree, his bare feet dangling. He was probably in his late twenties, but the magic rain told me he was a little older than that.

"Who are you?" I tried to keep my voice steady, but somehow a squeak made its way in.

"I am Frey, young goddess." His deep voice was filled with amusement.

Ugh, great. Wait, Frey? Freyja's brother. Wasn't he Gurd's—Oh shit.

"Hi," I said it almost as a question. "I'm Aspen."

"That is your current name." He dropped gracefully from the tree and the rain stopped. "We both know you have another name."

I wrung out the water from my hair and sent him an exasperated glare. "I don't know what that other name is yet, okay? The other day they were pretty convinced I was Fulla."

He laughed again and I turned away from him as he continued. "You failed at bargaining with the fae. Something Fulla would never have done."

He was close, very close. I suddenly realized that his shirt was one of those loose old-fashioned ones. You know, like the one that David Bowie wore in *Labyrinth*. Those really, horribly sexy shirts. He had everything to fill it out. I narrowed my eyes. If all the gods and goddesses were this drop dead gorgeous, my inferiority complex was going to rear its head.

I stared into his eyes, deep blue with an even brighter ring of blue around them, trying to find something that screamed 'asshole' or even 'fraud'. He raised a hand and tucked a flyaway strand of hair behind my ear and I shivered. It had stopped raining and now the air chilled slightly. Of course that's why I shivered.

It wasn't because he was more in my personal space than even Loki had been before—oh no.

I took a step back and he followed me, causing me to take another. I almost slipped when my foot came upon the root of the tree, my back against the trunk. "Get back," I hissed as he leaned closer to me. "I'm a biter."

He seemed to realize the position we were in and backed up. I relaxed my grip on the keys in my pocket, but I didn't let them go.

"What do you want?" I demanded. "Or are all gods perverted assholes?"

"I am merely seeing if you are Gurd," he explained, still way too much in my personal space. "I didn't mean to frighten you, Aspen. She understood me in ways no one else does."

I sidestepped him, wanting to put a few trees between us. "Aren't you and Freyja twins? Doesn't she understand you?"

He didn't follow, keeping a more respectable distance. "My dear sister is always close to my heart. I am a man, after all."

"Then use the bathroom," I snapped. "Don't get so cozy with someone you don't know."

His head snapped back and then he burst into laughter. "Okay, young goddess, okay." He did as I asked and finally backed away, moving so swiftly and smoothly he appeared to be floating.

I took that as his cue that he was leaving, but I wasn't so lucky.

"If you're Gurd, I've got my work cut out for me." His tone was jovial with a patient and pleased look on his face.

"What is that supposed to mean?" I jabbed my finger toward his face. "That you'll, what? Court me? Woo me if I'm Gurd? Well, let's hope for the sake of us both that I'm someone with no power."

He smiled, his white teeth straight and perfectly annoying. "I could woo you regardless. It's been so long, and with scores of goddesses yet to be reborn, meeting Gurd again may only happen in the next world."

There had to be another way to get information than interrogating gods and reading ancient texts. "The next world? Is that a thing, then?"

"No one told you about Hel?"

"I know all about Hell." I ticked things off my fingers. "Firey, demons, pitchforks, souls."

"No, young goddess." The name was no longer a compliment. "Hel is where souls of the judged reside, ones who were not brought to a hall of another god after death. Those who didn't die a death of valor, such as war or childbirth." At my startled look, he shrugged. "There's been a lot lost. Frigg was the goddess of childbirth, and anyone who died under her watch would be sent to wherever they wanted in the afterlife. The number that took up shields in Valhalla, Odin's hall of warriors who died in a glorious battle, would surprise you. Or maybe not. Maybe you're a hippy."

"That's my grandma, but yeah, it's in the veins." I finally relaxed more as he paced up and down, putting more space between us. "So, look, Frey, is that all you came here today for? To see if I was your wife?"

His lips curled into a smile as he reached out, tucking hair behind my ear again. "Yes, but darling goddess, I think this is going to be very interesting, no matter who you are." He looked me up and down and his smile did not falter.

I sighed, trying to keep my temper in check. "Look, I'm not going to sleep with you. If you were mortal—"

"I don't think I asked." He took a step forward and took my hand in his. I gaped as he brushed his lips against the back of my hand. My eyebrows met my hairline and I tried to pull away, but he held firm before backing away, that dumb smirk on his face. "You can put your hand down now."

I mutely squeezed my hands into fists at my side, hoping he hadn't noticed how red my face was turning, or that I was frozen solid from nerves.

"It is impossible to see the future in the past." With those words, he vanished.

Chapter Eighteen

"I mean—am I a magnet to them?" I asked Isa later that night.

Currently, I was in bed, my notebook open and ready to take notes on whatever Isa and I could brainstorm over the phone. I had earlier been listening to more of the book while Carrie wandered between spots in my room, trying to figure out where she belonged with the door closed. Isa's call to catch up had changed that. Well, at least my activities, Carrie continued to wander.

"You might be," Isa said between bites of her dinner. "I'm not surprised. Didn't they say it'd been hundreds of years between rebirths or something?"

"Yeah," I said. "Eir was the most recent."

I imagined Isa tapping her glasses as she thought about this. "Maybe they're trying to get a reaction out of your magic."

"Testing me?"

"Your magic is probably unique to who you are. If you were to, say, get pissed off and lash out with magic it would tell them who you were."

Okay, but... "What's your basis for this?"

"*Frozen. October Daye. Inuyasha. Circle of Magic.* Basically, anything involving magic ever. Before you say this isn't a movie, it doesn't mean people aren't simply people. When we're provoked to anger—" Isa stopped mid-sentence at my groan. "What? You think fundamental psychology isn't going to be present with magic? So far, it seems to be. 'Loki' is all I will say to that."

I did not want to talk about Loki and his penchant for mischief. Mischief at *best*. Carrie wove her way around my torso and nestled her into my arms. Putting the phone on speaker, I turned it down so our conversation wouldn't carry all over the house. Praying, I decided to change the subject to something I hadn't wanted to bring up before, but it had been on my mind. I needed a fresh perspective.

"I think Nana predicted my future with her morning tarot card reading."

It worked. "Wait, you mean you've been paying attention when she talks about that?" She sounded amazed.

I couldn't blame her for that "Well, that one she did for me. I'm almost scared to ask for a real one now."

"Wow."

"Something about refusing to let go and indecision, and then coming into power. And that all happened. I was holding onto Marc, and something about parental influence, it was all there.

"You haven't come into power."

"Maybe not, but everything else came true so far."

"You need to ask her for another one," she insisted.

"You think so? Oh!" I snapped up, glad we were finally on the phone instead of over text so I could tell her my news. "I got the first exciting step in my career by doing real magical field work."

"You rode Slide Rock," she deadpanned.

I deflated and frowned at the screen. "Who told you?"

"Charlie came in for some dinner today. She's really nice. Good tipper."

Charlie. Of course. "Well," I pressed on, "I was on the sidelines when someone was suspiciously held underwater."

She sighed and I pumped my fist in triumph. Carrie glared at me and moved over to the windowsill. "I'll accept that as magical. Though, keep to the sidelines like you're supposed to next time."

Her tone wasn't anything like Sif's. She threatened me with the real title of Magical Paper Pusher. Seeing that Lolita-styled woman verging on enraged was not something I wanted to repeat. Ever.

"So anyway, you think that was what this reading was telling you about? So it's over and done with now?"

"I mean, I think it has. There's enough to satisfy the other things. Like open hostility in the workplace—that's Charlie—and not focusing enough on my mental health. Which I'm back to journaling, so I'm totally doing that."

"Then yeah, it's totally over."

I wasn't sure if she was joking or not, and she didn't elaborate, either.

I had a few days off from work and I took Mom to PT one more time. We did exercises at the house every day, too. My next workday arrived with the scent of apple blossoms on the wind. The gray, drizzling day brought the temperatures down enough that I rolled down my windows on my way to work. I hoped it wouldn't be as exciting as my last few days, but those hopes were quickly crushed.

The waiting room practically buzzed with the sound of wings and non-Charlie noises. Because one of the 'people' had a flying pet. It stared blankly at the wall ahead, giving it the look of a slightly off flying rabbit with long floppy ears, a tail, and somehow managed to be bright pink with freaking gossamer wings on its back. There were two humans in the room—they were the ones who couldn't keep their eyes off it.

I closed the door behind me and walked up to Charlie's desk, glancing at the fluffy animal. "What is that?" I asked softly, hoping I didn't let the fae know I was talking about their pet. "Why can the humans see it?"

Charlie snapped gum and put down her book, which had no title or dust jacket. Today her ensemble included a blush pink lipstick to match her pink tennis shoes and bag. "Humans can see anything that fae want them to see, and most don't bother hiding in safe spaces. The humans are here because they have their own magical problems. Separately."

I furrowed my brow. "I thought cases like the other day happened only every couple of weeks."

"Usually." Her voice didn't change, but face clouded over the longer we talked.

Trying to find the courage to ask another question, I glanced around the more crowded than usual room. However, she was already dismissing me by going back to her book. Damn. I took a deep breath before putting on my big girl pants and walking to the back. As I got to the door, it swung open and Sif showed someone into the waiting room.

"Thank you very much for coming in today, Mrs. Schmeling," she said, leading the tracksuit-clad older woman to Charlie's desk. "Charlie will check you out today, and we'll get this figured out soon. Aspen, you're here." She beamed at me, her bouncy curls a little less so than usual. "Why don't we get you settled? Then we'll be with our next client shortly," she announced to the room.

All three of the clients in the waiting room, who had seemed angry before, now looked pissed when she said that. I gulped, scurrying back before anyone said anything. Sif did the same, leaving this to Charlie, which suited me—and now that I think about it, probably her too.

Sif leaned back against the door and blew her hair out. "Oh my gods," she said. "They will not stop."

"What do you mean? What's been happening?"

Eir handed Sif a mug with 'badass goddess' printed on it and she took a gulp as she went over to her desk. Her typical Lolita-style skirt and a frilly, ruffled shirt made her look adorable, but absolutely out of place.

"It's been like this for the past few days." Jord spoke up from her desk. She ran her fingers through her frazzled brown hair. "We slept here."

"Yeah," Eir said. "All three hours of sleep we got." She had on a black skirt and a black tank top under her red blazer. She sighed and fanned herself with a folder, enjoying the silence.

I looked between them and my heart sank.

"Why didn't you call me?"

My voice always gives away more than I want, and sure enough, it cracked on the 'me.' Eir crossed the floor so fast I jumped away. Instead of charging me, she grabbed my hand and my insecurities stayed, but the feeling of self-loathing fizzled.

"We didn't want you to miss your mom's physical therapy." Sif's voice held a note of 'well, duh' in it and confusion.

Wow. An employer who realized that people outside the company existed. "Thank you for the consideration," I mumbled.

Sif smiled, though she seemed far off and sad. "We don't have the luxury of family."

I furrowed my brow. Their families would have to be dead. Long dead. My stomach tightened, now unsure of what to say or how to say. Jord took my arm and pulled me to her desk.

"We don't have long. We have two more to see that we know of."

"Three," Sif moaned from her desk.

"Three? When did—never mind." For a brief second, I thought Jord was going to freak out, but she coolly collected herself and piled folders into my hands, explaining each one as she went. "This one saw a ghost in a nearby restaurant. That has since been confirmed by these three other cases. This one we think could be Jotun, so it gets bumped up in priority."

My head snapped up and my heart skipped a beat as she laid that folder on top. "A Jotun?" I squeaked out. "Giants?" Images filled my head of twenty-foot-tall men made of ice, using their superior strength and magic to mow down trees that had stood for generations.

Jord quickly waved it off. "Not a powerful one. If it were, we'd already be dealing with it."

She went through each of the half dozen folders with quick instructions on what I needed to do with each human presenting their case. Apparently, we believed the fae without question, which I think I was okay with. No telling what would happen if you pissed off a powerful fae, and I didn't want to ask.

Humans had to be background checked in ways that were borderline unlawful. First, I would match photocopies of their IDs with public records. Then we would take that information and if something came up, like a family member working at a new age store, that's when the securitization began. I put one case to the side because of that. It wasn't an automatic dismissal, but we would do even more work before following up. There were interviews to set up, statements to verify, and after all that we would do the investigation at the site.

After that, we would go to exorcise the magical creature, like Eir and I did before.

"Most don't move in with humans. That was one weird fae," Eir reassured me as I took over her desk to get my work done. I expected her to throw a fit over me using her space, but she honestly seemed relieved.

I hadn't even started my first internet search when the next customer was ushered in. The fae.

Tall and slender, their translucent skin gave them an ethereal, almost blinding glow. It didn't seem to rattle any of the goddesses. Sif ushered them into the room and sat them in the comfy chairs but didn't bring them any food or tea.

Its flying rabbit-thing was nowhere to be seen and I wondered if Charlie would survive taking care of it.

"Who is the eldest?" the fae asked, their voice holding a faint echo, a whisper at the end.

Jord stepped forward at the same moment Eir and Sif stepped back. The fae smiled with a mouthful of pointed canines.

Sif shuffled backwards but was careful not to turn around as she moved until she stopped next to me at Eir's desk. "That is called a Fae Wyn. They never give their names; that's their title. Most won't tell you anything about them because they believe information is power. If we get this case, it will be a first. They aren't always known to leave survivors."

I faced the not-quite-real person commanding the attention of the goddesses. Like back at the vortex, the hair on my arms stood on end and there was an odd taste in my mouth. It wasn't a bad one, but it was new, different. Something I hadn't tasted before but had always known.

Magic.

"They're almost like a demigod," Sif continued, "because they don't answer to the courts. They'll occasionally help the gods, though. Pay attention."

"Someone is trespassing in my territory," the Fae Wyn said. "Someone who can pass through the veils of worlds without leaving a mark. Even a fae will leave a scent. A ripple." They reached out and touched Jord's hair, plucking a strand from it. She didn't seem fazed and let the fae keep talking as it held her hair up to examine it. Sif returned to the sitting area with the others. "They come, take what is mine, they are tapping into my lands magicks and leaving again. Only when I am gone. There is no scent. Not a footprint."

I casually did my search, or pretended to, and listened in as the ladies questioned the fae about where they lived—one of our state parks to the northeast—and tried to parse together what was going on. After about twenty minutes of back and forth, all four of them rose and the goddesses and fae bowed to each other, just a slight tip of the head.

Jord held her arm out and the Fae Wyn took it, letting her lead them to the door. "I hope you understand, Great One of the River," not a name, but a title, "that you are not alone. Humans have seen an unusual number of—"

The Great One of the River whipped around and their clothing, which I now realized was water dripping down around them, sloshed out of place to wet the furniture. It constantly fell from their impossibly long hair and covered them in a dress of cascading water.

"I do not care of the affairs of humans, goddesses." A pin prick of black appeared in their otherwise pupilless left eye, but it quickly vanished as their temperament calmed. "I expect this matter to be dealt with swiftly."

They crossed both of their arms in front of them in an 'X' and instead of leaving through the door, they exploded into a million drops of water and evaporated out of sight.

Eir's mouth pressed into a thin line and Sif sighed. Jord, however, seemed only a little put out by the situation.

"Uh, was that a problem?" I asked, turning away from the computer.

"That Fae Wyn's territory is north of here," Jord started slowly. "And if they say someone is passing through worlds there?" Her brow furrowed. "It doesn't make sense with everything else that is happening so much closer to the vortex. Why north?"

"North has fewer people. Maybe someone or something is driving magic further south?" Eir suggested.

Sif shook her head. "We would detect something like that. Whatever is happening can only be felt by the fae so far."

After a few minutes I turned back to my work, finding their debates fascinating, but also a lot of it was going over my head. If fae could feel it, and fae were the spirits of nature, who else would be able to if nature goddesses couldn't?

Who had more power than that?

Chapter Nineteen

"**A**re you sure about this?" Isa asked me for the millionth time as I led her to the garden.

My mind was made up. I'd had the last two days at a very busy workplace to think about this, and we spent hours talking before I made this choice. Usually when we thought about doing something stupid, I would garden and she would help me out with minor tasks while we debated our options. Instead, we paced and read mythology together, the wood for my new planters untouched.

Educational on the past, but it didn't have the answers I needed.

Now two other gods had shown up to 'see who I was.' Sure, it made sense, I guess, for Frey. Maybe he wanted to become reacquainted with Gurd or something. And Loki... well, he's just a dick. He wanted to know, too. I still didn't know what made me keep my mouth shut about it. He hadn't asked me to, but his inability to speak made my gut twist.

"No, I'm not sure."

In the end, we came up with nothing. I needed answers.

"Then why are we doing this?"

It was almost midnight and we had been talking since dusk. Tomorrow I would have my next shift at the agency and I wanted to go in more prepared. I wanted to have something, anything, that would make recent events make sense.

Sometimes that meant going for broke and doing exactly what you'd been told not to do with your best friend riding shotgun at your side.

"Because," I began ticking the answers off on my fingers. "I need answers before someone finds me in the shower, or worse, in front of an audience, and I start talking about magic and gods and goddesses. They'll think I'm in a cult or something. Second—"

"Well," Isa cut me off "if they do the same things Loki did, I'm sure they'll believe you're not."

I snorted, containing my sarcasm by some miracle.

Isa sat down on the bench and folded her arms in weary defiance. "That doesn't mean we have to call the beings you were specifically told not to call."

"I need to know what I'm getting into and if I even want to get into it." I huffed. It had nothing to do with my burning desire to know more about the past, my past. Or to know more about how the berries worked.

Not even a little.

"Besides," I continued. "They said if you called them without a purpose was when you would regret it."

Isa's shoulders slumped and she looked to the sky, her face a mask of 'Why do I bother?'

"Fine. Let the record show I am here only for moral support."

"Sure, sure. No time like the present to start that."

She gave me a scathing look. "You don't have any idea what you're doing, do you?"

I smiled in what was, I'm sure, an entirely convincing way. "I thought we just had to say their names?"

Isa snorted and pulled her sweatshirt off from around her waist, pulling it over her head. "What, because every college professor who teaches Norse myths doesn't say 'Skuld' and 'Norn' regularly? I've used those words before in conversation!"

I gave my own snort. "Sure. Like right there?" I pulled my jacket around me and shivered. While it was currently the dead of night, it shouldn't be so cold. It felt much colder than normal for May. We were in the grove of trees, far from the house. So far out I couldn't see the outline of Nana's soon-to-be-home. Even the stars weren't out tonight, making the trees brighter than anything else around us.

"I don't know how this works," Isa said with an edge in her voice. "I'm listening to you!"

"I'm repeating what Jord told me!"

In fact, I couldn't see any of the solar lights I installed in the garden. Wow, those were cheap.

"Shut up, Aspen. Did it just get really dark?"

Okay, it wasn't just me.

"Aspen? Aspen who? Oh, it's you," an unfamiliar female voice said.

Isa and I turned around. I swear she screamed. I promise I didn't.

There were three females standing there. Well, I wouldn't call them women. One was around twelve years old. And I couldn't say girls because another looked so ancient a stiff breeze would send her to see her ancestors. The other? Somewhere between thirty and fifty. It was hard to tell because around them there was no light.

Not as in it was dark, but as though the surrounding light didn't exist. I had never seen anything so dark that it wouldn't have cast a shadow, but I think these goddesses were exactly what I was asking for.

"Shit, did I just call you?" Isa asked. "I wasn't serious! That wasn't supposed to work!"

"It worked," the little girl said, her lips a coral pink. "We don't come to everyone who calls us, just those who can."

"They're just mortals, Urd," the oldest said, her clothes shockingly modern for her age. "They won't understand how this works."

"Hey, I'm not a mortal!" I protested. "Kinda."

"You haven't eaten a single fruit," the middle one said, shaking a bejeweled finger at me. "You cannot be immortal if you refuse to be."

I hated being stumped by logic. "Okay, so what happens if I eat the fruit? Do I become immortal? Or do I become something else? Why did Loki take the fruit?"

"So many questions," the young one said. Her pear-green streaked blonde hair fell into her face. "Answers come when something is given in return."

Isa gave me her Look, and I took it as my cue to stay silent.

"So," the middle one said, twirling a lock of her bottle blonde hair in her finger. "What's it going to be, children?"

"What can we exchange with you?" Isa offered.

My jaw dropped and I stomped over to her. "You said to never bargain with a fae!"

Isa grabbed my arm and yanked me into a huddle with her. "I'm not, dummy. I'm bargaining with goddesses of the past, present, and future. They can see into time like we see books. If the legends are true."

"They're true," the eldest—Skuld—said, her shriveled lips turning to a cruel smile. She studied both Isa and me for a moment before shaking her head. "You have nothing we want, so we cannot bargain."

Isa, dear sweet Isa, challenged her. "If we don't bargain, how do you know what we're offering?"

The youngest—Urd—clucked her tongue and then blew a bright yellow bubble, which popped just as loudly. "Have you come with a potion? Or a spell? A rune? Anything of actual value?"

I threw my hands into the air in frustration. This was going so well letting Isa take charge. Last time things went this well I let her talk to my mother about the explosion we caused in the oven. I was banned from baking and she had been forced to write an essay by my mother about lying.

"Can you tell us why Loki was dodging Aspen's questions?"

"Did he?" The middle—Verdandi—queried. "Then I suppose we shall dodge them, too."

"What?" I gasped.

"We cannot leave without getting to know each other better," Skuld said with a tsk in her voice. "A gift, perhaps, to promise that we see each other again."

"No," I blurted. "You really don't have to—"

"We insist," Verdandi said.

"A gift," Urd agreed. "Ten moons remain."

"Ten times more will you claim kinship," Verdandi continued cruelly.

"Ten times will you feel the pain of the past," Skuld finished.

I latched onto the only thing I could. "Hey, why did the future lady say the past part?"

All three glared at me, and I swear if looks could kill, I'd have been riding into Hel that second.

"But," Isa protested, "we call each other sisters all the time. My extended family thought my mom was going to adopt her."

"Yeah. What does that mean, anyway? What did you—"

"Look to the future in the past," Skuld said, her voice echoing slightly as they vanished, disappearing as though they had never been there.

Suddenly I could hear crickets, and the stars were out in the sky again.

I don't know how long we stood there, but I saw a light in the distance and realized that someone had turned on the floodlights in the backyard. Everyone had been in bed, so I didn't know who it could be. If anyone came for us now...

"Come on," I said, rolling the words around in my head. "We'll write it down inside and see who's awake."

"That was freaky, Aspen. Just freaky."

"Yeah."

We trudged through the trees, coming out to the other side where the floodlights were on like I suspected. Once on the porch, I turned them off and Isa opened the door into the kitchen, the light there also on. Someone was probably hungry and hit the outside lights on accident.

I crept into the doorway and then stopped short, my heart in my throat and my blood running cold. Mom was on the floor, twisting, twitching, her open eyes unseeing. I smelled urine and waste. Isa swore and whipped out her phone.

"Aspen, roll her on her side! She's having a seizure!"

Chapter Twenty

E veryone said it, but that didn't mean I believed it.

   'It's not your fault, Aspen.'

After the paramedics stabilized her, they took Mom to Flagstaff Medical Center. Cora Alma's small hospital was apparently packed and the consensus to take her the extra forty-five minutes worried me.

By the time the doctors were ready to let her come home, my internal mess of shame, guilt, and fear peaked. Externally I did something that I hadn't done in a few years: I masked. I put on a fake show that I was doing fine, coping with Mom's seizure like any other day.

I don't know what I would have done if Isa hadn't been with me. They rarely tell you that there are four Fs in the 'flight or fight' function of your brain. There's obviously flight or fight, but the one that I did, freeze, is the other more common one.

What's the last one? Well, fornicate, to put it in the PG context.

No, that's really it.

Personally, I've never run into that last one as a problem, but I've had several clinical workers bring it up, so I tried not to discount it.

I knew, deep down, that my reaction was normal. Hell, it was healthy even, to freeze when presented with the injury of a parent. Or so my previous therapist told me when I called her in tears. Luckily we parted on good terms, with her promising to help me out in emergencies until I got a new therapist. I don't think she expected the sobbing mess call so soon.

She listened, soothed, and reassured. While I still felt the shame and guilt, I could put them in a place to deal with them later—when I was ready to confront them.

My knotted stomach felt queasy while all three of us—me, Dad, and Nana—listened to the doctor.

"She's declining faster than we thought," the doctor said with a grim note. "She needs rest, but she also needs her physical therapy to keep moving. I know it's contradictory." The doctor's soft tone was laced with serious concern. "Contradictory can be true. Make sure she takes her medicine, does her physical therapy at home and with the therapist. Don't let her wear herself out. Knowing her, that will probably be harder than the other two."

Dad and Nana chuckled good-naturedly. I didn't. I was back to 'frozen.' We had been doing all of this. Why? Why was she getting worse?

My mind jumped back to the fruit in my freezer, the Norns' taunting words and Charlie's shrug of 'they didn't die from disease' when talking about the gods.

I didn't think Mom wanted to live forever—that is, I didn't want to give her immortality without asking her first. I didn't know how to do that without talking about the crazy-sounding fact that I was now running around solving mystical cases with reborn Norse goddesses.

"I'll see you at her checkup appointment in two weeks, Bob."

They must have finished talking while I was feeling weepy. Great. I'd have to ask Nana about this later. Dad drove me up there the first night, then went back for Nana the next day.

"Come on, sweetie," Nana cooed at me. She put her hands on my shoulders and squeezed. "We're going to leave now so we can have things ready for your mama when she gets home. Right?"

I nodded; my throat too constricted to do more than that. Somehow, I managed a "Thank you, Doctor," as Nana pulled me to the hallway. I let myself be pulled and concentrated on something very important: the next thing.

"Tell your brain to shut up."

I glanced over and Nana was trying her best to look brave through her tears. "You're twisting your hands." Hands that she grabbed and held still, bringing those thoughts to a grinding halt. Somehow, she knew. She always knew. "If we worry about the future too much, or fret about our past, we miss what we have. What your mom has right now is time." We stopped in front of the elevator and she tipped my chin up. "Now, we're going to do what we can with that time. There's a very good chance this will never happen again. But it might. We won't stay there, though. Right now, she's coming home to rest. And so are you."

I swallowed back my tears. Nana, as always, was right. Okay, so the 'as always' part wasn't usually there, but how was I supposed to know that palmistry was real?

We rode the elevator downstairs in silence. The mid-morning sun beat down on us in a calmer manner than it would in Phoenix, making the short walk bearable. Nana got into the driver's seat and I slid in on the other side, buckling up and hoping to not come back to this place for a few years at least.

Ha.

Driving with Nana is a lot of fun, especially when she brings up any tarot readings that she does these days. I've been listening with fresh interest, which I think she's taking as me being more open to her experiences. She hadn't invited me to meet her psychic yet, but it would be an interesting way to determine if the woman was a fraud or not.

"I talked to my psychic about you yesterday." Her voice seemed hesitant, but I encouraged her.

"Oh yeah? Anything good?" I teased. "Come on, that last one was pretty good about me getting into grad school."

Nana grinned back at me. Her hennaed hair caught the sun, reminding me of the color of molten lava. Fire. "Your dad told me how you were feeling, and I wanted to see what good news is in your future."

I still chuckled like I was only half-believing it. First, I'd take good news, and second, what if she wasn't a fraud? I couldn't afford to discount my belief in anything anymore.

Nana pulled onto the I-17, taking the boring but easy route back to Cora Alma and my gardening beds that needed tending. With the interruptions I had been getting, maybe I'd be ready for next spring's planting season.

She continued once we were sailing along at 80 mph. "She said there was a change of fortune in your future. That you were going to find something that you couldn't, or wouldn't, have been able to before. She saw a lot of foliage. So I thought, maybe your garden is going to be a big deal."

I contemplated that, at the same time counting off my mystical experiences. First the doe, then Frey and the Norns? My garden had become quite a magical place all on its own.

"Part of manifesting the future is that you have to do the steps," Nana chattered. "Maybe Flo and I could help clean out the garden and with that kind of land, we might even be able to sell the leftovers for some extra money at the farmers' market."

She jumped onto the topic of the farmers' market, babbling about who had the best jams and honey this year. I tuned her out, watching the other cars pass us by, my nerves tingling as though electricity flowed through me.

The things I had been thinking about were the past and Nana asked about the future. Something green, probably the garden? What if that was about the berries?

Semis passed us by and I kept my gaze unfocused out the window, my mind turning.

Yes, the berries. What if they didn't just make you immortal? What if I could cross breed their seeds with something from this time that would give it the healing properties, while not giving some others? Was there a way to isolate that? Probably. I mean, there had to be.

As I planned, my fingers itched for a notebook to brainstorm in. If I could find the right fruit to cross it with, if I could contact Marc... no, Aspen, you'll have to do this on your own. Maybe the rent out a community college lab, or better yet, one from NAU, wasn't too bad.

There were so many possibilities, and there was a lot I would have to do. Not as much to learn so much as to try. Trying was going to take time. So if it meant saving Mom from this pain, I had to hurry.

Chapter Twenty-One

After skipping my morning routine the past few days, my mental health was showing cracks. Okay, maybe Mom being in the hospital was part of it, but that was where the suffocating guilt was coming from. The point is, I felt good doing the routines. Let me have my comfort.

I made my list. Another day off work, another short list to keep it light and easy. Before I jumped into breakfast, I had important work to start today. Stealthy work.

Tucking my microscope under my hoodie, completely inconspicuous, I clomped down the stairs with Carrie at my heels. I scratched her head while she wound around my legs on the stairs, trying to send me flying, of course. We completed the game of don't step on the cat, grabbed the frozen berries, and ducked out without making my matcha.

I had a purpose. I had to figure this out. Things were going to be different, and I was the one who was going to change them. I power walked to the backyard and put the scope in the most dilapidated of the greenhouses. I could move it, but if anyone found it, I would have some explaining to do.

I ran back to the house to make my matcha and get started for the day without looking too out of the ordinary. Flipping on the coffeepot, I then heated the milk on the stove and went for my blend. I wanted to say that I knew this plan would work, but I didn't want to get my hopes up. Before, I crossbred flowers to see if it was possible. I didn't know what I was going to create here.

My milk was just boiling when the kitchen door swung open and Mom did her normal shuffle to the coffeepot. I hid my smile because this shuffle, while a little slower than last week, was completely normal. Her red hair stuck up and she looked like a candle wrapped in her white robe.

"Good morning."

She mumbled something that might have been 'good morning' or 'get bent' and honestly, either was a good chance. Her coffee wasn't ready yet, so she sighed and shuffled over to the kitchen table to wait for it.

I sighed in contentment. "I'll make you some matcha."

She made a face at me. She loved matcha but in the morning she wanted *coffee*. No exceptions, no substitutions, and don't you dare bring her the lie water called decaf.

I poured my completed drink into a tumbler, wanting to get outside this morning and dig into that alyssum, literally. Before I moved, my phone buzzed and the default jingle played. Frowning, I didn't recognize the number. I almost sent it to voicemail, but it was a local number, so I slid the button with a shrug to Mom's unasked question.

"Hello?"

This had better be good.

"Aspen?" A slightly familiar voice on the end of the line asked.

I tried to place the voice but only paced the length of the table before I had to give in for the sake of politeness. "Yeah. Who is this?"

"It's Sif."

Damn.

"Uh, Linda, hello." I looked over at Mom, who was eyeing me with interest. Who do you think I get my rampant curiosity from?

She sighed on the other side, obviously realizing that she could be overheard. "There's an emergency." Her sugary voice became more like hardened resin. Something felt off. "If you can get here by 10AM for this, I'll pay you double time. In cash."

I almost choked on my matcha. That meant no reporting which... slightly illegal, but hey, was the government going to perform whatever service I was about to do? I think not.

Meanwhile, I waved my mom off and wiped my shirt. "Do I need to do anything special?"

"We'll go over it when you get here. You'll be sidelined, but we need extra hands and Charlie got drunk last night so she's out."

The knots in my stomach loosened. "Nothing too big then, got it."

"Call me when you're in your car. I'll give you more instructions then."

Sif hung up without saying goodbye and the ice started to creep into my stomach again.

"Work?"

My mind still reeled with the possibilities of that kind of pay, but I snapped out of it quickly. "Yeah. They said to get there by ten, but going now would give a great impression." And more pay! I quickly went through my contacts and brought up Nana. She was a morning person, so at least she wasn't going to bite my head off when I called. "I'll get Nana to come here for the day."

Mom's shoulders dropped and she frowned at me. "Really?" she asked, her voice with an edge to it. "I'm not a child. I'm your mother."

I didn't want to fight with her, but I would not be responsible for her getting hurt. "Yeah, and I'm supposed to watch over you, My Beloved Mother."

She gave me The Mother Look. "Don't try to sweet talk your way out of this."

I sighed and prayed for patience for her stubbornness. Which I definitely didn't have. "Come on, Mom. You haven't even been home for twenty-four hours. No one else is home. Please, let me call Nana."

Mom chewed her lower lip, and I gave her the greatest pout manageable before she heaved a sigh. "Fine. But she doesn't need to rush over. I'll be fine until she gets some food in her."

"Deal."

I got dressed quickly and gave Carrie a scritch before heading off. She meowed a pitiful sound at me as I left. I called into the house asking Mom to feed her, realizing with a pang of guilt that I probably hadn't. I got a yelled affirmative, so I shut the door, threw Bessie into gear and headed to Cora Alma.

Not even thirty seconds in the car, I called Sif using my Bluetooth. She picked up after one ring.

"Is anyone around?" Her voice was lower than earlier.

"No. Why are you whispering?" I asked.

Her voice rose. "Just in case you were around someone again. I need you to hurry and get to the road between Sedona and Cora Alma. We have an emergency."

Alarm bells were going off in my head. "Which one?"

"89A."

I suppressed a groan. 89A again.

"This will be dangerous, Aspen," Sif continued. "There are drastic changes in temperature, destruction, and magic every-where. This could be a Jotun."

"A Jotun? A giant?" I squeaked, making sure I heard right. My pulse thudded in my ears and suddenly my mind was blank as I absorbed her next words.

"Frost giants, to be specific."

"Giants," I deadpanned. "Like twenty-foot-tall monsters?"

"Those are the ones," Sif chirped. "Though these are only about ten feet. Better hurry, they still move pretty damn fast. I'll text you where."

The line clicked and I stared at my phone with my mouth agape.

Well, at least this time I wouldn't have a cat and plant cuttings with me as I hurried.

A giant. A freaking giant was loose in the woods. Her text said I would know when I got there, but so far there weren't even any other cars on this road. Her voice had been steady, firm, with a note in it I couldn't quite place. Earlier they'd told me that giants happened, but I hadn't thought I'd face one so quickly.

So much I didn't know.

Wisps of white fog whipped around the car, dampening the sun's rays. It became so thick that I had to squint to see the lines on the road, and after a few minutes in it, I could barely see ten feet in front of me. I pulled over, coming to a halt for two reasons. One being that there was a tug inside of me to stop. A tug to turn around, possibly while screaming. And two: there were about ten other cars and trucks, all pulling off for the same reason. The fog became so thick there was nothing in front of it. It stretched dozens of feet high, far onto each side of the highway.

I pulled my car over, marveling at the white wall before me. It stretched beyond the forest of pines and oaks, so far on either side I couldn't see where it stopped or started. The closer to the wall you got, the more frost appeared on the ground until white ground met white wall.

A group of people who didn't seem to know each other from all walks of life conversed together. A trucker, a delivery person, several people who looked like they were dressed for work, and a couple of families no doubt starting their day of sightseeing.

A tapping on my window made me jump, but it was only Eir in a black jumpsuit instead of her normal garb. She had on the same dark against pale makeup and a slight smile on her face when I rolled the window down.

"Hey Erin." We were within hearing distance of the others. "I thought you'd be in there."

"Nope, not yet," she said. "We were waiting for you when the Frost Giant noticed us. They put up the fog. It's impossible to do anything but walk through. Unless you're a mortal." She gestured to the people before us. One put their hand in and walked forward, only to be pushed back. "You had the urge to stop, right?"

"Yeah. Wait, is that their magic?"

"Yep. Come on, let's get ready."

I got out of the car and a shiver caught my skin, chilling me to my core in an unnatural cold. The hair on my arms stood on end, and once again I tasted what I now identified as magic.

Eir led the way down the side of the highway into the forest. Some of the people were watching us, but no one followed as the trees swallowed us. Our voices would easily echo, so I held my tongue until I was sure we were far enough away.

"Where are we going?" I whispered. The thick blanket of the sequoia and ash covered my voice.

"Not much further." Her voice was no louder than mine.

We pressed on, stepping around large rocks, boulders, and vegetation as we did so. As she promised, it wasn't more than another hundred feet until we arrived where Jord and Sif were waiting. Each carried their weapon but were dressed a little differently than when they were in the office.

"This is so above my paygrade," I muttered as they strapped small knives and other weapons I couldn't identify onto their bodies.

"Not for extra like this, it isn't," Sif said as I joined them. She had two swords strapped to her hips, and I realized that an intricately woven pattern decorated her black, red, and pink—yes, pink—leather clothes. Runes maybe? But... hey! If they got weapons, what would I do?

"Double time and a half and I'll get behind that," I muttered.

"Double time and a half it is," Jord agreed as she joined us, wearing a similar jumpsuit but in a toned-down brown, green, and purple. On her, it looked regal. In her hand she held a tall staff with a blue-green orb swirling like a snow globe at the top.

Eir strapped a long knife to her shin, and I couldn't help myself.

"Do I get one?"

I winced at how hopeful I sounded. Sif laughed, but Jord answered. "You'll get one that works with your magic."

"Whenever that is," Eir muttered, but I ignored her.

The trees rustled in the breeze and Jord closed her eyes. Then she knelt, using her staff as a guide before she touched the earth, splaying her palm on the ground.

I heard the whispers of the trees and the grass, but as always, nothing decipherable, only the sounds of soft over-lapping voices. It calmed me, soothed me. My tension melted away, but I remained on my guard. The songs of the plants were enough to remind me of my desire to know magic and to learn of this unseen world.

Jord's surprised gasp broke me out of my trance. "The trees won't talk to me."

"Do they usually talk?" I asked, the sound of disembodied singing still echoing for me. Eir nodded, worry etched in her face. I bit my lip, wondering if this was the time to tell them, but before I opened my mouth, Sif and Eir stopped and turned to Jord so fast I heard a 'crack' in the air.

"Won't talk, or magically can't?" Eir asked.

Jord, her palm still flat on the ground, shook her head. "Won't. The dirt is telling me to go southeast and the trees are... laughing?"

"Well, that's rude." Sif glared at the trees, which honestly was hard to not laugh at. "Are they gossiping again?"

"No, they say they don't want to talk to me. That's odd. We'll have to go in with only what the dirt can tell us."

"Great, a direction," Eir said with a huff. "Nothing else? Not even how many?"

Jord stood and didn't brush the dirt off her hand. "We've gone into worse with less."

"Wait, what am I doing?" I asked as Eir handed out small bottles with green liquid. "If you're not giving me a weapon, and we're going into the fog, what am I going to do?"

"Aspen, you aren't going in the fog," Eir said, continuing to disperse different colored vials. "You're going to keep this off of the internet and the news."

"Okay. How?" There were a dozen people who all had phones, which means they had cameras. "Someone's going to say something."

Eir put two vials in my hands. "You'll think of something. Now, the green one is not to be ingested, okay?"

"Okay?" I studied the small bottle and was grateful I wouldn't have to drink something that probably came from Nickelodeon.

"If the Jotun comes out, pour it over your head and it will make you invisible." I wasn't sure if it was the cold fog or her words that caused my stomach to turn to ice. "The blue one is fire smoke." She continued to explain before I asked. "It's more than enough to cover all the people out there for a minute if the Jotun comes out. It's not perfect, but it'll give us a chance to catch up." She hesitated for a moment before pulling out a larger magenta bottle and handing it to me. "This is a healing potion. There are about three doses in that. It's extremely hard to make, so don't take it for an upset stomach."

I stared at the bottle in my hand. "What can't it heal?"

"Mostly gaping wounds, neurological problems, the common cold, and chronic disease." She smiled proudly. "It's my own special blend, it can even take care of hangovers! But again, be careful when you use it. And if all else fails, use a circle of salt."

"Salt? Really?"

Sif gently nudged me and continued to smile. "Salt absorbs magic, especially negative and dark magicks. Table salt isn't the best, but it'll do in a pinch."

"Does anything else do that?"

"The usual things. Garlic. Holy water. It depends on the magic in play, but most holy purifiers will work."

"Really?" I asked in shock. I wouldn't have thought about any of that.

Jord put her hand on my shoulder. She smiled in her reassuring way. "Don't worry, this won't take too long. Frost Giants have a lot of power, but so do we."

"So, what would I be doing for triple time?"

"You don't wanna know." Sif laughed, putting away the last of the potions.

"Ah," I said, unsure of what else to say or do. They were going to fight, to use their magic in ways I could only imagine. It was going to be so amazing and there was fog keeping me from seeing it.

Come on." Sif started toward the fog, gesturing for the others to follow her. "We have to get in there before some idiot up there does."

They pushed forward and with a final wave from Sif, the fog enveloped them. Not even the shine of Sif's sword or the gleam of the globe on Jord's staff or the shiny black bow on Eir's head lasted more than a second before vanishing. I cast one last glance at where they stood before hiking back to the road, my pocket jingling with potions and my heart heavy as I thought—no, worried—about the worst that could happen to them, not knowing if I was capable of even imagining the worst now.

Chapter Twenty-Two

I trudged up the side of the slope back to the line of cars, which had almost doubled since I left. Most people's faces were somewhere between confused and angry. However, some of them were trying to push past the feeling of staying away, including trying to go into the fog. A woman in heels and a suit power-walked forward with a look of confidence.

Then she ended up thrown backwards by the unseen force of magic. The back of my mouth had that sweet taste that I was coming to associate with power as soon as the fog expelled her onto her butt. She quickly rose, a look of disbelief on her face as she and a few others continued to cautiously approach the fog.

It wouldn't take long before someone actually pushed in and broke through, or worse, had some unknown magic and found themselves on the wrong end of a sword. I racked my brain with different scenarios. Police and fire training. Aliens. With the variety of ages and other factors at play, I wasn't sure what to say that would capture their attention and be believable.

Shit. Why was I so bad at this?

"Listen to this! I'm stuck outside of Cora Alma, Arizona, right now." An unfamiliar male voice rose above the chatter. "We were making good time when suddenly this white fog, see this, blew up on the road and brought everything to a complete stop." The voices quieted down, listening to the narration. "No one is moving, and every fool, including this one, is out of their cars!"

Someone was live streaming this? Already?

I pushed my way past, scanning the crowds. I don't know what I expected, but when I walked to the front and saw a tall, lean, and handsome man, I stopped, looking like a yokel. He was toned and athletic, with a runner's body that didn't lack muscle. A pair of loose jeans left everything to the imagination, and I glimpsed a chain and charm around his neck. A blue ball cap rounded out anything interesting about him. He held his phone slightly up and walked up and down the perimeter of the fog, his umber face showing... amusement?

Okay, that I hadn't expected. Confusion, anger maybe. His voice showed those things, so why was he on the verge of laughter? I pressed my lips together and tried not to make a noise of desperation. In the end, there's only one way to get people away from a spectacle.

Be a bigger one.

"Hey, what are you doing?" I yelled at him, putting on my best annoyed customer voice. "You can't film here; don't you know what's going on?" That's right, Aspen, get a little attitude.

The man turned almost unworldly green eyes toward me, and he had the decency to look confused, but mirth soon entered his gaze again.

"No?" He kept his voice light and flashed me a grin with perfect teeth.

Holy shit, no one should look this hot.

"Yeah, uh..." I stumbled, trying to think of something. Great, had to go in half-cocked, didn't you, Aspen? "You can't film, because—because Michael Bay is filming his latest block-buster in there."

Oh yeah, he's gonna believe that one.

Some chuckling came from the other onlookers around me. Mr. Green Eyes only smiled wider. "Oh?"

"No, I swear!" I doubled down. "There's a scene from his latest movie being filmed right now, and if you leak it on the internet, he is going to sue your ass so fast."

The man turned to the fog. "Michael Bay is in there directing a movie. What's it called?"

I held firm, raising my chin in defiance. "Giving out spoilers is above my paygrade."

"Is it a Transformers movie?" a young child in the small crowd half-yelled. I whipped around to face the voice and saw a red-haired boy, his wide-eyed, slack-jawed face filled with hope.

Thank God for small children.

"Hey now, kid," I fully turned around. "I said I can't say. But—"

An inhuman scream muffled by the thick fog echoed. Then flashes of light, blue, purple, and red lit up in the distance. I caught myself on Mr. Green Eyes when the ground rumbled beneath us.

"It IS!" the boy squealed.

"Yeah," I muttered as the sounds of muffled battle reached my ears. "It's Transformers."

The man, who had thankfully stopped streaming, now watched the light show with interest. His complexion paled and he twitched, his phone disappearing. A scream cut through the air, louder than anything that had come through yet. My heart stopped because that scream was very human.

"Sif!"

The man yanked his necklace off and charged into the fog.

"Wait!" I yelled, reaching for him, only to have his shirt slip through my fingers. He didn't look back.

He didn't bounce back as expected. Instead, he glided into the gray cloud silently and so suddenly it was as though he was never there.

"Damn it," I hissed.

How had he gotten through? I was a growing goddess, so I had a guess why I could pass. What was this guy?

Wait, he said 'Sif'.

I fought a war in me. Maybe he knew Sif. Maybe. And maybe he had latent magic from birth. I had some weapons on me, the potions Eir gave me. If this guy got himself killed because I couldn't keep him in one place... I threw myself in after him, only to be swallowed up by the white mist. No resistance for me, either. People yelled behind us and I looked back just in time to see someone deflected away. All around me the fog was so thick and cold that I was drenched just from running after the man.

"Stop!" I yelled, trying to catch up. He outpaced me as though he was riding the wind. It was all I could do to keep him in my sight. I wanted to hope he wasn't heading toward the battle, but the flashes were getting brighter, with sounds like thunder occasionally accompanying them.

After a few seconds, I came out into a frozen wonderland.

Everything from the road to the trees and even the little mile marker was covered in ice. I almost slipped on the road but kept my balance by grabbing on to a piece of ice jutting out of the ground. I wished I'd grabbed my hoodie from the car because sweat turned to ice on my arms, and I saw the air in little puffs before me.

I cautiously took my steps, putting one foot in front of the other, following the tracks in the snow. I still slid a little, but the crunched snow gave me traction.

"Hey," I whispered in a hiss. "Hey, Stupid Guy, where are you?"

Even so, my voice echoed.

I got no answer from Stupid Guy, and it was getting harder to move the longer I stood searching for him in this frozen, fogless area. I marveled the domed clearing that stretched about a hundred feet in either direction. I considered going back. I mean, maybe Stupid Guy hadn't actually run toward the battle and he was still lost in the fog. Maybe he'd ended up on the other side and the Jotun had splattered him already.

The only breeze in the unnatural cold was my own breathing as I shuddered in my jeans and T-shirt. My lungs constricted painfully against the chilled air and each time I thought I heard a rustle, I jumped.

There was never any sound except my footsteps as they crunched on the new snow.

"Look out!" Stupid Guy yelled as he came careening from behind me, yanking me down and pulling me across the frozen ground so fast ice and dirt sprayed. As he did so, white ice flew over our heads, wind whipping so strong it stung every exposed part of me. I didn't have time to recover as a deafening, unearthly roar split the air into violent fragments of sound that pierced me deep in my core. My head pulsing as though I was the clapper in a bell, I stared at the man—well, not a man but humanoid—figure as it lumbered forward.

Stupid Guy helped me up and he threw his arms in front of me in a protective stance when I slipped again, bruising my knee as I did so. I was both flattered and burning with embarrassment as he stood in front of me, as solid as a statue.

But I was a goddess, damn it!

"What the hell are you doing, coming in here?" he demand-ed, never letting his eyes leave the monster.

"What about you?" I stumbled, my heart beating in my throat. I tried to match his height, but he towered more than a foot over me, matching my angry stare.

"Look out!"

The humanoid giant white thing—that I now assumed was the Jotun—roared again. I pushed my hands over my ears, but I still felt it painfully in my chest as though we were at a too-loud rock concert. Its spindly arms blurred impossibly fast for a creature of its size, and a wave of wind and ice rushed toward us.

I flinched, bracing for the hit, praying that my parents would never find out how I died. It never came. When I looked up, I hoped to see several goddesses glaring at me. I did not expect to see Stupid Guy holding a wooden plaque the size of my palm in front of him deflecting ice in every direction around us.

I stared at him, but something felt oddly normal about this. Had I met him before? No, not in this lifetime at least.

"What are your powers?" Stupid Guy—who might be a god—asked, his attention focused on the Jotun and the spell he was casting.

"Stunned dismay and sarcasm."

"You have no magic?!"

"I thought you had no magic!"

"What are you doing here, you stupid mortal? How did you pass through the magic barrier?"

The ice storm grew through our bickering. My jeans were frozen to my skin. The exposed skin on my arms and face were being pricked by pins, freezing me to the spot. The pain didn't let up. As I tried to move my legs, the fabric of my jeans ripped and a scream tore from my throat.

A string of words shouted in a language I didn't know by a voice I never thought I'd be so happy to hear—changed the tides.

Through the blinding blizzard I made out Eir's right hand raised up to chest level, glowing bright blue. Her left arm hung limply at her side, blood trickling from an unseen wound.

The Jotun let out another high-pitched shriek, one of its legs shattering out from underneath it. Fractals of ice burst in all directions, peppering my face with cold. It continued to scream as Jord and Sif came from the same direction Eir had, spells glowing at the ready.

Mr. Maybe a God (I can't call him 'stupid'; he just saved my life) took a cautious step closer to the goddesses holding a hammer with a short handle.

I knew of only one hammer in Norse mythology with that sort of description. That isn't to say I'm an expert, but I couldn't help but feel relief and dismay that it was Thor, *that* Thor, who saved my sorry butt.

"Sif!" the probable Thor guy yelled. "Are you alright?"

Embarrassment swirled through me and heat rising to the tips of my hair. I had yelled at Thor. And called him stupid. This wasn't just some idiot—this was the most famous person in Norse mythology. I had yelled at him. Still shivering, I saw that Sif was bleeding from a head wound, one sword in her hand, her eyes blazing and her face a promise of future pain. She nodded, but then winced from the movement.

"Jotun, you're surrounded." Jord's voice was, as always, calm, but there was a hard edge to it. "No further harm will come to you if you come with us quietly back to Jotunheim. We also won't make a complaint against your lord and master for coming to Midgard and breaking the fragile peace."

The Jotun laughed boisterously and spoke, its words like glass. I covered my ears to stop the shredding. Just when I thought I couldn't stand another second, the words became intelligible in my mind.

I'm not some child you can bully, Earth God-dess. I am only the beginning. You cannot stop us.

The Jotun took advantage of the collective inattention of the other four, and turned toward me, a bright white spell glowing in his hand.

I think I screamed, but I threw my hands up in front of my face. I prayed for it to be quick.

I heard a familiar sound, the sound of shifting soil—only much heavier and louder—followed by a sickening thud. I glanced past my thrown-up hands to the dark piece of earth protruding in front of me.

Well, that definitely hadn't been there a second ago.

Touching the cold rock that had saved me from the Jotun's attack caused fear and elation to shudder down my spine. The battle continued to rage outside of my safe cubby for only a moment longer. I heard the Jotun's inhuman scream once more and then silence. Light flashed and the earth in front of me crumbled back into place, except for the part where the actual concrete had been. That lay cracked and damaged in an uneven semi-circle as the only proof that something had changed.

Air blew around me and when I was able to focus again, I saw Sif held a sword stained with silver blood. Eir held the same type of containment sphere she had the other day with the pixie, but now it held a small white goblin-looking creature in it. It had a hard, knotted nose and was otherwise rather short and stocky.

"Is that the Jotun?" I stumbled forward, my legs shaky from the cold. The rest of my body burned from adrenaline.

"Yeah." Sif wiped her blade off on a black cloth. "You okay? Excellent cover there, Jord."

"That wasn't me." Jord didn't sound worried. In fact, she sounded pleased. The fog started to dissipate and she looked around. "Come on, we need to get out of here before the humans get here."

All five of us hobbled together and climbed over the guardrail, slowly sliding to the actual ground about five feet down on the other side. My shin burned and I wasn't looking forward to seeing the damage.

"That wasn't me," Jord looked confused for a split second. "Either someone else is looking out for Aspen or"—she smiled—"your powers are awakening."

I slowed my walk as the thought of having the ability to move the earth, of being so strong that I broke through concrete when I panicked, made me feel somehow more complete. Like I should have known what to do all along. Even though... "I didn't do anything."

We were approaching the cars. Most people had already driven off with the thinning fog. A few were still chatting on the side of the road, probably about this being a publicity stunt about the movie I'd made up or something.

May as well let them do that.

Keeping ourselves hidden behind the goddesses' SUV, I took stock of everyone's injuries. Eir's left arm was probably broken, Sif was blotting her head, and Jord had a hand pressed to her side, covering a small trickle of blood.

"What can I do?" I pleaded. "I haven't taken anything but basic first aid but—"

Eir leaned against a tree and closed her eyes, her face even paler than usual. "Don't worry about it. Thor, it's in the—" She stopped as he approached with a small blue first aid kit. Relief melted onto her face. "Thanks."

I kept off to the side and watched, fascinated, as Eir poured a clear liquid over her broken arm. The blood washed away and her face relaxed.

"You really are new," Thor said, his grin back. So was the chain and hammer charm around his neck. He stood next to me, his arms crossed. "Eir's good with healing potions. That one stops the bleeding and helps with pain." He pointed at Jord. "She's using the same one, and Sif is... well, dabbing at it with her shirt. Which I highly approve of," he said with an appreciative nod to her bare midriff.

She glared at him, a look I expected to be filled with anger. Instead, she simply marched over to Eir and grabbed gauze from the blue bag to dab at her head.

Thor chuckled, a mix between acceptance and exasperation.

I relaxed and leaned against the SUV, watching them as they worked.

"What are you doing, girl? Why aren't you treating your wounds?" Thor demanded, handing another potion to Eir, this one the same shocking pink as the one she had given me. She paused and looked me up and down, then swore.

I started out of my stupor and then stared at my leg where blood stained my right pant leg below the knee. Pain creeped into my understanding and I suddenly remembered what I had just gone through.

"Thor! Shit!" Sif snapped as she and Jord made their way toward me.

I moved to pull up my pant leg, but Eir grabbed my arm, stopping me. "You're not going to want to see that," she said. I saw her no longer broken arm and words failed me.

"Thor, Jord, keep her busy," Sif instructed—no ordered—before helping me into a safe sitting position.

Eir was pulling things out from the blue bag, way too much for that bag to carry.

"Internal Expansion spell," Sif explained, turning my face to face hers. "Unless you've seen skin shredded from asphalt before, you don't want to see this." I believed her, swallowing down my voice. She booped my nose and winked at me. "Atta girl."

From that moment on all I knew was Thor and Jord. They talked casually to me about what, I didn't know, because the buzzing in my ears grew louder and louder as more time passed. I couldn't feel the pain anymore and that worried me.

Our healing took so long that when they said I was safe to drive, the only signs that anything had happened here were dew on the ground and the circle where magic had been. I could barely see it from the side of the road. The goddesses packed up their cases of weapons and heavy potion kits into their SUV.

"Hey, Sif," Thor called. "Got any room for me? I got dropped off."

The look she sent him could have scorched the Sahara, but he somehow survived. "Aspen," she said, her voice sugary sweet, "you get triple time if you bring Thor back to the office with you."

And that's how I took my family out for a nice Italian dinner that night.

Chapter
Twenty-Three

After easing into traffic from my place on the shoulder, and a quick turnaround, Thor and I were on our way back to Cora Alma. None the worse for wear, but much more concerned about how giants were getting to earth.

"Still no idea who you are?" Thor fiddled with his chain and I kept my mouth set, a little unsure of him. I'd never seen Sif look so upset. "We all start like that, you know? Looks like you got your first clue."

I took the bait. "I guess I'm an earth goddess. Last week I thought I was Frigg's handmaiden. I thought that would have been cool."

"Ah, Fulla," Thor said with a nod. "Well, we can't have everything. There're more than a few Earth goddesses left. Most well-known would be Gurd, Gefjun, Vor, or several others. We all know who Bragi is, I think the word is 'rooting' for."

The name rang a bell, but I couldn't remember anything specific. Biting my lip and not taking my eyes off the road, I asked a question I hadn't thought of until now. "Thor," I started cautiously, "what does magic feel like?"

I expected him to scoff at my casual inquiry, or maybe even not understand it. That feeling continued as he mulled over his answer for what I considered too long for someone who talked so much.

"It's a strange thing to explain. You have magic. You can call upon it to do anything in your power. From the smallest spark"—he snapped his fingers and green light crackled at his fingertips— "to the greatest fire. Unless you're doing something that drains your magic to where your well is empty, you don't feel it more than breathing. It just is."

"'Your well is empty?'"

"When you have no magic left."

I turned toward him, horrified, but he pointed to the road and I snapped back before I drifted too far out of my lane. The idea that something so much a part of you could leave... it felt like it shouldn't be possible.

"Is that a thing? To use up your magic completely?"

His voice continued to be casual with a hint of smugness. "Your legs stop working after you walk too much. Why wouldn't magic do the same?"

"Can you die if you use your magic too much?"

He was silent again before whispering his answer. "Yes."

He didn't elaborate, so instead of pressing, I went on with a safer topic. "Who's Bragi?"

"Idunn's husband."

A memory sparked from my reading the Norsewikia and other sources. "He tried to get Loki to stop being an asshole once."

"Once?" Thor scoffed. "From the way Freyja tells it, they were constantly sparring."

I checked my mirror and changed lanes. "Who is Bragi 'rooting' for?"

"His wife, Idunn, of course. He's been reborn, and like many of us feels kinship to people and places from the past. His poetry was legendary."

"Really?"

"Haven't you read your mythology?"

I winced. I'd been busy since this dropped in my lap. A lot busier than I expected it to be. "Some of it. Come on, there's a lot to learn behind it."

"True," he grunted, also checking the mirrors.

We lapsed into an uncomfortable silence, and I ran through topics to bring up. His original home. His current one. His current alias—Hasan. Sports. At least twenty things danced around but I couldn't pick a topic. We were still several miles from the office and if the silence kept on, I felt like I might burst. This would be the perfect time to ask questions. Thor was open and he seemed friendly enough now.

"So, what's up with you and Sif?" The words were out of my mouth before I could stop them. Damn my inability to filter when it was actually important.

Thor laughed and fingered the probable Mjolnir around his neck. "Sif, well, she doesn't want to have a relationship. I do." I didn't turn away from the road again, but it took restraint. "There's a big problem, though," he continued.

"What is it?"

"She's a lesbian."

I snorted, trying to contain my giggles. I signaled to get off the freeway while trying not to burst out into laughter at the same time. I snorted again and then failed.

Thor joined me in laughing and shook his head. "I know, I know," he said. "It's pretty pathetic."

"I guess that means you'd have to have a sex change to date her."

Thor chuckled. "Not something I'm gonna do. The gist is I didn't realize that when we first met centuries ago. Anyway, she ran, I pursued. She hit me. I pursued with flowers."

"That didn't end well, I'm sure."

"I eventually learned. Now if I get the finger from her, I consider it a good interaction."

Yipes.

"There's the office." I pointed and changed the subject off this uncomfortable topic I'd brought us to. I eased into one of the nearby parking spaces, collected my things, Sif's ex, and we made our way to the rune inscribed door.

Charlie waited for us, her headphones on with a new fashion magazine that I hadn't seen before. When Thor followed me into the room, she lit up in a way I had never seen before.

"Thor!" she squealed. "Thor, Thor, Thoooor!"

"Charlie!" Thor opened his arms and he squashed her to his chest. "Charlie, you should have seen the Jotun that Sif killed. It was almost twelve feet tall!"

"Yeah, but I bet you helped," Charlie teased, probably already knowing full well that he didn't do much. The door banged open and Charlie frowned. "Hey, we're closed. Oh. Hey, guys," she greeted the goddesses as they walked in. "Sorry, thought you were another customer."

"Another?" Eir gasped, grabbing the messages out of Charlie's hands. "Were any of them overlapping?"

Charlie was already talking to Thor, ignoring Eir and everyone else. Oooh. I got it. Someone had a crush.

"So did the newbie do anything?" Charlie asked Thor, still ignoring the goddesses' requests for information.

"Actually, she did." Sif turned to me, her smile almost back to its usual brightness. "You are definitely not Fulla."

"Nope," Jord agreed with a headshake. "I'm not surprised your powers presented themselves. However," she frowned, "that's odd. It's just odd. What did you feel?"

I blinked a few times, conjuring the image of the Jotun screaming and barreling toward me. Its teeth bared and powerful, crystalized legs coming at me too fast. "When that happened? I mean, nothing? I was... I was praying? Or hoping, I guess, that something would save me from the Jotun."

Come to think of it, I hadn't done anything out of the ordinary for someone in danger. Unless people were way more collected than the internet portrayed them to be.

"Prayers are powerful magic," Thor said seriously, and everyone, including Charlie, nodded thoughtfully. I must have looked less thoughtful than the others, because he continued. "Praying is putting faith outside of yourself."

"I thought magic was inside us?"

"It is," Thor agreed, talking with his hands as much as his voice. "It's also around us. When you don't know what it is, you're putting faith in something you don't understand, aren't you?"

Jord peered at me, scanning me as though she had never seen me before. She studied me with a frown on her face. "There's too many goddesses and Valkyrie who are associated with earth. I couldn't start guessing."

"Others have." Everyone focused on me and I chewed my lower lip, cursing my slip up.

"Others?" Jord prompted, not frowning or betraying her emotions, just interested. "Who?"

Too late now, I decided not to lie. "Frey showed up the other night. And"—I bit my tongue before I spilled what might be an important secret—"and he said that he thinks I'm Gurd."

That doesn't mean that I told them everything.

Jord's face crumbled just slighting, her look one of knowledge, almost one of pity. "He's lonely."

I glared at her. "'Lonely?' Tell him to log onto a dating website then. It was creepy as hell at first."

If Thor had hair, his eyebrows would have disappeared.

"You should have told us Lord Frey appeared before you." Jord led us back into the office, closing the door on Charlie when she tried to follow us in.

"Look, I know you said not everyone can be trusted, but you also said I would have to judge that for myself. Why would it matter?" I asked, keeping my tone inquisitive and light.

"It doesn't matter," Sif interjected, glaring at Jord and looping arms with me. "You have no powers. Well, not much. If someone intends to harm you, you have no way to protect yourself."

"Why would I need to worry about someone harming me? Have you been fully honest with me?" I waited for one of them to answer, but even Thor looked away. I crossed my arms. "Didn't think so."

"Aspen, please," Jord's soothing, honey voice vanished. "We don't know who you are because the Ns wouldn't tell us. Something is blocking Freyja from knowing, and the only way for us to know is to wait it out. And without the fruit that you're not eating—"

Meeting Jord's kind, but stern, gaze gave rise to embarrassment, and I avoided hers, trying not to look guilty.

"—they won't awaken any more than if you were a minor witch."

"I moved the earth," I reminded her.

"The spell was strong, but easy. Not eating enough would be a terrible misstep."

"What?" I uncrossed my arms and looked between all four of them. "I thought the fruit made you immortal? Can it also hurt you?"

"No, it can't hurt you. At least... I don't think so. It makes you immortal while also waking up whatever dormant powers we have," Thor explained, his voice even and brow furrowed. "If you don't eat it, you can't awaken."

"What have you done with the fruit?" Jord asked.

I paused for a moment and then shrugged. "Nothing, I just haven't eaten it. I'm taking my time, okay? This is a big deal to me. Maybe I don't want to be twenty-three forever."

"I'm sorry, Aspen, you're right." Jord took a seat and stretched. "Sometimes I forget that mortals are different."

Eir came up behind me, a fragrant cup of tea in her hand. Her lips pressed into a thin line. "It's made of dried fruit," she explained, thrusting it into my hands.

I guess that explains how some of my powers were coming out. It had to be the tea.

"You didn't throw the fruit away or anything, did you?" A worried tremble echoed in her voice.

Each of them now wore a similar expression of apprehension. "No?"

"When Loki did what he always does," Sif sighed. "He destroyed a lot of the fruit stores and shoved some in his pockets on his way out."

Ice settled in my stomach and a sick feeling came with it. They talked about Loki like he was an annoying part of their lives. They always said he was responsible for Ragnarök, and that I would have to judge him for myself. He was a trickster, okay, an asshole to be sure, but I always thought that he was part of the same world.

"Loki isn't affiliated with you?"

"He's considered rogue," Jord said, her voice hard and cold. "We're under orders to bring him in, dead or alive."

Chapter Twenty-Four

Thor was apparently going to be staying in town because I got a call from Eir the next day. She informed me with an unusual soprano note in her voice, that his current name was 'Hasan.' I held my tongue about knowing that already. I didn't need to get on her worse side. She ended with a reminder to eat my fruit for the week.

After we hung up, I stared at the fruit they had given me on my way out the door, this one perhaps a blueberry. I held it up to the light of my bedroom lamp. It look like a dried blueberry should; it felt like it, but the thought of putting something a thousand years old into my mouth gave me the heebie-jeebies. Without it, I couldn't hope to be a goddess and keep up with work. Worst of all, no magical powers of my own without it.

Would being a goddess mean I saw other things? Would what I knew in the past come forward to help me now?

Grabbing my pillow and rolling over, the fruit still in one hand, I stared up at the ceiling. The unfamiliar patterns etched into the plaster didn't bring any answers. They did, however, bring a Carrie-like cat, balloons, and a warbly house. If I sat here thinking like this, turning everything over in my head, I would never find out. I couldn't move forward if I didn't take the step.

I pushed the berry into my mouth and tried to swallow it whole, only to gag and then chew it. Like an idiot I put it between my teeth and couldn't taste anything, but I wasn't expecting anything great out of something older than most of the knowledge in the world. When I bit directly down, a flavor exploded on my tongue, one I had never tasted, but something I had always wanted to know. So sweet and delicate, the finest dark chocolates mixed with melon and sweetened to perfection. It was... I moaned as I finished it off.

"That was so good," I whispered in awe, touching my lips as though that would bring it back. "They didn't tell me I'd be eating heaven!"

I closed my eyes, awaiting a difference, hoping to be swept up in a change in my body like nothing I experienced before. I anticipated the wind whipping my hair into my face and bright lights emanating from my body as I underwent a mysterious, but beautiful, change. Like when I used my magic earlier, there was no change even as the taste faded away. I opened one eye, then another. Heaving a sigh, I flopped back into my sheets, disturbing Carrie at the end of my bed. With a disapproving noise in my direction, she rolled over to the other side of the bed away from me.

Lost in my thoughts, I let my mind continue to drift, trying to sense anything different. But nothing came.

A bright light shone through my bedroom window and my chest tightened as I slowly sat up, drawn to the blue light. It passed over me, soothing me even more than the fruit, my muscles letting go of their tension. As it faded away, I tossed my pillow to the side and stood up, hurrying over to the glass, throwing the curtains the rest of the way open, my heart in my throat as I wondered who—or what—was out there.

I peered outside and I saw the light dimming into a smaller shape. I felt power—raw, unfiltered power—wash over me. It was like when the goddesses had taken me to Yggdrasil or being near the vortex. The hair on my arms stood on end and the aura almost pushed me to my knees. Someone was announcing their presence.

I pulled on my robe and wondered if I should take a baseball bat with me as I trudged out to my garden. These days, I never knew when another horny god would show up.

She was beautiful.

No, beautiful didn't begin to describe her. Glamorous. Extravagant. Radiant.

She was an aging beauty with a grace that I knew I would never have, goddess or no. Her golden hair was streaked with pure silver, held up in an intricate hairstyle of loops and curls that could only have been done by magic, with one long tail down almost to her waist. Her clothes were deep red with unfamiliar red-gold gems accenting the cuffs. It wrapped around her into a flowing pants suit. She wore flat shoes made of velvet in the same red-gold.

The goddess, or a monster in a wonderous disguise, awaited me at the line between the trees and the garden. She appeared to be taking in the overgrown beds and their state of shabbiness with the type of curiosity of an experienced gardener.

You know, lots of judgment.

I slowed my pace as I got closer, unsure of what to expect. I didn't want to piss off someone who threw their weight around so much. Maybe I hoped to sneak up on her, get some sort of upper hand, but when I was less than twenty feet away, the goddess spoke.

"Are you Aspen?"

Her voice was gentle, soothing, and held a matronly hum to it. Something told me everything was going to be okay.

"Yeah," I said as amazement kept me rooted in place next to the first pillar at the border of the garden. "I mean, yes. Sorry." I blushed, realizing I was staring. "Who are you?" I tried to keep my voice neutral.

"I am Freyja." She took several steps toward me, and I realized it was much brighter around us than it should be. She was radiating light so bright it reached almost ten feet away from her before petering out into darkness. She smiled and then chuckled. "I believe you have met my brother already."

Leaning casually against the pillar, my insides were screaming at me. The Queen of the Norse gods was in my backyard. I was certain she had been ready to throw her weight around, but the chuckle?

"Yeah, we-we, uh, chatted." I watched as she just shook her head and walked into the garden.

I wasn't going to mention that he approached me like a long-lost lover to start. Or that he was going to be watching me, which only creeped me out a little bit. She kneeled at the first bed and her long, slim fingers reached for the flowers, which seemed to lean in to get her touch first and she laughed.

"That's what I'm here to do. To 'chat.' Your flowers are quite content, but you need compost for your soil. It's quite old." She glided over to the bench in the middle of the yard and sat, the loose red-gold fabric flowing and glimmering around her. She patted the spot next to her and then smiled warmly when I hesitated. "I won't bite, you silly thing. I'm just here to talk."

What else would she be here for?

Her thousand-year-old power crawled up my arms and legs, and I shivered as it rolled off her in waves. It felt as heavy as flannel in a Phoenix summer.

"What are you here to talk about?" I asked. I sat on the bench, wishing desperately I had called for Isa to come back me up.

The slight wrinkles on her face crinkled with her smile, a look of contentment as though she routinely helped in the upheaval of mortal lives. Maybe she did. "I see you aren't one for small talk. I'll get right to the heart of it. Do you plan to join the gods, Aspen? Do you want to know more of where you come from?"

I probably must have looked like a fish, a dumb fish, as I floundered around for my voice.

Both of Freyja's hands grasped mine and at first I thought she had some sort of healing powers like Eir, but her grip only pulled me back to Earth. "I'm so sorry! Did I say something wrong?"

"I, uh, no. No, nothing *wrong*," I assured her. "I do have a lot of questions. A lot of blanks in my mind."

She smiled expectantly.

The doe. The gods popping in and out of my life like freaking meerkats. The goddesses almost pleading with me to take the fruit. There was too much going on. A guide would be great, but maybe that wasn't what I needed right now.

"Maybe it's better to keep things slow. I mean, I have a life here. My mom needs me." I glanced back to the house. "She needs me a lot."

"Mothers are important to daughters." She agreed with a nod. "Family is important. I hope that the gods will be a family again one day."

"Family?"

Freyja seemed to consider her answer. "Maybe family is too strong of a word for. However, your soul resonates with ours. That's how Eir helped you so easily when you first met. Your kinship is not in only your blood, but in your heart and spirit."

We sat there, Freyja the Queen of the Gods and Aspen Sommers, name otherwise unknown. Even with her light, I focused on the stars above me for I don't know how long. It was nice to enjoy the warmth of the night and the presence of a god who wasn't pushing me into marriage.

"You haven't been eating your fruit," Freyja stated. I started and faced her, gnawing at my lip. "Why? I'd like you to tell me the truth."

I mulled my answer, but quickly decided the truth was the way to go. "I want to study its healing purposes. Something like that is precious."

She seemed to consider me with a tap of her fingers against the cold stone beneath her before crafting her response. "Do you intend to give all humans immortality?"

"No. I want to heal disease. Not death."

Her smile came back, so that must have been a good enough answer. She stood and peered up at the moon and stars. "It's been so long since Ragnarök, Aspen. I don't know who you are yet, but I so look forward to who you become. Don't forget to eat some fruit, though, if you want to find out who you are."

Then with a flash, the wind whipped around me, her body quickly shrank and sprouted feathers from the red-gold cloth wrapped around her body. Freyja the raven flew off into the night and I blew a lock of hair out of my face.

What the actual hell was going on?

My morning routine changed.

I still got up at the crack of dawn, made my lists and did my journaling. I took my pills and sipped my matcha. I worked in the garden where I got dirty and sweaty and took a shower afterwards. My brain required that I not stop doing these things.

After I had my Me Time, it was time for Mom's daily physical therapy.

I would be lying if I said it was easy to do. Watching her go through this, gritting her teeth, pretending there was no pain... We worked on strengthening her core using a variety of tools, like balancing on a yoga ball. Or the stretchy band that I either held or tied for her to use to strengthen her legs and arms. Sometimes it took an hour, sometimes half that. It all depended on how Mom felt when she woke up.

Today, after forty minutes of good, sweaty exercise, my stomach made a noise that would have put Homer Simpson to shame. Mom almost let go of the band when she heard it but kept it together until the last two reps of the last exercise.

"Was that your stomach or a small bear?" she asked as she wiped her forehead with the back of her hand.

"Hey, everyone has days where they get really hungry," I retorted while hiding my blush.

Mom stood from the chair and stretched out. I heard a pop and she winced, holding her back. She twisted and waved me off when I tried to help. "How goes it with the garden so far?"

"I mean..." The truth was, I'd been so wrapped up in my job/apparent training, moving, and her illness that I'd spent a lot less time on the garden than I'd liked. "It's a lot of work and some planters need rebuilding in spots." Actually, a lot of them. "I might be able to get some things in before the end of planting season, but not much."

"There's always next year."

After physical therapy we grabbed a snack and vegged in front of the TV for a couple of hours watching 90s sitcoms and played "Mystery Science Theater 3000." After a few episodes of "Sabrina the Teenage Witch" Mom's head dropped down and a snore escaped her.

I scrambled up from the couch and hurried outside, grabbing the largest tree clippers we had from the storage shed. Dad had brought over all my gardening equipment from the other house and stuffed it into a shed he bought behind Nana's almost done suite.

With a bounce in my step, I wanted to focus on the positive, and not the weird. Definitely not the weird. My life fell into that category more and more often these days.

I bypassed the boxes and pillars today, gripping a pad of paper where I made all my notes. While touring the trees I did some simple cuts along the way. Dad and I would have to come out and really do this together or hire someone, which I hated doing. I enjoyed doing things myself until I absolutely couldn't. So far, none of the trees were so overgrown and knotted that I wouldn't be able to handle it. Just tall.

I was pretty deep in my work and enjoying the warm sun when the now familiar feeling of power washed over me. Less than what I'd felt with Freyja the other night, but whoever it was could have been holding back. In fact, when I turned and saw Loki smiling at me, his smug face too bright and cheerful, the cold dread that I was right settled in my stomach.

"Don't gods ever knock?" I asked with venom in my voice, snapping my notebook to my chest as though it were treasure. "I could have been dancing naked around here."

Loki, still smirking, replied, "I have had every opportunity to see you naked more times than I can count, but no desire."

My jaw dropped and with a blink I tried to retort, but his honesty left me literally speechless, even as every insult and swear I could think of ran through my head. "Well... I... that's..."

My brain screamed: *That stupid, overpowered, thoughtless, arrogant—*

He still smirked.

I was starting to get why the other gods didn't like him. I returned to my pruning, this time snipping harder and faster at the lemon tree as I tried to ignore him.

"You know," he said, his voice closer than I had left him. I jumped and swiveled to the right, my large shears only missing his throat by mere inches. He now had on overalls and a blue plaid shirt, complete with a floppy straw hat. "You could try being nice sometime, too."

I kept the shears in place, my threat clear: move and I'll get stabby. "So could you." I moved on to the next tree, pulling and cutting the lower branches without glancing his way. "You could also just tell me what you want."

"What fun would that be?" His voice came from over my head. His feet were now cheerfully dangling from the tree above me. I pursed my lips. "Hmm, not much at all, I think. You're going to have to figure me out yourself."

"Oh, joy." I threw my hands up and started back to the flowerbeds, my good mood in the toilet like so much other shit right now. "Just how I wanted to spend the next twenty years. Studying psychology to figure out if you're a sociopath or a psychopath."

Loki laughed and my anger flared as he vanished and then reappeared. As his laughter rang out, I wished I could try running him over again. He teleported in front of me, and I jumped back, barely containing a scream straight in his smirking face.

"You slimy prick!"

He didn't react to my insults. "It seems you abandoned being Fulla."

Back to business, as always. What was it with this guy? What did he want? Because if his goal was just to amuse himself, I was fighting a losing battle for information.

"I can't abandon something I never have been," I said when we reached the tree line. I pulled off my thick gloves and shoved them in the back pocket of my jeans. "The others said that Freyja couldn't see anything. And the N's gave me a lovely prophecy." I sighed and glared at him out of the corner of my eye. "It's like no one wants me to know. So why do you want to know?"

"I don't."

"Then why are you constantly—Oh, dear God. You have ideas about who I am!"

He pursed his lips together and his head wavered back and forth. "Close."

My stomach sank. "You already know."

He beamed in response.

"Tell me."

"Nope." He evaded me, walking backwards with a grace I can only describe as swan like, while I kept marching forward. "This is much too much fun. So, tell me, how goes your big case of too much magic driving fae out of hiding? Or are you not in on that, either?"

I don't think I've ever felt my blood boil as much as it did at that moment. Heat rose to my face and I let Loki have it.

I stopped, a foot away from his smirking, assholish face. Raising my finger I leveled it with his nose in anger. "You know, it would be nice if people would tell me what the hell is going on here. It took them almost two weeks to mention that you were still on the gods' bad side. It's like, what, certain topics are banned from me? And then you, you double down on it when I mention it because of the past?"

Loki clapped his hands together and laughed, one that echoed and seemed to be full of actual mirth, not the sarcasm he had been so eagerly displaying until now. After a moment, he stopped and a wistful look graced his features. "If only... if things were different, you would understand."

"I really don't like you."

He vanished before my eyes and his last words echoed in my mind. "You never have."

Chapter Twenty-Five

After a fitful night of sleep over Loki's words I went to work. How did he know? Did the goddesses? No, of course not. They wouldn't have bothered wasting their time on training and information if they did. They weren't like that. Now Loki, on the other hand, totally would have.

The asshole.

Before I pushed the rune-inscribed door open, it seemed like every other day outside. Downright nice out with the birds chirping their happiness to a few clouds. Inside, the lights were off. Only some light filtering from the ajar bathroom illuminated Charlie's outline at the desk. She was wearing a sleep mask with closed eyes and little tear drops on the sides over her face. She snuggled in her chair and wore pinky fluffy slippers, the tips of which were peeking out from under the blanket to round out the outfit. I bet she was in pajamas, too. The a few deep snores alerted to Charlie's asleep state and I tiptoed forward.

Shrugging, I left coffee for her, and tiptoed past, opening the door quickly and shutting it quietly.

"What's with Charlie?" I set the drinks on Sif's desk and jerked my thumb back to the entrance

Sif startled, her normally perfect skin a little shiny with visible bags under her eyes. She either hadn't put makeup on, or it had been a long, long couple of days. "She was up late going through a bunch of newspapers."

"That would be them?" I indicated a long table that had replaced the usual set of chairs in the extra space. The new tabletop was littered with headlines and clippings of print news articles. There were three distinct piles with a note card in front of each, reading 'No', 'Other', and 'Possible'. None of it made any sense to me, but I grabbed one from the 'Possible' pile and skimmed it.

The article had a picture attached to it. A man with an enormous smile, dimples, and what could only be describe as 'guns' for arms held the hand of a woman who had to be the same age and half his mass. They looked happy and perfectly normal. "'Dale Crayson, 34, of Peoria, was found to have died by secondary drowning in his bed—' Wait, secondary drowning? What's that?"

Eir, with her hands full of articles, frowned deeply. "It means a slow drowning. Dry drowning. It usually only happens after someone has a near-drowning experience. Their lungs become paralyzed from the damage." My eyes widened, horrified at the possibility that something like that existed.

Eir smiled in reassurance. "It's actually not common, but it usually happens in children, the elderly, that kind of thing. Still horrible, but it doesn't happen to healthy adults. Every single one of these people in the past year has dry drowned..." She trailed off, sadness in her voice. "These are just the ones Charlie found in Arizona. There's no telling how many tourists this could have happened to."

The possible pile, thankfully the smallest, was still big enough to constitute using the word 'pile'. "How many are there?"

"I didn't count them," Eir admitted. "We don't know if all these people went to Slide Rock, but two of the articles mention going there, according to Charlie. Some of these are regular drownings, probably. We have to rule them out and make some calls."

My stomach twisted in knots. Confrontation was something I'm good at—hooray for my curiosity teaching me to ask a lot of questions—but it wasn't something that ended well enough for me to say I was comfortable doing it. Confronting people with the hows and whys of the last days of their family members lives was going to be as pleasant as sitting on a cactus.

Eir read my mind. "Don't worry. Jord and I are going to do the calls. You're going to go over history and magic today with Sif."

Sif was currently standing at her desk, on the phone with someone. I'd had no time with her yet, and most of Jord's teaching had been about history, not magic. Maybe Sif would be different.

"Look, Daniels, I don't know what to tell you," Sif's strained voice floated over to me. I was not looking forward to getting Angry Sif after this. "You need to do some things yourself." She listened. "I don't know. Pull the answer out of your own ass this time." She slammed the phone down, it was a landline and I jumped at the bang. "Stupid git."

"She's ready for you now," Eir said with a cheerful ring in her voice.

Instead of glaring at her, I said a silent prayer, and left Jord and Eir to their job. Sif was sitting back at her desk, muttering to herself about 'Daniels'. I hovered off to the side before taking a step closer.

After a few moments, Sif turned and saw me standing there. "Is it my turn already?"

She didn't sound too happy. "Uh, yeah, Eir said—"

"Yeah." She sighed and stood up with a groan, her pressed and pleated clothes wrinkled from the time spent in the office. Stretching with a great yawn, she gave me a wan smile. "It's not you. It's this case. Come on. We're going for a lesson."

"Going?"

"Yeah. Don't wake up Charlie on the way out. She gets grumpy when provoked."

Sif's truck was one of those 2500 series that had a full cab backseat. A step came down to help me up when I opened the passenger door, making it a lot easier to climb into. Mud splattered the bottom half of the black paint, but it otherwise seemed in perfect condition. Inside still had the new car smell. I kinda felt bad having my dirty feet in such a new truck. We headed south, then west for a while before she turned off the road onto a smaller one. The road curved, then straightened, and I wondered as we drove if this was my new life. Going with the flow because no one would give me a straight answer.

There was more than one way to get information, and I had several other connections to the gods now. Too bad the strongest of those was Loki.

We turned off the road again, this time onto a dirt road past a sign that read 'Gyðjas Farms.' It took only a couple more minutes before we arrived because Sif stopped the truck and turned it off.

"Gyodjyas Farms? What is this?"

"'Gyðjas,'" she corrected gently, seemingly more relaxed. "It means 'goddess.'"

"In what language?"

"Icelandic," she said, her voice becoming thoughtful. "Icelandic is pretty much Norse with some new slang thrown in. Insular languages, am I right? This is where Eir, Jord, and I live." Her change of subject whiplashed me back to the present. She waved me over and started toward the big red barn off to the left. I jogged to catch up. The house, two stories, maybe three by the looks of it, had a neutral yellow paint with red accents, including the shutters. Half-windows poked out of the ground. The open garage housed Eir's sports car on the other side of the horseshoe driveway.

Near the barn, vast fields of various livestock grazing came into view. There were several goats, as well as a handful of cows. I counted four horses, more than a few chickens, and even some sheep.

On the other side, between the barn and the home, was their garden. Everything was in early growing days, but they had some of the normal things labeled: peas, carrots, lettuce. It also looked like they were growing flowers and herbs as companion plants in some places. Companion planting had seen a huge boom lately. It helped keep problem bugs away and had many other benefits, but I doubted they were only doing it after its 're-discovery.'

"You live there? All of you?" I asked, taking in the acres they owned, but following Sif's lead toward the field. "But"—I furrowed my brow and cocked my head to one side—"can't you disappear like the other gods back to... wherever you live now?"

"We all can," Sif confirmed. "The gods live in many worlds, but we report back to Freyja on Alfheim as often as needed. The thing is"—she grinned at me, amusement clear in face—"people have gotten suspicious of us before when we didn't have a place to live." She gazed at her house, her arms hanging to her side as the mood shifted. "Humans are so strange; they notice the oddest things. So now, when we take missions on Earth, we have homes. It's... not Asgard. Or Vanaheim. Or even Nidavilir. But it works. Having a home and showing up to it now and then, even one as rural as this, is enough for humans."

My questions stuck in my throat.

Come on, Aspen, this is the perfect time. Bring up Loki!

"So why are we here?"

Or don't. Your funeral, you coward.

"I needed a secluded place to show you different magicks." She turned to me, still smiling. "I'd put a lock on that stupid door, but I doubt it would do much good about motivated people."

"Probably not," I agreed, remembering Mr. Egert. "Going back to my magic... I thought we couldn't do anything about that until I started feeling it?"

She shrugged. "That doesn't mean I can't show you. Are you eating the fruit? Or are you letting them ferment further?"

I shifted and avoided looking at her. "Well, I've had one." I wanted one again. The taste, the texture, how it was the perfect level of sweetness. "But..."

"You aren't sure you want to be immortal."

My head snapped up. "How did you—"

Sif gave me a look. "I'm 350 years old, Aspen. Freyja is the only survivor. I still remember being mortal. Someone like her? She doesn't. If she ever was. If you don't question it now, you probably would within a decade or two." She looked off into the distance, an unreadable expression on her face. "It's... not the easiest thing to choose this path." Her voice grew soft. "When you do, there are things you have to do and things you're not allowed to do anymore."

"Like what?"

"Well." She stopped at the gate to the animal pen. "We're not supposed to have children with mortals. We're even supposed to do our best to stay out of mortal affairs. That's why we only take supernatural cases. We're not exactly going to look into cheating spouses."

I laughed. "Okay, but can I stop if I want to? Stop taking the berries?"

"Yeah. But no one ever wants to."

"Because of how amazing they taste?"

With a snort, Sif gave me a sly smile. "Well, there's always more than one reason."

Before I could ask another question, she opened the gate, and I gasped. "Are they all your animals?"

The creak of the gate opening had called several of said animals came over. Not only sheep and goats, but a couple of chickens even vied for attention. "Yep! Come on." Sif beckoned as she walked through mud into the field. Several bound up to Sif unafraid, head butting her in the knees or ankles to be petted, which she automatically did.

"Can I...?" I gestured to the fluffy white cotton ball in front of her.

She grinned and nodded.

I squealed, just a little, before I touched the sheep. It was soft, but also stiff and rough in the way wool is. I'd never been around farm animals before and couldn't help grinning as I switched and pet another one who came up and head butted my other hand for attention. I stroked them both a few more times before they bound off, baying as they went.

"Oh my God, that was so cute," I said way louder than I meant to. I dropped my voice and grinned sheepishly. Pardon the pun. "Sorry."

Sif laughed and smiled wider than normal. "Don't worry, they're good around people. We're going far in the pasture. They probably won't follow us too much." Going fast for someone in a skirt, she led me through the pen, but I kept up.

"Why so far?" I asked as we approached taller grasses that the animals didn't appear to have touched.

"Just in case," she said, continuing to lead me back.

She was taking this secrecy seriously. It made me feel bad for bringing Isa into this without consulting anyone about it first. But, a part of me countered, easier now than later.

I could always use an accomplice.

After about five minutes of walking, we were out of range of all the animals. It was impossible to see where we had parked from this distance. I closed my eyes and the wind whispered through the grass, calling to me, calming me with soothing words I couldn't understand, in a voice I was sure I had heard before. I reached down and brushed the grass through my fingers. Even now there was some dew still on the blades.

"Definitely an earth goddess," Sif said with a laugh. "I'm so sorry I made you think you were Fulla. That must have been awful."

"Why awful?" I asked.

"Being forced to be something you aren't always is. I just assume that was, too." Sif changed the subject. "Alright, so we're out here because we're of the earth. It's easier to get in touch with your power outside of the city. Outside of everything, even homes, to be honest. Cities, even long ago, deaden our connection with the earth because the process of humans gathering is a filthy mess. Although, let's not get into that. What we're here to do is get you in touch with your powers.

You haven't eaten much of the fruit, but you've had the tea, so that should be enough. I hope."

I sighed, feeling guilty again. While I wasn't sure about immortality, I would need more samples if I was going to study the fruits.

"There are things every god and goddess can do. We can all change planes. That means we can go from here to, say, Yggdrasil, like we did the first day we met," she quickly explained when I furrowed my brows. I guess I knew that since so many gods were deciding to pop in and out around me these days. "We can also connect with our elements and ideas that we symbolize and mold them. Here."

Sif waved a hand and the grass parted like the Red Sea. Then she leaned down and whispered, "Can you show her?"

The wind gusted, and the grass and wildflowers danced and bobbed before being snatched up into the air. They whirled around me and then blew up higher, almost like a vortex. Then it floated back to the ground in the shape of a star.

Sif had an enormous grin on her face when she turned back to me. "They wanted to show you that you can ask for things. Can you try it?"

They? Did she mean the plants? "What do I do?"

"It's inside you," she explained gently. I felt like I was in a church with something otherworldly unfolding about us, which I suppose there was. I'd never tried to access something like this before. "It's a power that has to grow."

Brushing my palm across the grass, I shuddered at the silk-like softness. "Has anyone had their powers develop without the berries?"

"Yeah. Great way to get burned at the stake prior to the 1800s, by the way. Do not recommend." My mouth dropped open in shock at the bitterness in her voice.

"Sif, do you know anyone who was...?"

"It was common. I saw more than one," she admitted, still dodging the question. "No one, and I mean no one, got to full power without the berries. You can be powerful, but you can't be immortal without them."

"More powerful than a witch?" I asked.

Sif stopped, growing thoughtful. "Way more powerful than a witch. All that burning at the stake through the centuries devastated magical lines. Those who could practiced in secret and safely kept some traditions alive. But more died out than were saved."

"Am I a witch now? Or like, equivalent? Since I called on some power?"

She shook her head and twirled her fingers around, causing even more flowers to sway to her magic. "Probably not. We checked as far back in your genealogy as possible, and there isn't anything. There might be something a lot further down that we don't know about. You don't have to be a witch to be a god."

I felt like my head was going to snap from all the nodding I did. "Can power leave you?"

"It can die, if you let it. So, come on! We're going to get in touch with your power!" Sif thumped me on the back, then she splayed her hands across the grass. "Would you mind? We need to sit."

The grass bent over and, I shit you not, it lay down on the ground, creating a blanket of woven blades for us to sit on.

"Thank you!" Sif chirped, fanning out her skirt and sitting cross-legged on the ground.

"Thank you," I mumbled as I stumbled forward and sat on the very much alive grass.

I swear I heard it say 'you're welcome,' but I'd also just learned about witches' bloodlines, so my brain was a little muddled.

"First, we're going to do some meditation, some deep breathing."

I almost groaned. I didn't mind yoga so much, but I only liked to meditate for my anxiety. I wasn't anxious right now; just crawling out of my skin with curiosity to learn a completely new skill. With a shake of my head, I curled my toes in my shoes several times and let my smile set on my face instead of jumping around. "Okay then."

"Let's close our eyes." She began as most meditations did, quiet and soft with a firmness to it. "I want you to inhale, two... three... four..."

I went through the exercises with her. We took deep breaths, inhaling the flowers and listening to the flap of butterfly wings and buzzing of bees. In those moments, I let myself be taken away to a world where I touched any flower and made it bloom. Where I whispered to the trees, and they would giggle and tell me secrets back. A world more alive and less restricted. A world where my crop harvests were always abundant and I never overwatered.

"Now come back," Sif instructed, her voice still as soothing as when we started. "When you're ready, open your eyes."

I never liked to wait when I heard that, so I opened them and didn't bother to stifle back a yawn.

Sif leaned over and plucked a small, closed-up bright orange wildflower. She offered it to me and said, "Open the flower."

I started to pry the flower open with my fingers, but she squealed. "Stop! Stop! I meant with your magic! Concentrate on it."

My ears burned with embarrassment. I did as she instructed for a solid two minutes. I stared at it so intently I think I embarrassed the damn flower.

"Think about it blooming. Think about how you want it to look when it's beautiful and showing its true self to the world."

I envisioned the flower in my head, blooming, flourishing, and growing taller. It opened and showed me all of its inner beauty. The damned flower sat there.

Sif set the flower on the side and grabbed another just as quickly. A different wild bloom glittered in dew in front of me.

"Again."

We repeated the process with five fresh flowers, and Sif's patience seemed to wear thin at about flower number four.

After number six's failure, she tossed the flower aside and snatched a handful of grass; her face a perfect mask of patience.

"There are some pretty easy tricks that all gods have, too. Like the ability to move things without touching them. Your basic telekinesis. Now..." She threw the grass in the air and instead of floating down or away, it hovered and then in a whip of wind the blades hit me in the face. I spat out the ones that made it into my mouth.

"Oops," Sif giggled and looked sheepish. "Sorry. It's not something I do a lot. I meant for it to go by your cheek in a very, well, Disney way."

I brushed the grass off my face and sighed. "So you want me to make something move?"

"Yep. Just wiggle it even. You don't have to make it float on your first try."

Fine. So I couldn't do something that probably any earth goddess alive did, like make plants bloom, but sure. Let's levitate shit.

There was nothing around much bigger than grass, and I didn't think it was possible to grab one tiny blade of grass in the wind. I snatched the original orange flower up and held it in my palm.

"What do I do?" I asked as I stared at it.

"Ask it to move, okay?" I sent her a look and she shrugged. "We all do it in our heads, but we gotta start somewhere. Just do it."

"Excuse me, Wildflower? Would you mind—oh, this is so stupid!" I threw the flower down, unable to look at it anymore. "Are you sure? I mean, are you sure that I have magic? That I can do this? That I was this person?"

"Freyja is certain," Sif said, her voice serious. She had a look on her face I couldn't decipher. Her lips were tight and her eyes were closed. She inhaled deeply before opening them. "If Freyja is sure, that's all we need."

I crossed and uncrossed my arms, trying to claw out a comeback that wasn't either 'Your mama' or 'Yeah, so?' neither of which would get me anywhere. "Fine. If I have real magic, the flower will hop right back up into my hand and I won't have t—"

I honestly didn't know what I thought would happen, because the next moment something soft brushed my fingers and the orange flower, which had done nothing before, now strained up off the ground, stretching for my hand with its petals and leaves. I gasped when my fingers gently closed around it in midair. The soft petals brushed me and a warm feeling spread from my hand to my heart when I heard the whisper:

Thank you...

Chapter Twenty-Six

"**Y**ou made it what?!"

We were in Vallejo's quietly eating breakfast burritos and drinking coffee and orange juice when Isa got the whole restaurant's attention with her outburst. Food almost fell out of her gaping mouth, her face a cross between astonishment and disbelief. Which I didn't blame her. It *was* magic.

My face was stuffed with eggs, cheese, about ten different veggies and some salsa, all wrapped in a homemade tortilla. I almost choked on my heavenly first bite and waved my hand to shush her.

"Sorry," she whispered, a flush spreading over her cheeks. "You made it levitate?" she repeated.

Chugging my orange juice to get that bite down, I nodded fervently. "Yep." I flexed my right hand, where I'd felt power concentrate. I made a fist and then let go, but nothing changed. "I wanted so badly to do something. I mean, I had only had one fruit. And some tea."

"Wonder what a dozen would get you?" Isa said, her voice low and amused. "Can you show me?"

I looked around at the crowded restaurant, then frowned at her, my mouth full by hopefully the look declaring all I needed to.

"Good point." She took another bite of her burrito. "Ya know," she said with her mouth full, "with there being so much to this mythology shit, I might change my major." She swallowed. "Anyone can be a vet. How many people learn gods are real and that ancient stories are true? And can talk to them about it?"

We started giggling together. It's impossible to live on a BA. One in mythology? Come on.

"Could you imagine that?" she asked. "It'd be so fun."

The sound of too high-pitched laughter broke through from a couple of tables over. I glanced behind me to see a woman older than my mom and with more makeup than a beauty pageant contestant at a table talking to a man half her age. He stood over her, his face away from me. She covered her mouth and blushed at his comments, still laughing way too loud.

Isa and I shared similarly disgusted looks.

"Some people are so weird. Anyway, what were you saying? Isa? Isa?"

Isa now stared beyond me. I turned to where she was looking, which was back to the really hot guy. He had left the older woman and was making his way past other tables. Dear God, was he gorgeous. Not lean like Thor, or even fairytale-like as Frey had been. This man could play Gaston at a theme park with the perfectness of his features. Though I felt bad comparing him with that kind of villain, it was true.

He was at least six-foot six with broad shoulders. His dark blond hair flowed with a slight wave to it. His eyes were the deepest, most piercing blue I had ever seen, and I couldn't help the rush of adrenaline that happened when he stopped at our table. His jeans hugged his hips, and he left the top button of his shirt undone enough to see the top of his chiseled chest.

What was this gorgeous hunk doing here?

Crumbles of food actually did fall from Isa's mouth this time, but she didn't seem to notice. The Hunk glanced between us before settling on me.

I wasn't one for one-night stands, quick flings, anything like that. But for this guy, I could be. Something inside of me stirred, something I wasn't sure I was ready to feel so closely after losing Marc... but what did I care about Marc, anyway?

"What is your name, beautiful one?" His voice, perfectly pitched, was almost lyrical and musical, all while being just low enough to rumble.

My heart skipped a beat and my mouth ran dry as I tried to speak. All I could do was smile and try and force my breathing to remain stable so I didn't hyperventilate into a puddle.

Wow.

"Ever young as the ancient forests yet bereft of speech in my presence to this day."

His eyes, deep pools of swirling ocean tides, held my gaze. I swallowed hard, barely noticing when he took my hand and brushed it against his lips.

"In ages past, we were the envy of all. Your beauty and power were known and those with a hope of creating came before me to beg for their abilities to be unlocked."

"How were we envied?" I asked softly, unable to tear myself away. A gnat buzzed in my ear and I shuddered.

"We were the power humanity craves in darkest times. A word to ease their pain and the knowledge of immortality itself so there was never pain again."

"Beautiful..." I murmured as he touched my cheek gently.

The annoying gnat got louder as it continued to buzz around me, drowning out part of what the hunk said. I swatted at it again, but this time my hand connected with something soft and fleshy.

"Ow! Aspen, what the hell? Wake up!" the little gnat—Isa—in my ear shrieked. "Wake up! He's Bragi!"

The air around me shattered and Mr. Hunk's face twisted, so much so that when I blinked and got a hold of my senses, Mr. Hunk seemed quite different. A little thinner, a little older, and with black hair instead of blond... but then the image snapped away and I was back in the restaurant, my breakfast burrito in a pile on my plate where I'd dropped it.

The restaurant buzzed around us, unaware of the space I had been trapped in. "What did you do to me?" I demanded, shaking and cold from how easily I had been drawn in. Now that I had stopped and had a chance to look Bragi over I saw that he was quite good looking, but I didn't usually have the urge to jump someone solely because they were hot.

"He's the god of poetry. Words are his power," Isa said.

Bragi, at first taken aback by her knowledge, recomposed himself and grinned at her. "They told me the newbie didn't know much, but not that someone attached to her did." All traces of eloquence were gone. Like the other gods, he didn't have an accent so I couldn't place where he came from. Other than his incredible hotness, which seemed to be a hallmark for them.

I withheld a groan of exasperation since he hadn't moved. I didn't want to piss a god off today. Great, what next? Loki was going to decide I was HIS wife, too?

Don't you dare answer that. I don't need this shit right now.

"My love, my light." Bragi kept going. I felt it happening again. This time I also felt the magic wrapping around me and pulling me into his world. He grabbed my hand and his soft lips brushed a kiss to my knuckles. I tried to pull my hand back, but he held firm, pulling me up to my feet with a jerk.

"Whoa!" I grabbed onto him as I lost all footing. Instead of falling back to my chair, he grabbed me and dipped me down low to the floor. Now he garnered attention from all the surrounding tables, many with women giving me absolutely scathing looks.

I've had boyfriends, lovers, what have you. Never had anyone done, well, this. Tongue-tied was simply a state of being in response to such romance. He stood me up properly and then let me go. I flopped back into my chair, blinking in shock.

"In days gone by you would stroke my hair, whisper sweet nothings in my ear, and in your hands you held the fruits of eternal life, eternal beauty, and godhood. Only you, my darling, my sweet Idunn, had the power of the gods." He went down on one knee and the embarrassment set in. "You and I could rule them, could be the ones with the power. My darling, you must awaken your powers. You must become Idunn."

"Get up!" I hissed at him when he went onto both knees, his arms in a dramatic pose as though he was preaching to the roof, and not me. He did so and I pushed him into the empty chair at our table for four. "What is your problem? Are you trying to draw attention to yourself?"

He looked around as though just now noticing that everyone stared at him. He still appeared puzzled when he turned back to me. "You don't want me to loudly profess my love? You used to enjoy it."

"Well, spoiler alert, I'm not Idunn." I grabbed a fork to try and salvage my meal. "Or I might be. Look, the thing is no one knows who I am, because no one who actually knows will say anything. So do you have proof that I'm Idunn, or are you just being hopeful?"

Bragi waved to another table full of women and all of them giggled and blushed. One waved back. He tilted his head. "I'm sorry. What did you say?"

I threw my napkin on the table, pushing my hand to my forehead. "Oh, dear God. How did any of you have children? You're all so self-centered and—and stubborn. You're not even listening to me!"

Bragi snapped back to attention from flirting with Random Girl Number 6. "Idunn, love, I am."

"I am NOT Idunn," I hissed. "If I was, I sure won't be hooking up with some asshole who flirts with other women in front of me."

Bragi's dancing smile froze. Cold descended around the table. My glass of orange juice iced over. Isa swore under her breath and I shrank back in my seat.

Great, I'd pissed off a god.

"My eye will never wander further than your door, good woman," he told me, his voice no longer teasing and warm. The cold continued seeping into my skin, causing me to shiver, but no one else in the restaurant seemed to take notice. "Idunn and I swore ourselves to each other. We promised nothing would part us. When death did, I came back, knowing I had to find her. A poet must have his inspiration."

I think he meant it to be romantic and not creepy. Let's face it, it was pretty creepy and over the top. I folded my hands together. "Ya know, uh, Bragi, I may not have any powers yet." He nodded earnestly. "I may not have them, but I know that whatever they are, whoever I am, we're gonna know soon. And when I know... what are you doing?"

He had cocked his head and was leaning on his elbow, getting comfortable. "I'm listening."

"When I know," I continued with less steam, "That is..." I shook my head, trying to think clearly. "I'll make you pay..." That sounded so much more threatening in my head.

Bragi smiled. "I suppose we are still learning about you. I am the least of your worries, no matter who you are." He stood. "Don't worry about your check, ladies. A gentleman always pays his debts."

With a final bow to us, he swept out the door, leaving sighing and gasping women in his wake.

Chapter Twenty-Seven

Streaming Saturday was a practice that we started right after my older sister Cypress went to college. Every last Saturday of the month was movie night, no matter how many of us were home. We always picked one new movie that no one, or most hadn't seen, snacked a lot, and then chose an old classic to wind down the night.

The only contact I'd had with the goddesses in the last few days was a text from Jord telling me they'd be in touch soon. Until there was something for me to focus on at work, I would do my own things, which included Streaming Saturday.

Dad and Nana were in the kitchen finishing up dinner and Mom's PT had taken more out of her than normal today, chasing her to her room afterwards. I lay across the couch, channel-surfing. The various gods and goddesses were on my mind, but without work, I hadn't had the chance to talk to any of the goddesses about it. I wasn't sure I wanted to. Two days since the call and not a word. Maybe if I had Charlie's number I could call her and ask if she knew anything.

I continued to flip.

Cooking show. Nope. Nature show that wasn't gardening. Nope. Nature show about gardening. Maybe. News. N—

Holy shit.

I jerked up on the couch and all my snacks from earlier in the day threatened to return on me. I turned up the channel, a familiar face filling the screen. It was the guy who I had seen a week ago at Slide Rock. There was no doubt about it with his smile and dimples. And he was dead.

The reporter was right outside of Slide Rock National Park, and her serious but calm tone filled me in. "Nathan Lanie was found in his room, dead of an apparent dry drowning incident. Now you may remember that we covered this not even a month ago when a high school quarterback was found under similar conditions. Both of them in their rooms, both of them had been acting strange for a few days. And both were recently seen enjoying Slide Rock."

I swore. Of course. If Charlie had found the connections then someone else would, too.

"To find out if there is any connection, we spoke with Detective Tawny Daniels of the Sedona Police Department," the reporter continued.

The screen flashed over to an interview with the detective and I almost fell off the couch in shock. I was tired of surprises. It was the same man from the office last week, teasing me about being the new kid.

"—we don't expect this to be any more than an unfortunate set of coincidences," Detective Daniels said. "There are no known connections, but we are going to investigate every potential lead."

"Just a shame," Nana said, setting down a plate on the table. "Turn that off, Aspen. The news is too depressing."

I changed from cable to the hub just as they started talking about a series of minor earthquakes near the San Francisco Peaks.

"Earthquakes outside of Flagstaff?" Nana tsked. "This old planet, I tell you. This old planet. Eat the charcuterie, honey."

It wasn't unheard of. Arizona wasn't on a major fault line, but we had enough extinct and dormant volcanoes to give Iceland a run for its money. I almost turned it back, but Nana kept talking as she brought in what I wouldn't classify as a charcuterie board so much as a cheese plate. My hands were busy reaching for Swiss and crackers.

"Cora Alma's away from the volcano fields, but we're not out of the woods for something like this altogether," Nana mused while arranging the cheese plate. "Flo! Bob! Get in here before we start *Wonder Woman* without you!"

I hid my giggle-snort, but only barely.

We had drawn today's movie from our to be watched pile and even though I saw it while at ASU—Marc loved superhero movies—I kept that to myself and planned to watch it like it was the first time.

The first time had been filled with me whispering about things I didn't understand—the gods for one—and some soft snuggling and kissing at the fade to black scene. I hugged a pillow tight and sighed wistfully as I remembered how that night ended, with us wrapped in each other's arms, giggling and trying to identify which stars were based on Greek myths later.

"We're coming, we're coming!" Mom called back as Dad came in holding a tray of sandwiches and veggies. She followed with her own tray of a chocolate monstrosity of a cake.

"I've been waiting to see this one," Mom said, patting my leg excitedly on her way to her recliner. After her nap she had a slight bounce in her step.

We filled our plates. Everyone went for the veggie tray and sandwiches first. I watched for a moment, my plate at the ready, when that delightful monster cake caught my eye again. I looked at the veggies, then the cake, and back a few more times before I gave in. Grabbing the cake server, I cut myself a decent—read here as large—piece and settled back.

"Aspen," Mom chided. "Eat dinner first. Come on, are you twelve?"

I pretended to think on it. "Will that allow me to have the cake?"

Exasperated, Mom gave me one of those looks that moms save for times like this, but it was crossed with amusement. I grinned back.

"I'll eat it next!"

"Come on guys," Dad said. "Let's get started." Dad dimmed the lights and I, still claiming the remote, queued up the movie.

Diana's voiceover began, and with ninja-like precision, I grabbed a second slice of cake now that no one could say anything. Nana nudged me and smirked, but I caught a glimpse of Mom shaking her head in my direction.

What? Sometimes we need to eat our feelings. Bragi definitely made me have some feelings. Though I wasn't sure what they were, beyond anger and confusion and sheer curiosity about the type of person he thought I used to be.

So what if I'm justifying things in an unhealthy manner? Who are you, my therapist?

As we reached the scene where Diana charges across No Man's Land, I saw a brief flash of light from the garden out of the window behind the TV. Each of my family members were still too engrossed in the movie. None of them moved or blinked. Even Carrie only stretched and curled into her favorite spot that wasn't my lap, my brother Doug's chair.

I stood and pretended to go to the bathroom but went into the kitchen instead, heading out the door to meet yet another god.

If this one tried to marry me, I'd kill them.

I didn't know if I was glad or worried when the new god I expected turned out to be Loki instead. So far, he hadn't done much to make me less weary around him. In fact, I think I was more on guard after my other meetings.

"Let me guess, you think I'm your wife, too, and that's why you won't leave me alone."

Loki looked puzzled at first, then burst out laughing. "Frey and Bragi? Interesting guys, am I right? They need those forever companions from ancient times." He shook his head and then laughed again. "They'll screw whoever, but they want that wife right beside them, waiting on them, always forgiving them."

The laughter died from his voice. "Sigyn was like that. I did think, briefly, that you might be her. But you aren't. She was so beaten down that I doubt she chose rebirth at all. I wouldn't if I was her."

I gasped, silence hanging in the air for far too long. "That's horrible."

Loki gave me a crooked smile, but then sighed. "I was a real bastard back then."

"You aren't now?"

He laughed lightly. "If only you knew, Aspen. If Sigyn is reborn, I will find her before any of the others. I don't think it's going to happen. She was tired, and I'm sure she now rests in whatever afterlife awaited her. A good one, I hope."

His voice grew softer as he spoke, so soft I strained to hear his last sentence. If I wasn't mistaken, the slight hiccup in his voice when he said her name, there was regret there.

Maybe people learn. But I wasn't here to be Loki's therapist, or to tease out his regrets.

"Why are you here, Loki?" I demanded, placing a hand on my hip. "Are you going to tell me who I am—who I was? Or are you here to make me think about why I'm not calling the goddesses and telling them the fruit thief is here?"

"They told you." A statement, not a question. His voice held no remorse, only certainty.

"You expected them not to?"

"It's not that. Listen"—he put his hands up in a gesture of peace—"I know they've probably told you every dirty, probably true thing they can. I need to know, right now, can you trust I want to help you?"

I pressed my mouth into a line, trying to stamp down the part of me that wanted to run forward and strangle him. "So why can't you just tell me?"

Loki grinned, relaxing back to his usual self. "Telling you would be too easy. Telling you would solve everything. It's amazing what people can't or won't tell you."

"So, you can't or won't tell me?" I tilted my head in thought. "Which is it?"

He hummed and shrugged at me, because that's totally enough of an answer. Great, so he couldn't tell me. I gasped. He *couldn't* tell me! Realization poured through my body, but I didn't dare say it aloud. If he couldn't, would something happen to me if I did?

Loki clapped his hands together and—get this—he danced. With absolutely no rhythm, he shook his butt and put his hands in the air. I cringed, glad that it was still dark and absolutely no one would be able to see us this far from the house or the road. When he kept going, I put my head in my hands and wondered if ignoring him would work.

When it didn't, I tried something else. "Okay, but why?" The question wasn't to him, because he couldn't answer that. He stopped dancing and I turned toward the horizon to Cora Alma proper. "Does it have to do with the people drowning, but not at Slide Rock?"

Loki started dancing again and I grabbed his arm. "Please don't. If I wanted to be tortured, there are other less painful ways of having it done."

He glared at me and I continued. "Okay, so Slide Rock is actually killing people. You can't tell me anything that I need to know. What about the goddesses?" This time, Loki merely tapped his nose. "Why?" He pressed his lips into a firm line. "Okay, you can't say that either. Is there anything you can say?" He remained silent. "Can we talk about Slide Rock?"

"Of course we can!" he burst out, and I gracefully kept myself from falling over at the outburst by catching myself on the pillar next to me. "I'd love to talk about Slide Rock."

We came to the first of the three greenhouses and I stopped, figuring we were far enough away that no one would stick their head out.

"Then tell me what's dragging people underwater."

"That I can't tell you. We can talk about other things." He didn't sound dangerous, he sounded delighted.

"Tell me about your relationship with the gods and goddesses. Please," I added after a second of silence.

Loki inspected the new wood and even took care to oversee the rows of alyssum that was still stubbornly planted. "Which ones?" he finally asked.

I grit my teeth and held in the slight scream I wanted to let out. He seemed to draw this out forever. I just wanted to know!

"The ones I know."

Loki considered his answer, calculating something. "I've been alive longer than Eir, but she was born after I broke from the gods. Sif, however, was between my different lifetimes and poisoned against me. Jord is... complicated. Does that help any?"

His gaze slid to the repainted pots on the pillars. I wanted to know what was in his head, or what he expected to find here with me. As long as he engaged with me, I could learn more.

"Okay, well, a little. What about Freyja? I know her—"

"You've met Freyja. You don't *know* her any more than you know the others who have appeared for you recently."

I clenched my jaw, hoping the cracking of my teeth was only audible to me. He probably wouldn't tell me anything about Frey or Bragi, either. I ran a hand through my hair, getting it tangled in the strands in my frustration. "Okay, so I get the first two, but what about Jord and complicated?"

His head bopped again and his lips remained closed. That couldn't be all. There had to be more. He had to be provoking me, mocking me. No wonder everyone wanted to kill him. I was getting there myself!

"Okay, what about the fruit? Why are they telling me to limit myself?"

Loki's lips curled into a smile. "Too much of a good thing will poison you, young Aspen." I glared at him, but he kept going. "Odin hung himself from Yggdrasil for nine days and nine nights to gain knowledge. Are you ready to die for it?" I shook my head stiffly. "Then you should gain your knowledge slowly."

He reached into his pocket and pulled out a small mason jar filled with pickled fruit. It was similar to the one that the goddesses kept in their fridge.

"Why are you here, Loki? The goddesses said you aren't aligned with them. And if all the other gods are together, why are you against them?"

Silence. He didn't deny it, but he didn't try to explain himself either.

"Why are you trying so hard to be like the you from the past?"

He threw back his head in laughter and I swear he was crying at whatever mirth this situation seemed to strike in him. I shook my head, wondering if he had told me anything of actual value.

A sharp prick at my neck caused me to freeze. I trained my gaze up the silver point of the blade to find Loki's dead hazel eyes staring straight through me and a dagger aimed at my throat. I wanted to jump back, but I was too scared to move or do much else but stand very, very still. The tip of the blade moved slightly and I whimpered, wondering if I would ever get to tell the goddesses about this while realizing that this man, this god, was not a mere pain in the ass.

"You don't know what you're talking about. Eat the fruit. If you don't, I'll come back and force feed it to you." He lowered his small dagger, and it disappeared as though it had never been there. "I don't want to hurt you."

"You want something."

"Well, duh, Aspen." Then he vanished, just like Freyja, but the jar of fruits remained.

My shaking hand went to my throat. He had kept his hand steady. There was no damage beyond the broken skin layer. I really tried not to let my anger get to me.

"Loki, you asshole! That wasn't an answer!" I cried into the night.

Nothing, not even his laughter, answered me.

Chapter Twenty-Eight

M arc leaned over me, brushing my cheek and whispering something in my ear. I giggled, warmth flooding me from head to toe as his lips tickled me. I sighed in contentment. How had I gotten here? Well, however it happened, this was paradise. Soft and warm. Then his gentle nuzzle turned into a lick and I squirmed away as a faint buzzing became a loud screeching in my ear.

My eyes flew open and I groaned.

My cat was licking me and my phone was going off. I was in bed at my parents' house. And I was alone.

Oh.

I fought back tears, reality crushing me as I pushed Carrie off my chest and grabbed my phone. Jord's picture flashed across the screen and I wondered if I was late for work before remembering they said they would call when they needed me next.

I fumbled, slid my finger over the screen and my mouth full of cotton. "Yeah?"

"Good morning, sunshine," Sif chirped on the other end. "Didn't figure you'd have picked up for anyone else."

I scratched my head and yawned. "Do you need me today? What time is it?"

"Three-thirty."

I sat up straight and jumped out of bed, which earned me a sleepy 'mwr mwr mwr' from Carrie, and pulled back the heavy blackout curtains that I had put up after Freyja's unexpected appearance. If another god made themselves comfortable in my backyard, they were going to have to *really* announce themselves now. I expected to find the day mostly over and wondered how I slept so long when I blinked at the darkness outside. The porch lights were off, but I could make out the outline of Nana's suite and a few of the nearby trees as my eyes focused into the night.

"Three-thirty *AM*?" Anger bubbled up in me. "Dear God, Sif. I'm going to—"

"Yeah, yeah. Blood bath, kill me, blah blah blah. Can you kill me later? The algae bloom story is only going to hold for so long, it's time to act. We're prepared now."

"This can't wait two or three hours? Really?"

"It probably could," she admitted, her voice less cheerful, but still too awake. "Cover of darkness is best. We're planning now and we need your help. When can you get here?"

I want to go on the record and say I hated this plan from the start. I tried to fight it but the goddesses unanimously outvoted me.

It still didn't stop me from crossing my arms and holding my position. "No."

"Come on," Sif begged. "We'll be right there with you the whole time."

"You're the only one who it won't be afraid of," Jord explained, her voice bordering on exasperation. Couldn't blame her. This had been going on for almost ten minutes. I still wouldn't agree.

"That's because I'm basically a bag of bones and meat with no magical powers. I am not doing it."

"Double time?" Jord said, and I glared at her, feeling the tug of my wallet.

I won't say that it wasn't a good plan, but I was allowed to be scared. I didn't want to be basically alone and defenseless against an unknown magical creature. Especially one in water.

"I am not dying for... how much would that be again? No, no. I am not dying."

"Exactly! You won't die," Eir said between gritted teeth.

I felt bad, I really did, but I also felt strongly about the unknown in water.

"The worst that will happen is it will grab you and you'll be underwater for a few seconds. Only a few seconds," she insisted. "Please, Aspen."

I stomped my foot in frustration. "Why can't Charlie be the bait?"

"Because," Eir continued, "Charlie is a practicing witch. Compared to her, you're a mosquito."

I grit my own teeth, counted to three, and tried to come up with a better argument. So far, they didn't seem to see my side of this. They couldn't seem to understand why, after at least a dozen confirmed drownings, I wouldn't want to get back into that water.

"And if we leave it, more people will die."

I deflated, knowing they were right. They'd been doing this a lot longer than me. Damn it. I refused to let more people die. "Triple time," I agreed. "With three weeks of paid vacation."

Eir started to protest, but Sif squealed: "Deal!" before throwing me in the car. leaving me to wondered if I should have negotiated for more.

By the time we reached Slide Rock, I knew I should have negotiated for more.

Light just touched the horizon, chasing away the scariest of shadows, but not the very real threat that lay beneath the water in Oak Creek. The water, usually so clear you see each individual rock on the bottom, was a murky green in the low light. A strange quiet settled in this area compared to my normal mornings; all I heard was the gentle babbling of the creek. No animals, not even a cricket.

The spot we picked was as narrow as the sliding area—the most trafficked—got. The red rock layers extended from the riverbanks all the way up the cliff on the other side, remnants of this area's last major seismic activity. The red rock was even under my shoes.

Near the banks both Jord and Sif walked a perimeter, taking measured steps and checking things occasionally in thick books bound with worn leather. They stopped, placing copper bowls about the size of tea saucers at their feet, adjusting them until they were in the right spot. Then they pulled packets of herbs out and emptied them into the bowls.

Eir motioned me over to where she stood at the riverbank and I left the goddesses to their strange ritual. The wind swept the smell of wildflowers and burning sage to my nose, and then Sif and Jord started chanting.

Oh, *spell* books.

I glanced behind me, but besides the wind and small whiff of smoke, there wasn't much to see. No bright lights, no shimmers, nothing showing anything special. Disappointed, I turned back to Eir just in time for a bright flash of light and a soft 'whoosh' to resonate from behind me.

"They already did the protection spell. Impressive," Eir said, her voice soft.

"I wanted to watch!" I exclaimed, moving back and forth, trying to get a better look at each side that was casting their spell.

Eir slapped her hand over my mouth and glared at me, her mouth firm and her finger over it. I glanced back and forth between all the goddesses, all of them frozen.

"Sorry," I whispered when Eir removed her hand. "I did want to watch."

"You'll have magic soon enough," she hissed back at me. "In the meantime, be a good little human, take off your shoes, and get in the damn water."

I slipped my shoes and socks off, thrust them at her, and she grabbed my hand one last time before I turned around. Courage and purpose flooded my veins and I gasped at the influx of power as she stared into me.

"Good luck, Aspen," she whispered, letting my hand fall from hers.

Hanging onto the feeling, reveling in it, I took two, then three steps toward the creek. I stepped one foot into the snow melt and a shiver ran through my body. Eir's courage still flowed through my veins as the water rose to my ankles. The brightening sky, now streaked with pink and orange, cast a rosy hue into the park, shimmering off the red rock in rainbows.

Not letting anything about the drownings in my mind lest I chicken out, I waded out to about waist deep. My feet held onto the smooth rocks underneath me while the current pushed against me. I marched in place to agitate the water, keep my body temperature up, and make my presence known.

Looking from one side of the bank to the other and every-where in between, I tried to stomp out the butterflies in my stomach. This thing was going to pull me under and there was nothing I could do to stop it.

Thirty seconds. A minute. I kept track through chattering teeth as the seconds ticked on.

Ninety seconds. Two minutes.

I stomped, I splashed my hands in the water, and I pushed the water away from me. Cold creek water splashed in my face and hair and dribbled down my back. I lost count.

I stopped splashing and turned to the goddesses on the sidelines, each standing at the ready. Sif had one of her swords out, her face hard and her eyes darting like mine. Eir had hers closed and her hands were in front of her as her staff rested against the inside crook of her arm. Jord looked to be in prayer.

"How long has it been?"

Jord sighed, her arms gracefully falling back to her sides. "Not long enough."

I dropped my head back and groaned in exasperation. Wading further into the water, I wrapped my arms around my body to warm myself up.

"If I stay in here much longer, I'll—"

I didn't feel the hand around my ankle at first. When I lifted my right foot, I felt the slightest of tugs... and then I was dragged down below the water.

Chapter Twenty-Nine

S pindly fingers gripped me by the ankle and every time I tried pushing out, the river, normally more like a trickle, roared over me like an ocean wave. It kept me pressed down like a weight settled on my chest. I kicked and flailed, barely gasping above water before being pulled back under. Hands grabbed at my arms, wrapping around me and pulling me across the rocks, splaying me for sacrifice. Music roared in my ears, a violin or some other stringed instrument.

As I choked back the reflex to inhale, feeling like it had been minutes and not seconds since I tasted air, a face flashed in front of mine. Child-like with a mouth full of sharp teeth. It grinned wickedly and I gasped, pulling in the water I had so desperately been trying not to. I kicked and pulled even harder, fighting every urge in me to take in a deep lungful of air.

It felt like there were clamps around my arms, more pressure, when I was hefted out of the water, causing the creature's hold to slip off. Sif dragged me out of the river, while Eir and Jord yelled words I didn't understand.

"Are you alright?" Sif asked, slapping me on the back as I gasped and heaved for air. I turned to the side and threw up the water that I'd swallowed, a burn in my throat and nose as a lingering reminder. My lungs hurt, scratchy from the inside after being starved for air.

Still coughing, I watched as the swirling cyclone of water held a creature aloft from the river. Its bowed arms and fingers, so long and thin that they looked as though they would break by gripping something, were nightmare fodder. Water dripped from it like it was made of water itself.

"What is it?" I coughed some more.

"A Nøkk." Sif's brow furrowed, deep lines betraying her calm tone. "They aren't from around here. Stay back, let us do this."

With that, she shouted an incantation and her sword emitted a green glow. With a cry, she sliced off the arm of the Nøkk and it shrieked a sound that made me want to throw up again as my entire world went wonky, almost upside down.

That moment gave the goddesses an edge. Jord planted her staff in the water, sending a ripple through the stream so strong it rose almost ten feet high and then broke, throwing the pint-size creature back down from the strike. Then Eir moved her hands in a pattern three times in rapid succession and a sphere formed around the Nøkk, trapping it in the water.

The Nøkk pushed and screamed and tore at the water's edges, but just like the pixie and the Jotun, it couldn't break free from Eir's trap. The water prison became smaller until it was just large enough to hold the creature. It shook the trappings as it continued to scream. Eir touched the sphere, murmured another incantation, and the sounds of the Nøkk stopped.

I scrambled into a standing position on the bank and rubbed my cold, bruised arms. Once again all I heard was the running of the creek and the panting of my co-workers.

"Is that it?" I received three nods. "What now?"

"Unfortunately we can't kill it," Sif said, her voice suggesting she would like that outcome. "We only have permission to kill Jotuns and monsters. This is a sprite."

"It drowned people!" I protested, tugging at the blanket that Eir had thrown over my shoulders. She then hushed me and grabbed my wrist, taking my pulse.

"Sprites do that," Jord said in resignation. "The good news is it can't follow you home and drown you on land now. But this is a known spot. They wouldn't come here normally. They prefer the quiet where they can lure people in. It makes no sense for one to make its home here. It's...not right."

Sif popped some gum in her mouth and offered a stick around like one would a cigarette. Each goddess took a piece. Why not? My near drowning sure felt like a celebration. "Not to mention they rarely leave Europe."

I studied the Nøkk. Its face was a curious mixture of child and monster. Its eyes, black, and unblinking, reflected my stunned face.

"So why would it be here?"

By the time we got back to headquarters, the Nøkk had gone from bashful watcher to baying at the top of its lungs again. The water sphere muffled it mostly, but not enough to stop it from going through the walls. My fresh warm clothes weren't enough for Eir, who wrapped me in another blanket. The cold water had given me a headache, and despite popping some Advil, the Nøkk did *not* help.

"If that thing screams again, I'm going to pull out Aspen's hair," Charlie snapped, coming in from the waiting room. "I can't read with that thing screaming."

I furrowed my brow and gave Charlie a withering look. "Pull out your own hair!"

"My hair is too fabulous to pull out. You will suffer for my pride." She was looking at me expectingly and I realized... she had cracked a joke. Charlie was joking with me.

I grinned at her, trying to not look *too* happy or dorky for that matter. One of the knots that had been holding in my stomach loosened. Now if only I could figure out Eir's problem.

"Hey, stop flirting with her, Charlie," Sif teased. "We have a real problem on our hands."

Charlie surveyed the Nøkk and poked at Eir's sphere, causing it to ripple. The Nøkk stopped screaming while it watched Charlie. Both of them were now quiet, surveying the other through the barrier.

Jord picked up where she left off. "I can't figure this out."

Which was to say, we were still at square one. We had a Nøkk—something that wasn't native—and no one knew how it had gotten so far from its home in Northern Europe or into such a populous area. And worse, they didn't know how long it had been there.

"We can keep looking into dry drownings?" Eir suggested, strangely uncertain of herself.

"People from all over the world visit Slide Rock," Sif moaned, scrubbing her face. "Sure, we found several cases. There could be dozens of other cases out of the state or country."

I mulled over the information. Who would bring something so deadly here? "What if someone had traveled with it?"

"Who, though? A human? A witch?" Jord shook her head. "Humans would never see it, and a witch would never survive it."

"Why not?" I asked.

"Witches are strong," Sif said. "Quite strong, to be honest. You need more power to deal with fae like we do. Our magic doesn't always require an incantation or a rune. We can still use those. You have to be quick to catch a fae like this. Or very lucky."

"What are we going to do?" I asked.

Sif shrugged her shoulders. "Guess we'll have to send it back. Thanks for the help today, Aspen. Why don't you go home and rest? Oh, and—" She walked over to her desk and grabbed an envelope off the top. "Try not to spend it all in one place," she said as she handed it to me. "Welcome to the team."

I held the envelope and bit my lip, waiting for something, anything else. An apology for taking so long to get to me? For allowing me to swallow water? With a rush of anger, I crushed it in my hand. "You don't get it, do you?" Sif jumped and I gestured to the Nøkk. "That thing almost drowned me. And it actually has drowned others. You said it yourself; there could be dozens!"

"Aspen," Jord started gently, "you weren't hurt. And we—"

My throat constricted, the soreness reminding me of what happened, of how close I had felt to death. "Maybe not much, but I might have been. You say you're here to help humans? To make sure humans survive the things that accidentally cross into our realm? You've forgotten what humans are. We're fragile. I'm sure Eir could have done something even if I had been unconscious, but that's not the point. You should think about things before, not after. I didn't like it and you still pushed me to do it."

I turned on my heel when Eir grabbed my arm. I whirled on her, expecting to find her using her magic to calm me. My anger surged again, but she pushed something into my hand. Two berries. I said nothing, just walked out, slamming the door to Charlie's waiting room and then the one that went to the outside, non-magical world.

After kicking Bessie's tires in frustration, I sat down in a huff and shoved the berries into my purse. The sun was now out and shining, people would soon begin to arrive for work, and I wouldn't go unnoticed. I went to shove the check into my purse as well, but stopped and decided I could get a nice boost of happiness from my first paycheck. I opened the crumbled check, and my mouth dropped, and all my dopamine receptors went off at once.

They hadn't just paid me triple time for the Jotun attack, but for the entire week that the paycheck covered.

"Huh..." A grin spread on my face and maybe I had a tear in my eye. Charlie and I were the only employees, so there was no way this was a computer mistake. In fact, the check was signed, not stamped, by 'Deolinda Serra-Costa.'

I threw the car into gear and started home, my thoughts continuously running to catch up with me.

Maybe I had been a little harsh, but I wasn't ready to forget yet. It would take a little more stewing and some discussions before I would be ready to take a risk like that again. If they had similar things happening all the time, I could leverage for hazard pay as long as I was mortal.

Mortal.

Chapter Thirty

My driving had been on complete autopilot as I mulled things over. I parked Bessie in the driveway when I arrived home, bypassed the front door and I went straight to the backyard. I passed Nana's home, made a beeline for the greenhouse, power-walking and eventually breaking into a jog. My mind raced, probably from the near-death experience.

Or maybe from the idea that I wouldn't die if I continued on my current path.

Would I?

Even though they had partaken of Idunn's fruits for who knows how long, the gods still died. Their eventual deaths were all violent; no one died of natural causes. Freyja had lived for over ten centuries after *that*, which seemed to prove that disease and long life wouldn't kill you if you had the fruit.

Did I want that? I tried so hard not to think of it, of what I might leave behind, how much things might change in the world. Or what if they didn't? What if the bad never got better, and I have to watch life for others get worse?

What if...

I almost slapped myself. I had spent years learning how to stop myself from spiraling, yet here I was. A bead of sweat made its way down my brow and my breathing became shallow. If I didn't take control, I would have a panic attack.

I stopped in front of the run-down shed, the cracked green paint on the door marking which one I chose. My hands shook when I reached for the door. Curling my fingers in, I forced the feelings down. I had come too far to let myself spiral out on something I could easily get clarity on. But they would need to take some responsibility, too.

After Loki's visit the other day, I had set up my lab in the old greenhouse, unsure of what I could do. He had a reason for giving me so much of the precious fruit. Right now, I needed to clear my mind.

My microscope sat ready with petri dishes and slides on the newly cleaned off shelf designated as a makeshift workbench. I had also put about twenty car air fresheners around the work area, hoping that airing it out would clear out musty stink that hung in the air.

I pulled out the fruits and divided them into species, or tried to. The strawberries and blackberries were easy enough. I even picked out lingonberries. There were three other types, at least, that were either unfamiliar, or possibly degraded. I set those back into the jar while laying out the dozen pieces of fruit I recognized. I wouldn't eat a single one of these, not even if the goddesses still gave me more.

I reached down to the shelf below and pulled out a notebook and pen I had stashed. Science wasn't easy, but the theorizing part of it was fun. I spent at least thirty minutes sketching out my plan—supplies needed, the basic idea, and my ideal result.

That result? To help Mom.

Could I cure the MS? Make it more tolerable? Maybe slow it down? I didn't know. I would try for any and all of it.

The far-off sound of sirens broke the quiet of my morning. I listened as they came closer and closer. Someone had probably crashed on the 89A, which wasn't too unusual. The climb was dangerous, even deadly, for law enforcement trying to get there quickly.

I continued writing, but they still came closer until they seemed to be almost on top of me, and then they stopped.

My heart dropped.

I abandoned my work and ran out of the garden, flying faster when I saw the ambulance pull into our driveway behind the firetruck.

I didn't listen to the paramedics as they called for me to stop. The air inside the house was warmer than outside. I followed the firefighters from the door to the kitchen, panting heavily from my run. Nana motioned for them to come closer.

She grabbed me before I had the chance to cross the threshold. Her mouth moved, but I only heard the roar of my blood in my ears. Then they came with the gurney and held the door open long enough for me to see her.

My mom lay sprawled on the kitchen floor in her robe and slippers, blood under her head.

I screamed.

For the second time in two weeks, I stood in Flagstaff Hospital, listening to a doctor detail exactly how careless leaving Mom alone could be. Every word felt like a sliver of glass shoving itself into my heart. I mean, he didn't say it so specifically. It came down to being more careful with her seizures. Basically, we were going to babysit her. And she would not like that.

This time everyone was here. Not just Nana and Dad, but Doug and Cypress, with baby Ivy, too. The only one missing from the immediate family was my brother-in-law, Jeremy, but he was on his way. The tiny room only held enough seats for a few people, so Doug and I stood with Cypress holding Ivy in her lap.

"The concussion isn't bad, but we need to keep her for a couple of days to monitor her," the doctor continued, his tone soothing. "She's already proving to be a handful for the nurses, so it could be as soon as tomorrow that she goes home."

Dad sagged forward, relief clear on his face. Nana squeezed his hand, but her face didn't change as she tried to be brave for everyone.

"What else?" Nana prompted.

"She needs rest. Her MS flare is much worse than her doctor thought last week. We can't predict how a body is going to react all the time. We can only take our best guess and plan for what we know. Since she's never had a flare this bad and the seizures are new, routines and extra precautions are going to be needed. Do you have stairs in your house?"

The doctor, Nana, and Dad talked for a few more minutes. The doctor was pleased that Mom lived on the ground floor and that we would make sure she wasn't left alone until the flare calmed. Whenever that would be. It could be months. When the doctor stood, we chorused our thanks and he closed the door behind him.

And then, my dear friends, everything went to shit.

"Why the hell did you leave Mom alone?" Cypress turned to me, calm, cold anger in her voice.

"Cy—" Dad started.

"No! She was supposed to be there. You came up here for what? So that you could run off and do whatever you wanted and leave Mom when she needed you? Were you in the garden again?"

Tears stung my eyes and my jaw quivered as I took her abuse. She was right. God, she was right. Dad tried talking again, but she plowed forward.

"She could be dead because you, what, were out playing with your plants again? If Nana hadn't come along... Why don't you grow up, Aspen?"

I hate myself. God, why can't I just die right now? Let me die. Please, let this end.

I started sobbing. Cypress stopped her yelling, and through my tears I tumbled down, far from the grip on reality I had held so close. I fell into myself and my insecurities because they were all true.

"I'm sorry! I'm so sorry. I—I don't deserve... I'm sorry. Daddy, Daddy please," I turned to him and then his arms were around me. I cried into his chest. "Mom's hurt and it's my fault," I cried. "It's my fault, it's my fault! I left and I shouldn't have. Daddy, please, I can't—I can't—Please! Don't let her die, she can't die."

Different arms were around me now. "She's not dying, sweetie. She's fine, it's okay, you need to calm down. Deep breaths. Deep breaths, Aspen," Nana coached me.

My sobs had become so intense that I could hardly suck in air. My chest was tight and I gasped for air, but at the same time, I also didn't care if I got it.

"Get the doctor back in here!" Doug yelled.

The world around me got darker and my breathing came faster and shallower as my still-sore throat reminded me that just that morning I had been underwater. Drowning. Now I drowned in my own fears and insecurities.

The world went sideways and dark.

Chapter Thirty-One

T he world came back slowly and when I finally had control of all of my senses I woke to a quiet, white room.
It took several dizzying seconds to figure out why my limbs
were so heavy while my chest ached.

"Are you awake, Aspen?" Doug asked. He sat in the chair
next to the scratchy hospital bed I was lying on. "We're in the
ER downstairs. Mom's awake now."

"How..." My mouth felt like someone stuffed hot garbage
down my throat and I'd gargled on the juice. Doug handed
me a cup of water, which I sipped before starting again. "How
long was I out?"

"Not even an hour. They gave you something at the height
of the meltdown." He shifted Ivy from his lap down to the
floor, where the toddler happily toddled to her toy bag and
sat down, pulling things out. I cocked my head at him having
Cypress' kid and he shrugged. "Nana gave her to me and told
me to follow you. On my way out she let Cypress have it. Then
Dad joined in. She's probably had enough of people telling her
she sucks, but I promise I'm going to anyway."

I forced a chuckle. Cypress had been out of line, but some
of what she said still rang true. They asked me to be around
for Mom, but I hadn't thought that meant I couldn't ever leave

the house, especially that early. I hadn't known Dad's job had run so late that he stayed over at a hotel with his team.

Bracing myself, I continued to take stock of my situation. They hadn't changed my clothes, and I wasn't cuffed to the bed. That meant they weren't taking me to a behavioral health hospital for my panic-induced meltdown.

"Aspen," Doug said, his voice gentler than ever as he juggled the toddler. "Are you feeling okay? You said some things during your panic attack that I think you should mention to your therapist." His tone was full of concern. "I'm not getting on your case. I'm just checking in."

"I don't have a therapist anymore," I mumbled. "I was seeing someone at school and now that I'm out, I'm waiting to get back to the doctor to find a new one."

He seemed to consider that and then asked the question they always asked. "Have you been taking your medicine? On schedule?"

I blew out some loose hair around my head before giving him an affirmative. "Of course. I promise."

"I know this is against everything you're supposed to do, but while Mom's in the hospital, I need you to stay strong for her. I need you to hold it in until you're home, and—"

Doug didn't finish the sentence and instead dropped to one knee with a grunt as the earth roiled beneath us. The entire room shook, my metal bedframe scraping along the ground, wheels locked, as we swayed back and forth in what I thought must be an earthquake. Ivy burst into tears and screamed. Doug covered her as the cabinets opened, some of their items shuffling along the shelves and crashing to the ground as everything continued to vibrate.

I jumped out of bed and threw myself over the other side of Ivy, praying that nothing fell on us, praying harder that the ground would stop moving. It slowed, then stopped. It took Ivy pushing herself even further into me to realize it was over.

It didn't take long for the injured to begin arriving at the hospital. The change in the air was palpable, thick with worry and the unknown. The hospital released me within twenty minutes of the first earthquake victim showing up. The quake was confirmed as being a 5.8 on the Richter scale, a terrible strength for a place that doesn't get them. A earthquake that size in Arizona was rarer than water, rarer than snow, and even rarer than hurricanes in this state.

Don't look at me like that. We get hit by tropical storms and hurricane remnants all the time. Pay attention.

A tech ushered me from the hospital room, thrusting my discharge papers in my face. The hallways were filling with victims. A man, whose torso and right arm were covered up with a bloody towel that didn't hide that something had fallen on top of him, took over the space without them even wiping it down.

I kept my face to the ground, my mind replaying what had possibly happened to the man. I gulped. How many more were like that?

The news blared from every TV on our way to Mom's room upstairs. When we got there, Mom was sitting up, her head bandaged. She probably wanted to fall asleep right there with her droopy grey eyes.

I leaned down and kissed her cheek, and she patted my hand with a soft smile on her face. "I had to wake up for the earthquake. Just had to."

"Good job, Mom."

"Pretty scary stuff," Cypress said as she brought Ivy up to give her grandma a kiss.

"Scay," Ivy repeated, clapping her hands together with a laugh. If only we all forgot everything after five minutes and a cookie.

Cypress looked like she wanted to say something, maybe thank me for getting her daughter though a 'scay' situation, but she kept her mouth closed.

Nana took Ivy from Mom and sat with her in the chair next to the bed. I expected us to talk about Mom's care, but everyone focused on the television as they reported on the earthquake. I shrugged and stood off to the side, leaning against a wall and out of the way, feeling shaky from the lorazepam, but more so from adrenaline. We could always talk later.

"We're getting more information that there were three simultaneous earthquakes, and not just the two epicenters up north, which were felt even down in Phoenix," the local news anchor said, her tone cool and serious. Her quick makeup job showed everyone's panic.

"Two epicenters?" I repeated.

"Three, actually," Cypress muttered, pointing at the screen which showed where the three epicenters were.

The first in Tucson had been much lower on the Richter scale at a 2.6. Then the one closest to us in Sedona, was a 3.9, followed by one up north of us, in a state park of some sort, which was the 5.8.

"Isn't that unusual?" I asked.

"This is all unusual," Dad said, his lips tight. "I can't remember the last time we could feel an earthquake here. And three? It's..."

"It's the vortexes," Nana said, certainty in her voice. "It has to be. Those are three of many places in this state that have them. See, there's Sedona and the Tucson Mountains, of course. I bet that's the San Francisco Mountains."

The vortexes? Why would that matter? The remaining fog in my head cleared and the blood drained from my face. I grabbed the rail of Mom's bed so I wouldn't fall over from the wooziness. Oh, God. Or gods, in this case.

"Aspen? Are you alright?" Cypress touched my arm, concern in her voice. "Do we need to go get a doctor? Doug, go get a doctor. She's going to fall over."

"I'm fine," I said in a dazed tone. Then I nodded firmly and swallowed hard. "I have to make a call. It shouldn't take long it's just to work."

"You have work tonight, don't you?" Mom asked, giving me the out I needed. "You should go. Don't stay for me."

I didn't before, but I definitely did now.

"Yeah, I should get to my job, but only if you're okay with it."

I kept my eyes on her, happy when no one came forward to say I'd just worked through a panic attack. Not even Nana, who gave me a warning look. I played along as Mom continued to reassure me she'd be okay.

"I have everyone else, and I don't want you to get fired after only working there a couple of weeks." She waved me off. "I'll be fine, honey."

I kissed Mom on the cheek again and with a quick goodbye, I was out the door and on my phone.

Pick up, Sif, please pick up.

"Aspen?"

"Sif!" I reached my car in under two minutes, somehow making it through the craziness of people and reporters who were, I'm sure, just doing their jobs when I almost bowled them over.

"Where the hell are you?" she asked. "Are you okay?"

"Yeah, fine." Now wasn't the time to make a big deal about leaving the hospital. I fumbled for my keys and eventually grabbed them with my shaking hands. "Did you see the earth-quake had three different points of origin?"

"What? That's not even possible. And... Hold on." I scram-bled into my car, watching as several ambulances pulled up to the emergency room. From my vantage point they brought one person out on a stretcher, their clothes stained with blood.

I wanted them to not be related to the earthquake, but as the second stretcher got out, this time with a father holding a towel to a crying baby's head, fear settled in my heart. Fear that there were more like that baby, or worse.

"Jord says they weren't earthquakes." Sif's voice held a note of uncertainty. "She's been trying to figure it out, but our divination keeps coming up with nothing."

I kept my attention on the ambulance bay. "Eir said the vortexes are ways of getting to other realms?"

"Yeah? What does—"

I cut her off. "What if someone from another realm wants to come here? Not just a pixie or a Nøkk, but something like a god? What would happen if a god opened a vortex?"

"Not this. This would only happen if someone tried to open the Bifrost. You know, the portal between realms? Even then only one place."

I groaned in my head and tried not to let the sound leak into my voice. "Okay, so someone's doing that! What if—"

"You need a vortex and a literal volcano to open it. Not to mention Heimdall." Sif was clearly exasperated.

I went quiet. Sedona, Tucson Mountains, AND the Volcanic Fields?

"Does the volcano have to be active?"

"I think so. I don't know."

I jumped at her uncertainty. "What if it doesn't? What if someone's been testing the vortexes by sending creatures through? And what if that was just to be sure it worked? There are extinct volcanoes all over the state. Hell, Sif, not just the Volcanic Fields."

She swore in a language I wasn't familiar with. Then she swore in a different language, followed by a third.

"Uh..."

"You stay home," she barked. "We're going to check this out." She hung up on me.

I blinked at the phone, astonished that she not only hung up, but that she thought I would listen. After a moment or two of what I will only be calling fretting, I called the only person who could help me now.

"How's Auntie? Is everything going okay? Did you feel that earthquake?" Isa said in a rush.

"She's fine, but everything is not okay. I need your help."

Chapter Thirty-Two

I didn't drive home. I bet that surprises you.

My drive was going to be the opposite way of home. Before going anywhere, I reached into my pocket and felt the pickled fruits I hadn't taken back to the freezer after getting home. They were warm and a little squished in their bag, but if I ate one, I'd be that much closer to being a goddess. If legends were true it would 'restore my vitality'.

If I didn't at least try, if I didn't eat it and this was some sort of Jotun or pixie invasion...

I huffed and chided myself. What was I so afraid of? I wanted this, I wanted to know these things. I wasn't going to get answers to my questions if I remained mortal. I had choices before me, but only as a goddess.

Something had changed and if we left it unchecked, it would bleed into the mortal world. This wasn't only affecting the supernatural anymore, but my family.

And no one messed with my family.

The berry touched my tongue, and I tasted the perfect chocolate covered strawberry fields of my childhood that existed nowhere except in the blur of my fondest memories and dreams. I had to stop and savor, wishing this taste would last forever.

With renewed vigor I sped on.

When I reached the signs that signaled the turnoff for Sunset Crater, the only place I could think of that would possibly be volcanically active in the Fields. The electronic sign over the highway indicated the area was closed. There would be only one reason they were closed right now, and I pushed Bessie for all that little '98 engine of hers was worth, going much faster than I normally dared for an extended amount of time.

Sunset Crater, a cinder cone, was probably one of the youngest volcanoes in the Arizona desert. According to Native stories the volcano erupted almost a thousand years ago, give or take a few decades. It changed how people farmed and worked, like many of the other chutes that had opened up over the last several hundred thousand years.

I drove through the entrance and followed the signs until I reached one of the easiest and closest trails to Sunset Crater, A'a Trail. My flat shoes were woefully inadequate for the desert landscape with craggy, black basalt volcanic flows that made up the land. Not only were the majestic fields dotted with wildlife, but I got a fantastic glimpse of the volcano caldera itself, which rose up out of the forest, dotted with greenery up its side.

Pulling into the parking lot for the trail, I turned off Bessie and waited. While I waited, I realized I had no idea what would be waiting for me. A Jotun, a god, pixies, fae, monsters, it might be anything.

I wasn't going to go in unarmed. Gazing into the distance, ignoring the beauty around me, I waited with my arms crossed over Bessie's steering wheel and soon Isa pulled up behind me.

She frantically jumped out. "Are you out of gas again?" Then she gasped. "Is Loki here?"

I went over to her car to help her unload. "Even if I knew how to call Loki—which I don't—do you think I would after the last time?"

"No, but I thought it'd be funny to remind you of it." She grinned at me from the other side of the car. "Especially since you asked me to bring..." She opened the door to the back seat. "I got salt and holy water, no problem. I didn't have any garlic, though."

"Wait, garlic was the problem here?" I double checked to be sure. "Not the holy water?"

She stopped rummaging around and her eyes bore straight through me before she answered. "I went and got it from Granny's house. She had a lot of questions that I then lied about. I don't think she believe me."

Her granny, a staunch enough Catholic to give a Cardinal a lecture on the Bible, supported Isa and me in most things we did. Like my Nana, 'weird' often got thrown around to describe her.

"Do we have any weapons?" I asked, opening the back door.

"Just some softball bats." She reached in and then handed me a metal one. "I don't know what you think we're going to do."

Since I could only go off what I had been learning from other sources, like the goddesses and long-dead Snorri, I had no idea either. I knew the others worked as purifiers, so I threw in garlic for its purifying properties.

We slammed the car doors shut and faced A'a Trailhead. "We're just here to back up the goddesses. If we find something, we call them. It might not even be here. Maybe it's down in the Tucson Mountains."

"How will we know?" Isa asked.

"Probably because they'll show up and tell you off for specifically going against orders," Sif said from behind me.

"Are Jord and Eir behind me, too?" I asked a pale Isa.

"Oh, yeah. And, uh, some bald guy?"

"Don't think I'll be any help," Thor said.

We turned and faced the goddesses and Thor, all scowling. I tried to look at the ground like I was ashamed of myself, but unfortunately, I had Isa with me. She cocked a hip at them in challenge.

"What are you doing here? With"—Eir reached into Isa's backpack on her back—"salt and a baseball bat? Really?"

"Well, it's not like you ever prepared me for this!"

"Yes, we did," Eir said. She all but threw the salt back at us. "We told you to stay home. That's how we prepared you for this. You're not a goddess. You were ready to walk away after this morning."

"I didn't like being bait."

"Goody, now you're not bait. Now leave. Whatever this is, it's gonna be dangerous for you *mortals*." Eir spat out the word.

"We're not going anywhere." Isa planted her feet, crossed her arms, and stared at the goddesses and Thor, daring them to move the girl who skipped junior high and went right straight into high school from sixth grade.

Thor looked between the tiny Hispanic girl and then me, a grin on his face.

"Thor, she's got bigger balls than you," I said.

He winked at Isa. "Well, if said balls are going to come with us, then you'd better pick up your baseball bats. Those you might need."

"Thor!" Sif's head snapped to the god. "They can't—"

"Come off it, Sif. They drove here on their own. They were prepared to fight. Am I right?" I nodded and Thor kept going. "So there. If all of us are right, this is where the Fae Wyld spoke of. I think we can put everything aside until later. They could be helpful."

Sif hesitated. "They could also get in the way."

Jord placed a hand on Sif's shoulder and shared a meaningful look with Eir.

Sif put her hand on her sword and sighed. "You know you might get hurt?"

"Yes," I responded.

"Yeah." Isa sighed.

"You know you could die? Or worse?"

"What's worse than death?" Isa shared a look with me. "I mean... you're dead."

"Some monsters will eat the souls of their victims." Eir rummaged around her crossbody bag, keeping her eyes on me as she searched for something.

I swallowed and met Isa's gaze. She had gone a little paler, but I saw the same thing I felt burning in my chest: determination.

We both nodded.

Eir came up and handed us each a vial of liquid. "Smoke bombs," she explained. "They have cayenne inside them, amongst other things, so they're going to *hurt* if you don't run immediately."

Jord raised her swirling staff and tapped the bulb on my head, then Isa's. A white light bloomed in front of my vision before exploding in a small green firework just above my eyes. I blinked rapidly and Isa was waving her hand in front of her face to get the small amount of smoke away.

"A protection spell," she explained, her voice serious. "It will last one hour and should keep you untouched by most small magicks."

"What'll it do against medium magicks? Or big ones?" Isa asked as she rubbed her skin, seemingly trying to feel a difference as the green glow faded.

Jord shook her head and pursed her lips before Eir answered for her. "It might save your life. Don't depend on it. Do you still have those potions I gave you?"

"Uh, yeah?" I held up the smoke bomb.

Eir glared at me. "I mean the ones you didn't use to save your life with the Jotun."

My head snapped up. I'd totally forgotten about those. "They're in the trunk!"

Running over to Bessie, I unlocked the trunk, feeling almost obscenely grateful to every god in existence that I had moved recently. I stopped short of saying it out loud for obvious reasons. I had cleaned my trunk out before moving, so the brightly colored bottles stood out. I scooped them up and gave the healing one to Isa, keeping the firebomb for myself, tucking it into the opposite pocket from the smoke bomb.

"First, don't ever drive around with a firebomb in a glass bottle in your trunk. If you'd been rear ended, you would have been blown up. Second... good job keeping them around even if stored inadequately."

A tingly feeling filled me. Praise? From Eir?

Sif threw her hands up in the air again. "Fine. But if you get hurt, you can't sue us. Okay, well, first things first. Thor?"

Thor winked at me and pulled at the chain holding Mjolnir off his neck. The hammer grew until it fit securely in his hand, the runes and other markings all glowing faintly purple. I expected a mighty roar or something, but he quietly raised it above his bald head.

A few seconds later, the clouds which had been sparse and fluffy morphed. Storms were known for popping up all the time during the monsoon season, which we were not in, but it wasn't a normal storm forming. This was Thor's power.

The clouds built up and changed from fluffy white to menacing onyx. Before long, the sky roared and flashed and a downpour took the surrounding valley. Rain drops fell, and I smelled the damp dirt, but by Thor's magic, we were dry in our little circle extending out about twenty feet. I didn't see where the magic began; the faint shimmer around us almost obscured by the near darkness that the storm provided. I walked to the edge and put my hand out, amazed when I passed through the barrier without resistance into a hard, steady rain.

Before we took a step, Sif trotted back to her car and came back with a pair of boots tucked under her arms, socks rolled into them. She thrust them at me and they waited patiently for me to lace them up.

We took the short trail to where we would have an unimpeded view of Sunset Crater so we would know when it was safe to go in. Right now, all we could do was wait.

The scientists, probably from ASU, U of A, or NAU, packed up their sensitive equipment and at first tried to wait out the storm under canopies and inside cars.

"Give me a break. Thor?" Sif cocked an eyebrow at our meteorologist, who obliged her flirt.

The gale grew in intensity, the wind whipping so fast and hard that the rain descended at an angle. The howling intensified; the rain splattered into mud around the barrier. This time, I stuck my hand out more cautiously and then retreated quickly, shaking it and swearing.

"Like that?" Thor wiggled his eyebrows as though to be funny. "Stinging rain. Humans hate it."

"No kidding. Does it feel like a massage to you?"

Laughing, Thor clapped me on the shoulder, pushing me down from the force of his 'gentle' pat. "No, it stings me, too. Just not as hard as it does for a mortal."

I didn't see Sif's eyeroll so much as I heard it.

Finally, after what seemed like hours but might have only been twenty minutes, a convoy of trucks and cars left. The police kept the barricade up, but they even left in the deluge. We waited until their taillights faded before heading to the flats, trudging through the mud of the A'a trail.

The storm stopped so abruptly that Isa startled when the sunshine peeked out of the sky in a small patch. As soon as the sun started to shine, Thor summoned fog to shelter the entirety of the valley just as easily as he called the storm. Power from the vortex prickled on my skin we moved, the sweet tang of it on my tongue. Even Isa rubbed her arms as though she were cold.

We were in the right place at least.

With the park completely empty of mortals, we trekked across the rocky terrain, careful of the low brush and surrounding trees. The Volcanic Flats contained over six hundred extinct and slow-acting volcanoes, including Sunset Crater, which had erupted so long ago.

About the time of Ragnarök.

The rocks changed from small and desert-quality pebbles to black and craggy. The lava flows were hundreds of thousands of years old in some places, but that didn't make it any easier to not trip over them.

However, after Sif tripped over the lava flows for the third time she turned to Thor and hissed, "I can't see six inches in front of me, you un-cocky codpiece."

I scrunched up my face as I tried to keep myself from laughing too loud. Isa snorted and grabbed me for support.

"Sif, that one hurt," Thor pouted.

"So does my ankle. Thin the damn fog!" she snapped.

"Okay, okay."

I didn't notice the change at first, but the dimmed purple light of Mjolnir glowed in front of me. Before long I could make out the shapes of my comrades, but not their faces. The glowing runes stopped as Thor lowered his hammer. In a smooth but cocky motion, he turned to Sif and saluted her with Mjolnir.

Sif pushed in front of Thor to get back in the lead, probably while rolling her eyes, and he chuckled before falling in line behind her.

We got all of thirty feet when Sif raised her hand and put a finger to her lips. In a soft whisper, she said, "Form ranks around the mortals."

The god(esses) switched where and how they were walking in a practiced movement of years past. As it ended, Isa and I were being escorted like we were movie stars at a premiere, which would have been impressive if it didn't feel like we were walking to our potential deaths.

"What was that for?" Isa asked as she slowed down.

Ahead of us through the mist, an outline of pure light protruded like a crystal. The unnatural glow was enough to see, but not enough to shine in the dense air.

We crept at the speed of a sloth covered in tar during a January snow. Isa and I had our bats ready to go, the potions within easy reach in our pockets. I expected something to come jumping out at us, or maybe running toward us? The only reason we had our bats ready was because of the goddesses and Thor, who now carried Mjolnir in one hand and a half-staff in his other.

We drew closer to the shining void until finally the fog cleared and for the first time, I saw the true power of a vortex.

It opened on the side of one of the dormant calderas, towering over even Thor. With reds and greens occasionally streaking through pitch black, it swirled like so many starry nights. Nothing else inside of it, only inky nothingness.

Were we too late? Could it be the Bifrost?

Sif raised her sword and chanted. Eir joined in and Jord spoke softly in English, as she knelt to the ground, her palms flat as though she were worshiping.

"Mother, please, we ask that you—"

A massive paw, like something out of a rottweiler's most vivid wet dream crashed out of the vortex with a tremor to the ground. Then another appeared, black and massive, with glowing magic trailing after it. The head, now visible as drool dripped from its jaws, was as large as any shark. Isa grabbed my hand in fear. I gripped back.

"A Hel Hound?" Jord gasped.

"What?" Thor's head snapped between the 'dog' and us poor mortals. "No, that can't be." He sounded confused and shocked before his demeanor shifted entirely. "Use the salt! Whatever you do, don't let it break the circle." He gripped my shoulder and our eyes met, fear undeniably in his. "It will eat your soul!"

I didn't get the chance to ask anything—after all, they'd just made fun of me for it—because the gargantuan dog leapt out of the vortex and charged at us.

The gods broke ranks and Isa and I were left alone.

"Hurry!" I snapped at Isa as she fumbled with her canister.

"I don't see you helping!"

I ripped the salt out of her bag, sending it flying everywhere, and then as carefully as I could, shook it out and enclosed us in a circle. Next, I grabbed one bottle of holy water—holy shit, she had over a dozen of them. What the hell did you need that much holy water for? Was Granny planning for an invasion of the undead?

I pushed a vial of water into Isa's hands and she handed me one of the baseball bats.

"Here, eat this." I thrust the pickled fruit into her hand and she blanched when she saw it. "It's one of Idunn's fruits. I don't know what it'll do to you, but maybe you won't die. I've already had one today." I thrust the fruit out to her again.

She took the berry, hesitating only briefly before popping it in her mouth and chewing. Her eyes closed and her mouth slowed as the taste, of only her favorite things I assumed, consumed her.

"Damn. That was delicious," she whispered, her hands to her lips. "Got another? I want to savor that."

"Isa!"

"Sorry, sorry."

And then... we watched.

There were two deep calderas next to each other. The one we were on mostly sunk into the earth and the second fissure broke the surface right beside it, as we were standing where one met the other. Sif pointed to the second one, getting a nod from everyone before they focused on the massive problem at hand. The Hel Hound moved slowly and deliberately toward the gods, who showed no fear.

Isa and I gripped hands and she muttered prayers. In the midst of all those prayers, I wished I hadn't called her.

Neither party moved closer. In fact, the gods were backing up, not into us, but toward the second caldera with careful, slow steps. Each time they would back up or try and turn, the Hel Hound would follow and push them a step or two further and turn them back toward the small woods that lined the side of the volcano. It was either smarter than the average dog—possible—or being controlled by someone else—also possible—because it came after them in a perverse game of follow the leader.

Then it lunged, with teeth bared and a growl that rumbled in my chest, hitching my breath in my throat.

It went for Sif first, but she rolled out of the way and then ran up the caldera to keep the beast away from the stupid, helpless mortals. When it couldn't get her, it switched to Jord, who merely waved her hand and a large boulder smashed into the Hel Hound's jaw from below. With another, more complicated wave, she used the earth to take her up past the fissure line that separated the two calderas, riding the rock like a wave.

Thor lifted Mjolnir and with a roar, directed a bolt of lightning down into the monster. Its inhuman cry echoed in the dark, but it didn't stop. Instead, it charged again, moving too fast for them to stop it from dragging Eir forward with it down below the fissure.

"Aspen!" Isa gasped, grabbing onto my shirt and shaking me.

I tore myself away from the battle, which was now regulated to flashes of light and unintelligible yells. Two massive black paws were visible as another Hel Hound stepped out of the vortex, just as big and ugly as the first one, the pools of darkness where its eyes should have been searched before landing squarely on me and Isa.

I don't know if both of us screamed or only me, but I didn't stop until the Hel Hound harmlessly bounced off an invisible barrier in front of us. The barrier reached as far out as the salt line and I let out a trembling, almost disbelieving breath. I clutched the holy water in my palm, renewed hope in my chest. With only a prayer, I threw it in the demon's direction, a perfect arc that I can only say happened due to my adrenaline. With accuracy that I'd never been capable of for track tryouts, the jar arched, bounced right off the beast, and fell to the ground.

Uh, okay. Thanks for not using cheap jars, Granny?

Isa swore viciously and tore the lid from the jar in her hand, I reached for another one to try again, my target getting closer and closer with each heartbeat. The Hel Hound growled and lunged at the barrier again, and this time, it bent from the force before throwing the creature back.

Isa threw the open holy water jar at the monstrosity, landing square in its chest. An unholy cry came out as a deafening whine, and I lost the jar in my hand to the ground as I pushed my palms into my ears. Even though it was only a small bit, the visible burns smoldered and spread as the holy water dribbled down.

She threw another and I threw my first. Again it cried out and whimpered as parts of its fur were caught by the flying water. We had a few more of those, but they weren't doing enough damage to really hurt the thing. Burns and pain couldn't be the solution.

"Close your eyes!" Isa barked.

"Wha—?"

Smoke and the smell of pepper filled the air as Isa's smoke bomb exploded right on the Hel Hound. Once more it howled, scraping at its muzzle with one of its massive paws. Isa cheered but I trembled. I was amazed at her bravery, but also terrified and on the verge of hyperventilating.

She had had one berry; would it be enough to save her?

Would it save *me*?

The ground shook and I tore my eyes from my best friend to the monster, who charged us again. My heart leapt into my throat as the barrier folded and pushed it back once more. Isa let out another triumphant noise, but the hound simply charged a fourth time.

With my mind made up and holy water in one hand, my baseball bat in another, I bolted from the safety of the salt and ran into the forest of trees on the other side of the lava line. Isa called after me, but I fished in my pockets and grabbed one of the bombs and smashed it right behind me.

A roar and heat at my back were all I knew of the fireball and I pushed forward, praying it would buy me—and more importantly, Isa—time.

The pounding of paws rumbled behind me as the Hel Hound charged after me, through the fire. It slowed as soon as it reached the trees. Hoping and wishing that it wouldn't enter, I looked for a place to hide. With a sniff and another growl, it did. Softly, delicately.

I shimmied up the nearest palo verde tree, dropping my bat as I did so. It wouldn't save me, but it would give me a few seconds to think of a plan. I slipped on the next branch up and came crashing out of the tree with a cry and a loud thud. The air whooshed from my lungs as I hit the ground hard.

Get up stupid, get up!

I took a few shuddered gasps and sat up slowly. After two quick gulps of air I was back on my feet, just in time for the Hel Hound to come back into view. I reached for my baseball bat, but it had rolled away. Instead, I held a large branch out in front of me. I backed up into the tree, the beast panting and growling with foul breath as it advanced.

Chapter Thirty-Three

This is where you all came in, isn't it?

Scared for my life? Abandoned my best friend? Possible dead co-workers in the distance?

Check. Check. Triple check.

Would any of their lives—or souls—be in danger if I hadn't been here? If I hadn't worked at Goddesses, Inc.? Or called them to this place?

What good had I done? Bringing myself and another mortal had only caused everything to be worse. I was going to die and it would all be meaningless. The gods could have done this without me and Isa.

However, if there was death in my future, I would face it and be brave. I touched the tree behind me, hoping it had been a person for a moment, thinking I felt warmth and the heartbeat of someone. There was just bark, dirt, and guilt as I began to hyperventilate and tears trickled down my cheeks.

The Hel Hound charged.

I screamed again, this time so loudly and with so much energy that I hoped I could push the damn beast back to Hel with the air in my lungs. My eyes squeezed shut of their own accord, but I felt wind, a rapid breeze and the sound of wood creaking.

THUNK.

Five seconds passed, and I wasn't dead.

I think.

I opened one eye enough to know it was darker than it had been moments ago. Also a lot greener. I gasped and tried to take in what had happened around me.

It was like being inside a tree house, that is, a house made inside of a tree. All around me rooted branches had come together like a fence, entwining and reinforcing each other. Several trees mixed green and brown branches in an interlocking system that the Hel Hound pawed, sniffed, and growled at—but wasn't able to get through.

The trees, several of which I noted were my namesake, weren't budging. They held strong as I sank to the ground, my knees clacking together in relief.

"Thank you," I whispered, wrapping my hands into the earth next to me. "Thank you."

No, a high-pitched voice I didn't recognize whispered back. *There is no need for thanks, Great Goddess.*

No need...

No need...

Great Goddess...

Goddess!

Something unfamiliar, tangible, but unlike anything I had experienced before filled me. As I sat in the stillness of my fortress I tasted nostalgia for this feeling.

Peace.

Goddess!

"Well," a new deep voice rumbled from inside my barrier. "I must say I didn't expect that. Did you pray, goddess?"

I gasped and turned my face up to see a man, no, definitely a god, towering over me. His sleek black hair came almost to his waist, as though it had never been cut in his life. Brown irises peered out of almond-shaped assessing eyes. He was dressed in similar leather armor as my coworkers with two different swords—one long and thin, one short and wide—strapped to each side. His armor had less damage than the goddesses but showed a similar make to it.9

I tried to stand, but as I did my knees locked and he pushed me back down before I regained my balance. I hit my head on the tree and stared up at him, rubbing the back of my head. "What—"

"You weren't supposed to awaken," he growled. "So damn stubborn, so ready to step into someone else's business."

That sounded like me. "Who are you?" I tried to sound threatening but instead made a sound more akin to the newly cracking voice of a preteen boy.

He chuckled. "I am Heimdall."

I paled. I had been right about the Bifrost. And of course who would be with it but Heimdall? He was its keeper after all. He unsheathed his thinner sword—a rapier?—and held it under my chin, the tip touching my skin. He pushed me so far back against the tree that I had nowhere for me to go safely. Instead, I took shallow breaths and tried not to swallow or tremble too much, just like I had back when Loki held his dagger to my throat.

"What do you want?" I finally asked. "Why are the Hel Hounds here?"

"To take care of any humans who get in the way. Make it look like a wild animal caused it." He seemed to struggle with something before he removed his sword and crouched down next to me. Taking my face in his hand, he studied me. "That's quite the protection spell. Yes, there's Sif or maybe

Jord and...something else. Yes, yes, I can see it. In your pocket," he clarified at my puzzled look, not explaining anything. "Unfortunately, you brought the goddesses here, so..." He sighed and let go of me. "I suppose it's up to the Hel Hound. I don't need more uncomfortable questions anyway. And you won't be able to tell anyone even in death once it's done with you."

I whimpered.

The creaking of branches reminded me that the Hel Hound's efforts hadn't stopped. As it snarled I started to panic, my heart beating too fast within my chest.

"What, like you did this yourself?" I bit out, figuring one way or another I wasn't getting out of here.

"Close."

I sat up straighter. The first small branch broke with a creaking sound as it folded over. "Why now? What changed?"

He glared at me, clearly exasperated. "Yes. Let me detail my plan to you so that your friends know exactly who is causing this, in case you miraculously survive."

I shrugged because, honestly, you can't blame a girl for trying. "What is 'this?'"

Or trying again.

Heimdall chuckled again, disappearing from view, slower than Freyja and Loki had.

"Good luck, fledgling goddess." His sarcastic salute faded with the rest of him and all I heard was the snarling and creaking as the Hel Hound pushed and pulled on the branches, begging for entrance.

I felt the sobs coming on, and I then started doing what I should have done before. I stopped.

What would crying do now?

Outside I heard the renewed efforts of the Hel Hound, scratching and snarling. I tried to keep myself focused, tried to think, but nothing came and I collapsed back against the ground.

I clutched the earth under me and broke it in my palms. It was so... alive. Never had I stuck my hands into the ground and felt so much inside of me. Breath, the very foundation of life, and thoughts that weren't mine washed over me. The trees strained to hold me inside this bubble and worry swept through my heart at the thought of them dying for me. The wood against my back reverberated with a promise:

We will not lose those who fight for us.

The air around me was new, fresh, and beneath me I felt Yggdrasil's breath, but this time so much closer, so much more than before. These trees knew me.

"Do I fight for you?" I asked aloud, my voice breaking as the Hel Hound continued to pace. It wouldn't be long now.

You always have, always...

Since seeds of seeds of other seeds...

"You mean... seeds that have evolved? Seeds that have traveled?"

Yes.

The pawing stopped, but the light shifted through the trees as the Hel Hound prowled.

You are the original.

"The original? The original what?" I asked, keeping the hound within my sights. I stood up and let the earth fall from my hand. "Who am I?"

The Ever Young

One Who Rejuvenates

The Golden Touch

With a smile, I understood and sank back to the ground. It all fit, it all made sense, and as tears ran down my cheeks, I whispered: "Idunn."

Even with the Hel Hound, the knowledge of my name, my real name, gave me strength. Inside me a memory tried to break through. More of a whisper, but when I put it together with what I knew now...

"Can you help me?" I begged, wiping my tears. "I don't have my power. I need your help, please," I whispered to the trees and ground and even the sky. Idunn had no domain there, but maybe Thor would hear me. Who knew?

Tell us.

Tell us, Goddess.

Help you...

Help.

I couldn't kill it. That is, I didn't want to. It was just a creature doing someone's bidding—Heimdall's bidding? Or Hel's?—and I wasn't sure it knew good from evil. I also wasn't gonna let the thing eat me. Let's get real. I still had my priorities straight and me going to another reincarnation wasn't on the agenda.

"Push it. Push it back to the portal!"

I didn't know what I would do when the trees near the portal thinned. Maybe Jord would show up. If I could just get it there...

The trees obeyed and whipped out of the ground, revealing me to the demon beast. It reared back, but before it launched at me, the branches enclosed around the Hel Hound's trunk-like legs, trapping it in place. It bit the tree limbs, but they were faster, thicker than teeth the size of my forearm.

Yipes.

Two green limbs of a palo verde reached and wrapped around its horns, pushing the head down and rearing it back the way we had come. Slowly, the surrounding structure wrapped around the beast and it fought, whimpered, and bit to get out. One Joshua tree branch came around its great mouth, shutting it, making it impossible to snap any more of the branches.

The pushing seeming to take ages with new trees joining as the first ones were pulled taunt to their breaking point. They would let go and slowly stand back up in their normal positions. I couldn't understand the Hel Hound; that is, there was nothing there for me to hear. It simply sounded like snarling to my ears. The trees spoke to each other: laughing, talking, giggling, and sharing how to best reinforce in their own way.

Up fast up fast
Hurry around
Cautious
Hold hold hold

The words were sparse, but they were meaningful to the other trees.

I reached the circle of salt and found my best friend just as I had left her, but with tears trailing down her dirt-smudged face. When she saw me her face no longer held fear, but simple amazement. She saw the trees and the Hel Hound and let out a whoop.

"You dumb bitch, I can't believe it!"

I let that one slide. I'm not dumb, I'm impulsive. I kept asking each new tree around me for help. Before I could ask they were already moving, taking another's place, never breaking the chain. They were almost done; we were almost there, they were stretching beyond what I thought possible.

The Hel Hound seemed to realize it, too. I expected renewed efforts to try and break the woven bands of branches, not the inhuman shriek it released from between its clenched teeth. My hands covered my ears, but my head snapped toward the distance as another one answered the call.

"The other one!" Isa shouted, taking a step out of the circle.

The hound wretched its two front paws free and struck the thickest of the trees at its middle.

"Get back in the circle!" I screamed at her. "Get back in! It can't get you there!"

She jumped back and the trees immediately regained control over the monstrous form, thick and thin branches alike wrapping around its legs. Some trees from behind and around the portal reached out and pulled the Hel Hound toward them and back to where it had come from.

Then it stopped, a monstrous tug-of-war at a standstill with only ten feet left to go.

I trembled and my blood roared in my ears. What was wrong? Why did it—

Too much...

Much!

Goddess!

Holding holding...

The voices wrapped in my mind and their struggles tingled in the air, almost sweet and fragrant. My magic. Wild magic.

"Then I'll give you more." This was the whisper. The idea that to give them more spoke to me beyond just a throw away possibility. It was how I—how Idunn—had given them life and growth before. I saw it in my head as though it were my own memory.

I tangled my hands into the nearest tree, soft leaves and rough bark at the same time. My magic welled up from inside me and I offered it to them, gave them what I could not yet control: my power.

From my hands purple power veined through the aspen tree and spread both upwards through its thick branches and outwards to the other trees, snaking and glowing ethereally.

I was glowing.

Holy shit, I was glowing?!

I almost fell over in shock, but forced myself to hold on to the trees, feeling the leaves tickle my hands and the little pieces of bark that bit into my palms.

"Aspen!"

Isa called my name, but my mind focused only on giving from this well inside of me while Thor's warning about overusing magic echoed. My mind went fuzzy, almost like I was drunk or high, but my magic entangled itself through every tree that touched the Hel Hound and with one final, magical push it was back where it came from, the trees holding it there.

With no way to close the stupid portal.

Damn it.

I couldn't hold the creature forever, but my mind blanked on what to do next.

Isa's scream reached my ears at the same time as the new awareness reached my senses. There wasn't a thought process connected to it, just knowledge. With my magic as the focal point, some of the trees held the Hel Hound back in the portal, while the others reached for the Hel Hound that had responded to the distress howl.

It was bloodied and beaten down, gashes across its face and what could have been magical burn marks on its body. I cocked my head, the thought of 'why' crossing my mind, but worry had no time to set in when Sif came running up, both swords in her hands as she pumped furiously toward us. The others followed and I turned my attention back to the Hel Hounds, uncertainty flooding me.

We can close the portal if you can hold them.

Jord's voice floated through my head and I glanced around the battlefield fervently, only to see her hanging back, kneeling on the ground with her hand gripping the earth, her eyes locked on me.

I smiled. The battered Hel Hound was similarly wrapped and pulled to the portal to join its friend.

The trees said this was almost over. Light tinged the edge of my vision and sweat poured down my face as I continued to hold one Hel Hound and fight the other. Sif and Eir were poised on either side of the portal, and the branches dragged the next Hel Hound through the darkness. First its paws, then its muscular body, followed by the growling head.

"Now!" Sif yelled, bringing her sword to the ground. Her voice echoed in a language I didn't understand, and with a last burst of wind the portal shrank, allowing each branch to release its creature without getting stuck or cut. They groaned as they returned to their original positions.

Thank you...

Goddess...

Goddess!

Thank you...

I fell into darkness.

Chapter Thirty-Four

L et's be clear, I don't like to lie. Sure, everyone tells their best friend that shade of lipstick looks great on them when they need to hear it, but in general I steered clear of an out-right lie. I didn't even own a bike; but between Isa, the goddesses, and my faint acknowledgments, my family believed I had heat exhaustion from bike riding with them. I'd been ordered to stay in bed all day after sleeping all night.

No questions asked.

As I stroked Carrie's fur and glanced out my window at the garden in the distance, I was glad for the quiet day. It wasn't much, but I had enough magic to hear plants, and they were able to do so much more than I ever thought possible.

I could be Poison Ivy from *Batman*!

No, no, wait, she wanted to overthrow world order, and I wasn't about to do that.

What I had now came after only two full exposures to the fruit. I had to wonder what else I was capable of. There was fear, but also a thrill. It was like it had always been there on the cusp, and I'd never been able to access it before.

A knock at the door brought me out of my thoughts. I stopped petting Carrie and she nipped at me for it. "Hey," I whispered before calling out, "Yes?"

Nana opened the door and peeked in, a bright smile on her face. She pushed the door open and balanced a tea tray on her hip. I moved to get up, but she just shook her head at me and grabbed the tray with both hands when she had the door open.

She set it on my bed and then took a seat in my desk chair. Meanwhile, I grabbed the first thing in front of me. It was either pumpkin bread or a pumpkin muffin. I ate it so quickly that I don't remember.

"Oh, my gaaaawd," I moaned as the sweet and savory of the pumpkin pranced around my tongue. "You and Mom have been busy." I then got a good look at the spread and gasped. "Oh, Nana!"

The tray was chockful of my favorites: half a loaf of pumpkin bread, zucchini muffins, a matcha latte, and not one, but two, peanut butter cookies the size of my hand.

"Don't get sick eating it all," she joked. "Your mama and I got the goods at the market this morning. She's feeling great today and wanted to do something for you. Of course, now she's tired and taking a nap." She stretched and yawned. "I feel like I want to do that, too."

I smiled, and then let it fade. "Nana, about the other day—"

"We didn't tell her, if that's what you want to know." Nana looked out the window, I'd pulled the curtains back so I could open it. A hammer pounded in the distance where her suite was visible. "I figure she's got enough going on that she doesn't need to know every little slip up that happens. We all fall, honey. It's getting back up that matters. You're never too old to learn something new."

"Not even you, eh?" I took a bite of zucchini muffin and groaned. So good.

Nana's grin returned. "I learn something new every time I go to my psychic."

I raised a skeptical eyebrow at her and then mentally smacked the side of my head. I had to remind myself, despite everything, that magic was real. The tarot was real, at least if the person knew what they were doing. I still needed to vet Nana's psychic. No idea how I would go about that, but I think I needed to do it to take anything they said seriously.

I shifted my weight and leaned forward. "What did you learn this time?"

"Well, we did another tarot reading for you." She sat on my bed and had her phone out faster than I could say 'Ragnarök'.

Groaning, I let my head fall back, hitting my headboard. "Nanaaaaa."

She hesitated. "You don't want to know?"

"No, it's not that. It's just..." It was my turn to hesitate while I collected my thoughts and rubbed my bruised head. "Why do you keep doing tarot readings about me?"

"I only do readings about what's in my heart." Nana's face softened even more and her smile returned. "You keep coming up these days, I can't help it."

Feeling about two inches tall, I sheepishly asked, "What did she tell you?"

"How do you like your new job?" Nana asked, her smile now a little wooden and fake.

"It's... fine. I mean, the detectives are lots of fun and not jerks. They let me have any time off for Mom that I need. I think it's a good fit."

She nodded and relaxed a bit. "Yes, they seem to be nice."

"Come on, Nana. Just tell me," I instructed as she started for her phone again.

"I pulled from the face cards like I always do, and I pulled The Empress. We decided to do a quick reading on where to go after the hospital."

I made a face at her vague reason, but she ignored me.

"First was the Eight of Swords and then the inverted Six of Swords. They both indicate that there's feelings of holding onto something. Not letting go when it's clearly time to." She frowned, but kept going, flipping through her phone for the pictures she'd taken this morning. "Then the inverted King of Cups... perhaps shaky boundaries or even emotional instability."

My heart pounded so hard I swear Nana heard it and just ignored the drumming as a courtesy to me.

"There's something in your way. Something is blocking you from the possible outcome. The Knight of Wands, which says the time is now. For whatever you're waiting for. It's time to overcome these things and act."

"On what?"

Nana put her phone away and leveled a shrug my way. "On whatever's blocking you, I guess. Maybe it even means on your mental health—"

"Nana..."

"Aspen."

I'd learned a lot lately with tarot being just one of the many pies my fingers were now in. "Nana, if it's not my energy, then it can't be all about me. Some of that could be transference."

Her mouth twisted into a pout, but she seemed to be listening.

Sure, even though the last one turned out to be mostly true, and this one made a lot of sense to both Aspen and Idunn, I sure hoped it meant I was longing for my ex-boyfriend and not my ex-husband.

She took one of my cookies before standing. "You're right." She spoke around a mouthful of cookie, "But it can be about what I've noticed. The things my old eyes see are different than yours."

My eyes were a lot older than Nana's—well, kinda—but I wasn't going to say that.

"But," she waved her hand around, "sometimes my psychic talks in riddles. I'm trying to figure it out. If you don't think it's about your mental health..." My lips thinned in response and she continued. "I think you're doing so much better. Like not blaming yourself for something you have no control of."

I smiled, praying that it never, ever made sense to her.

Nana poised to leave and kissed me on the forehead and sighed. "Well, sorry about putting that on you. I promised Flo I'd do the dishes, and they aren't gonna get any easier if I wait."

"They will if you eat, though." I picked up a muffin and waved it around like a wand. "Come on, Nana."

"Not all of us are addicted to your mom's cooking like that." She winked. "Call if you need me."

The door had scarcely closed when the wind brushed past me and I felt the rise of power in the room. Choking at the sudden change in pressure, I actually grabbed the nearest plant, ready to launch it at that bastard Loki when he appeared.

To my ultimate displeasure, on so many levels, it wasn't Loki who appeared.

"You know," Bragi said as he materialized in the middle of my room, his bare chest taunting all straight women and more than a few men to touch him, "she's so close that it would probably be physically painful for her to realize it's all true."

I scrambled out of bed faster than if another Hel Hound had materialized, still clutching my poor succulent in my hands. "Are you crazy?" I hissed, clicking the lock and then turning to face him. "What the hell are you doing here?" I crossed my arms in a desperate attempt to look intimidating in my shorts and tank top only to smack myself with the plant. I put it down and crossed my arms, definitely looking intimidating.

Bragi quickly closed the gap between us—too quickly—and I pivoted off the door back toward my bed, managing to barely catch myself on my bed post and straighten up just in time for him to grab my arm. Carrie hissed at Bragi and he jumped back. Her fur was on edge and tail perfectly straight and bushy.

"I'll take care of the mean man, Carrie," I soothed her. Then I whipped back on him. "Don't make me a liar to my baby. Get the hell out, Bragi. I didn't invite you."

Bragi snatched my hand in his and placed a kiss on it before I could pull away. I want to say I felt something, had a vision of him doing this in the past with his open shirt and chiseled good looks... but there was nothing. Okay, sure, he's hot. That wasn't all he was, hopefully. I glared at him, wishing that I could scream for help and explain this somehow. That would require a lot of explanations I wasn't ready for. I would have to deal with him myself.

"My lady Idunn, it has been far too long." He forced a bouquet of yellow and puffy white dandelions on me, the look on his face showing that he clearly expected something from me.

"Excuse me?" I asked before remembering exactly who Bragi was or had been. Shit. Well, wait a second...

"How did you know I was Idunn?"

"I will always know, my lady," he said bowing at the waist like something out of an old painting of the 1600s. "Your magic called to me."

"What?" I hadn't called anyone. Definitely not Señor Puffy Shirt.

"We were one before, we can be one again, Idunn."

Whoa, whoa, whoa. Back up.

I needed my own sword. Instead, I settled for the one thing every woman had going for her: a glare as cold as ice and a tone that would freeze over water. "My name is Aspen."

"But Idunn—"

"Aspen," I snapped.

Bragi pursed his lips, a pout marring his face. "Love, we must pick up where we left off."

"No. No, no, no." Each word was more punctuated than the last. "No. I already told you; I'm not interested in a boyfriend. I'm not interested in a lover. I'm certainly not interested in a dingbat who gets off on women fawning over him."

He took a step back in shock and I pushed forward. "If you want to—what was it you said—'pursue me?' Then you can try, but not by sneaking into my room and taking pointers from *Twilight*." I pointed to the window, not the door. He couldn't leave that way. He was welcome to jump.

I stomped down the part of me that screamed to touch that chest, or worse, let him complete the kiss next time.

Hormones are hell after a breakup.

Bragi's face crumbled. Then with a fire blazing I hadn't noticed before he approached me again. He was back in my space, his lips so close I saw he used some sort of lip balm. He merely smiled wider.

"As my lady wishes," he whispered, backing up and taking my hand once more, kissing it.

I didn't have a chance to rip it away before he turned around and disappeared with a gust of wind... which whipped the dandelions he had placed in my hand away, throwing the seeds in all directions.

As the white feathered seeds settled, I grit my teeth and yelled as loudly as I dared, "Who's gonna clean this shit up?"

"You're so nervous," Isa said as I pulled into the nearest parking spot we found to Goddesses, Inc.

I grunted—okay, whimpered—in response. Then I rolled out my shoulders and let them fall by several centimeters as the muscles in my neck wept in relief.

So what? I *was* nervous. "This is the first time seeing them as Idunn. I can't explain it. It's just weird."

Isa nodded, but the way her eyes darted to the side and her mouth turned down slightly made me think she didn't understand at all. We were now walking to the ugly yellow building, making a beeline for the rune-inscribed door.

"You got this," she whispered, pushing my hand onto the doorknob. "Go in, we look weird."

Snorting, I did as I was told and we quickly entered so as not to look weirder.

Charlie, as always, sat at her desk, large headphones on her head bopping to a beat I couldn't hear. The door closed behind us and Charlie perked up, something I wasn't used to seeing in my direction.

"Hey!" she exclaimed, grabbing a cup off her desk and holding it out to me. "You can get the next one." She turned to Isa. "I didn't know you were going to be here. Can I get you water?"

I took the offered cup and felt warmth in my hand. A quick sniff delivered a fragrant, earthy aroma with a hint of sweetness. I took a sip and savored the fresh taste on my tongue. "Matcha is best warm."

"Agreed," Charlie said, beaming. "Come on, they're in the back."

"Am I late?"

"No. I would think they all lived here if I didn't know about the damn farm."

I thought the farm was more of a secret than that. Then we followed Charlie to the back room.

Thor was notably absent, but the others were there, not a hair out of place despite the fact that Sif had been injured two days before. Her face was full of color, and she easily crossed the office to come see me, as though she hadn't lost a gallon of blood from a paw swipe two days ago.

"Where's Thor?" Isa asked.

"Why is she here?" Eir asked me, ignoring Isa's comment.

"I don't want to repeat everything later, so I just invited her to come." Isa and I took seats at the magically available sitting area.

Sif coughed to hide a laugh, but Jord's sigh was audible.

I think at that point Eir's eyes turned red, but I wasn't going to let them get the jump on me today. "What happened after I passed out? Do we know who sent the Hel Hounds?"

Eir pursed her lips before answering, just like she would have before, and after what I suspect was the longest she'd gone without yelling at me, she answered. "We don't know."

I reeled back in shock. They didn't know. After all that, after the pain, after nearly getting *killed...* they were as in the dark as I was. Actually, a thought tingled in the back of my mind, I knew more than they did.

"We can only make theories," Eir continued, her voice low and grumbling. "Hel is the only one who can control Hel Hounds, so it has to be her."

"But," Sif picked up from there, "she's never interfered in this realm. Not even in Ragnarök."

I mulled that over. Why would she start now? We were beyond the times of the old gods. "What about Heimdall?"

"Heimdall?" Jord said, her brow furrowed. "What about Heimdall?"

Confusion and fear trickled down my spine as the goddesses exchanged confused looks and peered at me as though contemplating a head injury.

"Heimdall," Isa repeated, her sarcasm growing with each moment. "You know, the guy that controls the Bifrost? The guy that almost got us all killed, that guy?"

Sif was the first to relax. "Heimdall? He's not in charge of the Bifrost right now. Even if he was," she continued as the others relaxed, too, seemingly over my misunderstanding. "There's no way he would have let someone use it like that. Or have aligned with Hel."

Something wasn't sitting right. "Who is in charge of the Bifrost?" I croaked out.

"We used to take turns." Jord's soft voice washed over me. "Now it's Frey's job. Without Heimdall's eyes, he can't prevent something outside of his vision."

I thought back to my encounter with Frey and there hadn't been anything too off about him. Not evil. Hell, not even Loki gave off an 'evil' vibe. Other ones though...

"As for after you passed out," Eir said, "we had to force feed you one of the healing potions after Isa stopped screaming. As it would be inappropriate for us to go to your house to interrogate you, we had to wait until now." She said the last word with a toothy, almost sadistic grin.

I opened my mouth to ask my next question, and reroute the conversation back to Heimdall, but Sif beat me to it. "What happened in that grove of trees, *Idunn*?"

I inhaled sharply, a sick feeling in my gut. How did they know? Bragi knew, but I assumed there was some magic around him and Idunn I didn't know about yet.

"Your magic awakened to everyone else," Jord explained, her voice airy, as though she would burst into song at any moment. "Well, everyone with Norse magic. We felt you become you. Become Idunn. Your magic is still here, it's in the air, it's in the spells of those who call on you."

"I don't feel that," I whispered. "I mean, I can feel my magic just under the surface." I concentrated on the warmth within me.

"What about your memories?" Sif asked.

"Who knows if I'll get those back. No one else has mentioned theirs."

Sif paled. Jord picked up where Eir couldn't continue because her jaw was still on the floor. "Who's talking to you?"

Time to put all of it out there. "Oh, y'know, just Bragi, Freyja, Frey. Also, there actually *was* this guy claiming to be Heimdall, who left me for a snack for the Hel Hound. In the grove. I don't think I missed anyone." Except Loki, but that was on purpose. Sparse information begets sparse information.

The room noticeably changed. Jord put her hand on Eir's shoulder while Sif clenched and unclenched her fists.

"What's wrong?" Isa asked.

"Most of that isn't a surprise," Eir said. "The gods like to check in on the new ones sometimes."

"But Heimdall has been missing for centuries," Jord said. Her expression twisted as she continued. "No one knows what happened to him, or why. He simply vanished one day." A pause. "Are you sure he was Heimdall?"

"That's who he introduced himself as when he left me for dead. I could be wrong, all the names sound alike."

"Very funny, Aspen," Eir snapped. "You have no idea what this means."

"That Hel is working with Heimdall?" I asked, drawing an obvious conclusion. "And if Hel is, then Loki might be, too?"

Eir glared at me. I managed to not stick my tongue out at her. I had hoped her attitude would change once my identity had been revealed. That maybe she just hated humans or something. So far that didn't check out.

"If we work on the theory that Heimdall attacked us for unknown reasons, why didn't he kill Aspen?" Sif asked.

"Oh, he said the protection spells on me stopped him."

It had taken some thinking before I remembered what the second spell was. The one I carried on me at my Nana's request; a small black onyx crystal jammed in the bottom of my pockets.

"Look, I'm not saying I don't want to do this, but I am saying I need to know the stakes. What am I getting into? Why are we even awakened? Isa's involved in this now. I can't get her killed."

"Then you shouldn't have involved her." Eir's snooty reply set my teeth on edge.

Isa touched my arm, stepping forward with swagger and purpose. "You're assuming that because I'm human I wouldn't have noticed the differences. People notice. And I'm a little smarter than the average person. So," she continued, addressing all three of the goddesses but mostly the steaming Eir, "just tell us what you do know."

Sif looked more relaxed that I'd ever seen her before, her shoulders actually sitting below her chin for a change. "It's always a choice. You aren't immortal yet. You've barely tapped into your powers..." she trailed off. "I'm sorry. I can't be sure of what's going on with the other gods. As for why we are awakened, I guess why not?"

"Okay. Does it have to do with magic, then?"

"We call magic 'sedir,'" Eir said softly. "You haven't given any of the gods that saw you anything, right? Because if you think making a bargain with a fae is a bad idea, wait until you piss off Odin."

"Luckily, I didn't have to see him." I shuddered just thinking of the once King of the Norse Gods. His power was literally legend. "You gave me a job, and I'll be honest, a lot of money and flexibility. It's meant the world to my family the last few days while I've been out of it. They've been raving about you. So if you'll keep teaching me, I'll keep showing up. Some things have to change, though."

"Are you going to eat your fruit to regain your powers?" Sif asked.

The three goddesses and Isa looked at me expectantly. I nodded curtly before voicing an idea that might keep them off my back, with even more leeway than before. "If I'm Idunn, what if I can recreate it? You said I'm the one who grew it, so shouldn't I be able to do that?"

Jord furrowed her brow. "It should be possible, but it could take years, or decades. You might have to be immortal for it to work."

My guts twisted at that: the thoughts I had purposely been ignoring. The expectant looks continued, so I and admitted it. My own unknown. "I don't know. I don't want to die, but... why did you all decide to be immortal?"

"Everyone's reason is personal," Sif said, her smile back on. "All of us faltered on it at some point. It's not an easy thought. Take all the time you need."

"What about Heimdall?"

"We'll tell Lady Freyja what you have told us," Jord said with a smile. "She is our most powerful lady of our lands. But understand that if Heimdall is working with Hel and Loki, we will need the help of all the gods we can get."

Chapter Thirty-Five

L ike a child waking up from a nightmare, I tiptoed into my mom's room while she slept. I wasn't a child anymore, and it was the middle of the day, so things were different. The thick blackout curtains were drawn, a newer addition since she had started taking naps so frequently.

She was lying on top of the covers, her red hair being a beacon and a reminder that she was *there*. Her chest rose and fell slowly, and I nodded before smacking myself for checking on her breathing. I sat in the chair next to the bed and just watched her for a bit. Somehow, things were going to change. Especially if I could remake those fruits. With even the slightest of chances to help her, I wouldn't give up. Maybe she wouldn't end up in a wheelchair or dying from hitting her head during a seizure.

Tears welled up and I tried to force them back. I would not let my thoughts go down that road right now.

"Aspen?"

Mom's eyes opened and she smiled at me. But there, behind the mirth, I saw an exhaustion that hadn't been there. Or maybe she'd never been allowed me to see it before.

"Hey, Mom."

She patted the bed next to her. "Hey. Come on. Lay down?"

I pretended to think about it and after a few seconds gave my own grin and climbed in next to her. Days of scrambling up into bed to be with her and Dad rushed back to me, a sense of home and belonging settling on me. We were both of us on our backs staring at the ceiling as light from the bathroom illuminated the room just enough to create strange patterns on the ceiling.

"It's been years since we last did this." Her voice soothed my frazzled nerves and I felt so much younger.

"Remember when we used to put the stars on the ceiling so we could name them?" She didn't say anything, but I babbled on. "I was eight. Doug was about five. Cypress thought it was stupid." I grinned. "She felt stupid the next semester when she had to study astronomy as part of her science class."

"Yeah," she whispered.

The silence was light, comfortable, and warm. After a few minutes, my eyelids drooped. If I wasn't careful, I'd sleep there myself.

"How is your bipolar and anxiety doing, Aspen?"

I groaned. I didn't mean to groan, but I did. She knew. Nana swore she didn't, but damn, she *knew*. I turned over, facing her scrutinizing but soft gaze and my voice ran away as soon as I opened my mouth.

She turned back to the ceiling, studying the invisible patterns. "The hospital called yesterday to follow up. I had your phone."

I waited to hear the disapproval in her voice, but it never came. Her hand squeezed mine tightly. My throat was thick like peanut butter and I felt a cry coming on. Right here, right now, I had nothing to cry about. It was all in the past or the future.

Even with so much unsettled, I could be honest with her about it. "It's hard, but I'm doing okay. The ladies at the detective agency are understanding."

"They sent me flowers, did you see?" Mom pointed to the corner of her room to a vase of colorful roses. When I say colorful, I mean one of every color of the rainbow two or three times over.

I wiped away the tears that did escape and scoffed. "Wow. Those jerks didn't send me flowers."

Mom laughed, and life came into me with that sound. It wasn't sick or strained, just full of joy.

"I keep thinking I'm not good enough, but then something happens, and I realize I am. Mostly. I know things in my brain but not always in my heart. If that makes any sense."

"I think I get it." She squeezed my hand again. Then she smacked my arm twice, getting my attention. "I think I'm going to have to get a new pair of boots and join you in the garden more often. My doctor said as long as I take it easy, gardening should be good for my dexterity. I think it's going to take more than just you to clean that garden up in time for planting next year."

"I'd like that."

Mom fell asleep pretty soon after that, and to be honest, the garden sounded good. Since awakening as Idunn—as a *goddess*—I'd had the urge to go outside and just sit and be with nature more often than before. Damn, it sounded like a great time right now.

Weird.

I changed into jeans and scritched Carrie's head before going out. It wasn't dark outside, but as I approached the garden, I noticed a light on in the broken-down greenhouse—my research shed.

Crouching on the ground, I put my hand to the earth which answered back who waited for me.

I threw open the shed door, ready to let Loki have it. He sat in a chair, feet up on a planter, reading a book with goddamn glasses resting on his nose. He looked almost quaint and cozy in the armchair he had magicked into the room.

"Interesting read?" The sarcasm was impossible to miss, but good ol' Loki plowed ahead like it wasn't there.

"I do love a good dystopian fantasy romance." His voice floated by with warmth for the story.

I... did not have an answer to that, and honestly knowing he liked romance novels made me uncomfortable, like Loki was an actual person. I changed the direction of the conversation and sat on the nearest cinderblock. "You knew who I am all along."

He snapped his book closed and it vanished in his hand. "I said I wasn't going to tell you."

"We almost died because I didn't have any powers."

Loki crossed his arms in an X. "Wrong. You were never in any real danger, and your friend shouldn't go into things that are above her paygrade." I shot to my feet and he held up his hands in surrender. "Look, I was there, okay? I admit, I almost stepped in when the trees reacted. You were okay."

"You asshole!" I yelled as he rolled his eyes and settled back in his much comfier looking chair. The cinderblock had been biting into my legs. "You were there the entire time? I almost died. I am going to kill you." I said the last part slower, with more clarity than anything else.

This time, Loki jumped up, the chair vanished and he backed away. "Ah-ah-ah, Aspen, I think you're trying to hide this from your family. Murdering me would mean you have to hide the body."

"There is a lot of ground in my backyard." I sat down again and groaned as the homicidal urges ebbed. "You are *such* a dickhead."

Loki laughed, delight lighting up his face. "So you've said multiple times. Have you been in contact with the others since this happened?"

"Why?"

"I'm concerned and I need you to be, too."

My stomach tightened and something pushed in the back of my head. Something near my magic, but not the magic itself. Maybe the past? "I ask again, why?"

"Because it appears my beloved daughter is involved. Hel Hounds aren't capable of weakening a vortex barrier. Not on their own, Aspen." He leaned forward and put his hands together in a prayer position. "If she's intending to do something..."

"They think that means you're involved," I told him as though he didn't know.

Loki glared right back at me. "I haven't seen Hel since the last time I died in the fourteenth century. I may be the enemy of the gods, but I am not an enemy of Midgard, Aspen."

I pinched the bridge of my nose, feeling a headache coming on.

"So," he continued slowly. "How far have you come in your cultivation of the fruits?" I fumed as I realized this set up had been specifically to make me uncomfortable as he whiplashed me through information with a great big grin on his face.

"You are the biggest asshole."

"Well?"

I threw my hands into the air. "All I've done is isolate the seeds. I don't know if they're capable of being planted at this point. They could all be dead. I've been too busy to do much else."

I could ask him. He hadn't lied to me so far. As much as I hated to say it, omission was not a lie. That's why there's a separate word for it. "I need the fruits to awaken Idunn's power."

"Idunn guarded her secrets closer than anyone in all of Asgard. She gave her fruit only to those who were kind to her and proved themselves to her.

"How did you get it?" I asked with a laugh.

"I have always been charming. Suave. Debonair." He bobbed his head back and forth, as though deciding to say something. "Also, Odin and I were blood brothers, and he had them first, so I suspect he asked you to do it as a favor."

Yeah. That tracked. "I'm regretting it now!" I sat back on my cinderblock in a huff, pressure in my head still begging me to know or understand something. "How do you know all this? Do you remember?" I snapped.

Loki continued giving me some precious morsels of information I was begging for. "Some of us remember, others never died. We have many first-hand accounts of things that others don't always remember. It's not perfect."

"Can you just answer the damn question?!"

My voice grew louder with each syllable. It was a wonder my parents didn't hear us. I was standing again, though I didn't remember getting up. He was infuriating. His riddles, his ridiculous insistence of taking up time with them was only costing us exactly that: Time.

"Listen to me, you little—"

"Uh, excuse me?"

My blood ran cold. I think I stopped breathing. I know I stopped thinking.

I know that voice. I know that voice.

Loki and I stopped arguing and faced the door where someone stood, his face partially obscured as he ducked inside. "I was driving by. I felt an eruption of power from here just a moment ago. Is everything okay?"

My heart beat fast, my mouth went dry and without thinking, I stepped away from Loki, my face coming into the sunlight. The man in the door reeled back, shock clear on his tanned face as he saw me.

"Aspen?" My ex-boyfriend said as it finally occurred to him that Loki might not be his real problem.

"Marc. What the fuck are you doing here?"

Thank You

D id you know one of the most amazing things you can do for authors is to review their book? Please scan below to quickly go to a list of websites where you can leave a review. Or if you'd like to stay on top of my updates about the next book in the series, and more, join my (free) ko-fi! Thank you for making it this far, I hope you enjoyed the book. Or at least you don't want to throw it across the room *too* much.

Acknowledgements

To say this book was a journey would be an understatement. I first conceived the idea of a character answering the phone in different ways to say "Goddesses, Inc!" while working at a Walden Books (no joke) circa 2004 or so. The idea sat with me, slowly developing into mini adventures and some very rudimentary characters.

When my Aunt Ruth died after a very brief fight with an extremely aggressive form of cancer in 2022, I was extremely depressed and had a hard time coping with the loss. After a few months, I had a sudden, painful, realization that she had supported me so much, and in the end she never saw a book by me, even though I had written several already. (God willing, most of that will never see the light of day.)

I was watching a lot of YouTube, and after finding the right people to encourage me, especially Sarra Cannon of Heart Breathings and Jenna Moreci, I found myself digging in my brain and dusting the cobwebs for anything I could think of that would work to write a book, and "Goddesses, Inc." popped right into my head. By the end of the year, the first draft of the book was ready for my editor.

However, that's about the time things changed. Without going into too much detail, I became a caregiver to my own mother unexpectedly. She, luckily, is well on the road to recovery as of writing this, but it was a long road. And it was incredibly hard even with all the help we had. I had never been a true caretaker like that before, and so I was surprised at how my life suddenly mimicked Aspen's in certain ways. The uncertainty, the feelings of failure when it could never have been my fault. I felt validated about certain things, but it also gave me more strength in others. Sadly that strength was not in the form of supernatural powers, but it was found in my friends and family—which is pretty awesome, too.

Speaking of those family and friends, I have so many thank yous!

To my mom, Debbie, I can't thank you enough for giving me the strength every day to keep going with this book. Even at her worst, she was always telling me to never give up. And my step-dad, Mike, for giving great advice on the book design, the cover, and everything in-between. To my younger brother, Tommy, for giving me a shoulder when I needed it, and also more *Simpsons* and Leslie Nielsen quotes than I ever will know what to do with. Don't worry, I ~~held my own~~ lost spectacularly in the quote-offs with him.

To my 'little sisters': Rachael and Wilmelyn: Rachael, you're my best friend and I'll never forget the support you have given me, especially over the last 3 years while this book has come into being, and a lot more in the last year. My Wil of All Trades, you forever have my thanks for keeping my online presence from falling apart before it started. And possibly my sanity, too. I'm not sure about that last one, but someone should get the credit. I love you both so much, it's probably ridiculous.

My 'big sisters' Kay Parquet for being your hilarious self every time we would have pain days together. And, of course, for cheering me on from the moment we met. And Trisha Thacker, for listening, cheering me on, and for not making me have a 'sorry jar'. Or a swear jar for that matter. And for also being a beta reader, even if it didn't seem like it to you.

This book would be more like three Minions in a trench coat if it weren't for my editor and book coach: Julia Stringham Allen of Better Than Spellcheck. With her help and guidance, and the occasional good-natured threat, this collection of ideas is now a full-fledged book.

Luckily I had two editors on this, because Sebastian Taylor found some really embarrassing mistakes on my part while they were doing the final proofread of the book. Thank you, Seb!

I must also give many thanks to the person who made the book into a series—and gave Aspen her true super power. Thank you Sara Fujimura, your excitement has kept me on my toes, and your kindness continues to inspire me, Obento Lady.

Meredith Sweet, for your advice and endless patience as my brain continues to work with what I have. Rachel D. Adams, without your input I would have wasted at least three days coming up with a (much) worse summary.

To my Aunt Carol, Aunt Donna, and Uncle Joe, I'll never, ever, say you didn't encourage me. The entire way. Not that my cousins (who are way too numerous to name) weren't also supportive and encouraging! I can't ever say I didn't have my family behind me. Thank you and I love you all so much.

My beta readers: Brenda, Dylan and Shannon—I hope the book got a lot better since you first read it! And I hope more you're ready for me to ask for your help again. We can't have a book one without a book two!

To every friend who has been along this journey with me and giving me encouragement, advice, and sometimes kites... you know who you are. Thank you for never actually going through with your threats, and for being another hand to help me hold my pen when things got tough. And to my family and friends who supported me, who wanted to see this and weren't able to, I hope I've made you proud. I miss you.

And finally, I have to thank the first person who ever looked at me and told me: "Yeah, sure, you can write a book!" My Dad, Chuck. Sure, I was 13, and it was actually Sailor Moon fanfiction, but it was everything I needed. I'm here now, and I love it. Time to not turn back.

About the Author

Stefanie Santone woke up at the age of 13 and decided to be a writer. For some reason, she thought a Literature BA looked less pretentious on paper than a Creative Writing one (which she got at Arizona State, so did she really need to worry?). She puts it to good use at her home in Mesa, Arizona, where she spends much of her time (not) writing. When her editor isn't whipping her into top form, one can find her either reading, journaling, playing Dungeons & Dragons, or playing with one of the four family cats while sipping coffee day or night.